THE TI

Neil doesn't unders
Thought Domain, b
For this weird place
person are organized
Unless Neil can destroy the wicked Gander, people everywhere will be unable to think properly, and catastrophe will inevitably follow.

So, with his unlikely companions, Shipshape and Shambles, Neil sets out across the vast plains of Thought. But before long his quest brings him face to face with the most frightful and deceitful of enemies, and he finds himself in many extraordinary situations – and some hilarious ones too! From encountering the foggiest idea to being lost in his own thoughts, Neil's mission is full of excitement and fascinating insights.

This brilliantly imaginative and original fantasy novel is immensely entertaining and, quite literally, thought-provoking.

Paul Stewart was born in London and studied English at Lancaster University. He has also studied creative writing at the University of East Anglia with Malcolm Bradbury and Angela Carter. He lived in Germany for several years but now teaches English as a foreign language in Brighton. Since *The Thought Domain* he has written another novel, *The Weather Witch*, which is soon to be published in Puffin.

Paul Stewart

THE THOUGHT DOMAIN

Illustrated by Jon Riley

PUFFIN BOOKS

For Julie

PUFFIN BOOKS

Published by the Penguin Group
27 Wrights Lane, London W8 5TZ, England
Viking Penguin Inc., 40 West 23rd Street, New York, New York 10010, USA
Penguin books Australia Ltd, Ringwood, Victoria, Australia
Penguin Books Canada Ltd, 2801 John Street, Markham, Ontario, Canada L3R 1B4
Penguin Books (NZ) Ltd 182–190 Wairau Road, Auckland 10, New Zealand

Penguin Books Ltd, Registered Offices: Harmondsworth, Middlesex, England

First published by Viking Kestrel 1988
Published in Puffin Books 1989
1 3 5 7 9 10 8 6 4 2

Made and printed in Great Britain by
Cox & Wyman Ltd, Reading
Filmset in Linotron 202 Baskerville

Introduction

So, you have just opened your copy of *The Thought Domain*. May I wish you good morning, or good afternoon, or good evening (I'm not sure what time it is with you at the moment!), and welcome to the curious events which happened to a twelve-and-a-half-year-old boy called Neil Davies on 8 December last year.

I'm very glad you're reading the book, of course, but I wonder if you can tell me why you are. Did you like the sound of the title? Or was it the cover which first drew your attention? Is it a library book? Or a present from someone: an aunt, your granny, your dad? I bet you'd be able to give a perfectly good reason for reading it – but I bet it wouldn't be the right one. Neil could tell you why, out of all the thousands of books around, you chose this one; although he would put it differently.

He would say that the book chose you.

How does that make you feel, hearing that this book chose *you* to be its reader? Doesn't it make you feel special? It did Neil. He told me that he felt completely different when he realized how and why people make choices. He said . . .

But I mustn't start in the middle of the tale. Like all stories, this one should start at the beginning, at the point just before everything began to go haywire. We must go into the kitchen of 38 Chenley Road, Newford, where Mr Davies, Mrs Davies and their son, Neil, are sitting at the table, eating their breakfast. It is twenty-five to eight.

Chapter 1

Out of the Normal Run of Things

'What a load of old rubbish!' said Neil's dad.

'It didn't ought to be allowed,' said his mum, nodding.

It looked as though his parents were agreeing with one another, but Neil knew better. Every morning they would read through the two newspapers, and every morning they would argue about the news they found in them. If Mr Davies said 'yes', Mrs Davies would say 'no'; if she argued for more, he would argue for less. Whatever one said, the other would have to claim the opposite. And because of this Neil knew that as they seemed to be in agreement, they must be reading different articles.

'Something'll *have* to be done,' shouted Mrs Davies.

'It's disgraceful!' said Mr Davies, thumping the table with his fist.

'What is?' asked Neil.

'You get on with your breakfast,' said his mum.

Neil shrugged. A typical morning. His head turned from left to right and back again as his parents continued to make their comments on what they were reading. The curious thing was that they both seemed so sure of what they were saying. It was no wonder that they never reached any conclusions: after all, they couldn't both be right, could they? Neil tried his best to find out which one was making the mistakes, but they'd never answer his questions properly.

'They should take it to arbitration,' said Mr Davies. 'Stands to reason.'

'Where's Arbitration?' asked Neil.

'Stop playing with your cereal and get it eaten,' said Mrs Davies. 'They shouldn't have a closed shop,' she replied to her husband.

'Shouldn't have a closed shop?' he repeated, as if unable to believe his ears. 'Where would we be without one? Workers back on the open market, lining up for jobs for a day, that's where.'

Why should a shop being shut be cause for an argument, wondered Neil. Either it's open, or it's shut, which can be annoying – especially if it's the video shop – but why argue about it? And what was all this about an open market? All markets are open. Perhaps you have to go to the market if the shops are shut. No, that probably wasn't it. Even when the words sounded familiar, Neil still couldn't understand what his parents were talking about. Perhaps, he thought, it's some secret code. Perhaps one day I'll suddenly be able to understand everything, and on that day I'll know that I've become a grown-up.

'If you ask me, it's undemocratic,' continued Mrs Davies.

'I didn't!' snapped Mr Davies.

'What's undemocratic mean?' asked Neil.

'Neil, if you don't stop stirring your cereal and start eating it, you can forget about going to the cinema on Saturday,' said Mr Davies.

And the craziest thing of all, he thought, as he spooned the cereal up, is that they never get anywhere. Round and round and round and round they go!

He looked at them sitting there, noses buried in their newspapers, concern wrinkled across their brows, and he realized how much he liked them both. His dad was tall and big with dark hair and a beard. An angry snake-like scar peeked out of his shirt sleeves, which were nearly always rolled up; he was a tool-maker and about three years earlier had cut himself badly on a factory lathe. His mum was also tall, with wavy brown hair and a pointed nose. Both of them wore glasses for reading. Neither of them looked as nice with glasses on – perhaps that was because they only wore them to read the newspapers and start their daily argument. Glasses meant arguing.

'It's the bosses' fault.'

'I blame the unions.'

'The government should intervene.'

'The government got us into this mess.'

The same phrases day after day after day.

'What ARE you talking about?' asked Neil, putting his spoon down. 'I just don't understand.'

'NEIL!' they shouted in unison. 'BREAKFAST!!'

Yes, sometimes it was Mrs Davies who didn't answer Neil's questions, sometimes it was Mr Davies, and on occasions they joined forces and didn't answer him together. They always seemed to find something more important to say to him, rather than giving him a straight answer to his straight questions.

'And as for the clampdown on secondary picketing,' said Mr Davies.

It was hopeless. None of the words seemed to mean anything. What was a clampdown? He'd done camels at school that week: bactrians and dromedaries. Maybe a secondary was another type of camel, one with three humps. He laughed to himself.

'I warned you,' said Mr Davies, laying the newspaper down and turning angrily towards him 'No cinema.'

'Oh, dad, dad,' pleaded Neil, spooning the cereal up as fast as he could.

'You heard what I said,' said Mr Davies.

'Da blobbyl grobber bloffs,' said Neil.

'And don't talk with your mouth full, Neil,' said Mrs Davies.

He swallowed. It sometimes seemed that you really couldn't win. He continued to shovel in the horrible breakfast cereal. It was all right with cold milk, but in the winter his mum always warmed it. And then it went all soggy and formed a skin, which made him feel sick. She said it would help him feel the benefit outside. And he'd never got a proper answer to what a benefit looked like either!

Finally his bowl was empty and, after a last gulp, so was his mouth.

'Pleeeease can I go? Everyone else in my class has seen it,' said Neil.

'We'll see,' they said, and as that generally meant yes, Neil went off to get his satchel feeling better again.

In many ways, he knew he was lucky. At least his mum and dad still liked each other. Terry Reynold's parents didn't. Neither did Helen Southey's. And Phillip Clarke's were getting divorced. And yet something definitely didn't seem to be quite right. He wanted so much to help them solve their daily differences so that they wouldn't argue over breakfast any more. He wanted to stop them going over the same old ground and getting nowhere. If only he could help them arrive somewhere.

Twenty to nine. If he didn't hurry, he was going to be late for school again. He put all thoughts of his parents aside for the moment and ran, arriving at the gates just as the bell was going. All through the morning lessons, his mind wandered. He thought of his father going off to work in the factory every day, of his mother working in the launderette. All that talk and nothing ever changed. He leant over to his best-friend, Marty.

'Do your parents argue?' he whispered.

'Course they do,' Marty replied.

'What about?'

'Money, mainly.'

'Be quiet, you two boys,' said Miss Beale. 'Pay attention.'

Neil looked up and pretended to be interested. He hated geography and he hated Miss Beale, with her crisp grey hair and smell of bananas and biscuits.

'Sorry, Miss Beale,' he lied.

'Money,' he thought. 'Well, that's different.' He couldn't remember hearing his parents discussing money at all, just the contents of the newspapers. Politics they called it. While Miss Beale was drawing some rainfall chart on the board, Neil turned round to Peter Allinson.

'Do your parents argue?' he asked.

Peter nodded.

'What about?'

'Us – me and my brothers,' he whispered.

Peter had six brothers. It seemed reasonable that the parents should talk about them.

'Anything else?' said Neil.

Peter thought for a moment. 'No,' he said, 'it's always the same.'

'Silence,' said Miss Beale severely, without turning round.

'And your parents?' said Neil to Dean, turning round the other way.

'They used to argue about sex,' said Dean.

All four of them sniggered.

'Before me mum walked out,' he added.

Miss Beale spun round.

'Neil,' she said, 'is that you again? I won't have you interrupting my lessons in this manner. What are you smirking about?'

'Nothing, Miss,' he said.

'Do you always sit there looking like a cat that's been at the cream over nothing?' she demanded to know.

'Sometimes, Miss,' said Neil, attempting to make his face look serious.

She glared at him.

'One more peep out of you . . .' she threatened.

'Yes, Miss. Sorry, Miss,' he said.

'Now, if you would all open your books at page twenty-seven and compare the picture at the bottom of the page with what's on the board.'

Neil looked down at the sketches of the water-level of a

reservoir at different times of the year; looked up at the chalk bar graph on the blackboard. He knew he would get into trouble if he asked. He knew it would be a mistake to push his luck too far. But the question was there and wouldn't go away. Perhaps because it was a geography lesson. Perhaps because it was Miss Beale's lesson. He hadn't yet learnt how choices and decisions get made and so was almost as surprised as everyone else when his hand suddenly shot up when Miss Beale asked if there were any questions.

'Yes, Neil,' she said, her eyes narrowing, as if to dare him to ask anything irrelevant.

'Miss,' said Neil. 'Where's Arbitration?'

'Where is . . .' began Miss Beale, sucking in her cheeks so that her lips formed two hard, narrow lines.

'Arbitration,' said Neil, and swallowed.

'My word,' said Miss Beale, 'you certainly are a most stupid boy at times.'

The others giggled behind their hands and turned round to look at Neil, who was becoming redder and redder with embarrassment and anger.

'No, I'm not,' he said.

'I've never known anyone throw so many red herrings into a lesson before,' she continued, ignoring him. 'What has arbitration got to do with this geography lesson?'

'I don't know, Miss Beale. That's why I asked,' said Neil.

'And I don't want any of your cheek,' she said.

The atmosphere in the classroom was becoming increasingly riotous. Miss Beale felt her grip on the situation weakening and knew she would have to have a show of strength or risk losing control altogether. Her nose thrust angrily towards him. But before she could speak, Neil was off again.

'Why don't any of you ever answer us?' he shouted. 'Why can't anyone take a couple of minutes to listen to us for a change? All we ever learn are the unimportant things, and anything we want to know is just ignored . . .' Suddenly aware of what he was saying, his voice faltered, his legs shook and he had to look away from the grey-white anger of Miss Beale.

'You disgustingly insolent little specimen,' she hissed. 'You wretched, revolting, repulsive, reptilious creature,' she roared, her voice reaching a shattering crescendo. 'HOW DARE YOU? GET OUT OF HERE THIS MINUTE. TO THE HEADMISTRESS WITH YOU! GO!!!'

Now he'd be for it. Mrs Pringle, the headmistress, was bound to write a letter to his parents and then he'd never get to see the film at the weekend. Sometimes everything seems to gang up on you. You start off with the best of intentions, thought Neil, and then, there you are, in the soup!

To get from Miss Beale's classroom to the headmistress's office, he had to cross the junior's playground. Walking past the wall, with its painted circles and cricket stumps, he got slower and slower, scuffing his shoes along the tarmac. He thought of the film he wouldn't now see. He imagined his dad opening the letter and could picture the disappointment on his mum's face. And as he was thinking of all the horrible things that would happen, and all the nice things that wouldn't, he found himself walking out of the school gates. Now, this was strictly forbidden during lesson-times but, well, Neil had by now built everything up into such a monster of a problem that even though he knew he was making things *even* worse by running off, this was what he did.

Straight out he went, turned left and ran down to the main road without once looking back. It was a warm day for the winter, overcast and windless, and everyone was out shopping, buying food and presents for Christmas. A thought, more horrible than all the others, suddenly occurred to him. Maybe he wouldn't get any presents! He didn't believe in Father Christmas now, of course, but it was great to discover the stockings stuffed full of things and see the Christmas tree surrounded by the heap of brightly wrapped and ribboned presents. As he imagined the scene, all the nice things disappeared. First the stockings, then the parcels, then the tree, and all he could see was his mum and dad sitting there reading the papers, glasses on, arguing, just like on everyotherday.

'You can't buy presents in a closed shop,' Mrs Davies was saying.

'You should have got them in the open market,' retorted Mr Davies.

Faced with this bleak vision of Christmas, Neil began to feel increasingly sorry for himself. He came to the park and, picking up a stick, he let it clatter along the railings. In summer the park was full all day, but now, apart from a couple of old women with poodles, it was deserted. It was a fairly typical recreation ground, with its slide, roundabout and swings, the paddling-pool with its peeling turquoise paint, a muddy area with goal posts for playing football, and wooden benches lining the paths, usually occupied by old age pensioners with their yappy dogs. For Neil the park had one saving grace, and that was an area over in the far corner which had been allowed to become completely overgrown and wild. It had once been part of the grounds of a Victorian mansion which had been bombed in the last war. Now the gardens were totally out of control and formed a labyrinth of brambles and vines, with moss-encrusted plum and pear trees which still bore fruit in autumn. Clambering through giant rhododendron and laurel bushes, and over the crumbling remains of outer walls, Neil came to a squared patch covered in a mosaic of leaved shrubs which smelled sweet when the sun shone. Neil had identified them as rosemary, lavender, thyme, mint and basil. There had once been a wall enclosing the tiny herb garden, but now all that remained was a single wrought-iron arch which had long ago given up trying to separate the overgrown weeds from the overgrown herbs.

This was Neil's favourite place of all. It was here that he had always come when he wanted to be on his own. He imagined himself as Lord of the Woods, as a valiant knight returning from battle; the brambles reminded him of the thorny thicket which surrounded the Sleeping Beauty. His imagination would run as wild as the plants and time seemed to lose its meaning. Sometimes he had been there for centuries and only an hour had passed.

The problem, as I see it, is that grown-ups just stop thinking. They seem to get one thing stuck in their heads and can't think about anything else. Politics, money, geography. It makes no difference what. And whenever we children ask them why, they tell us we're too young to understand. Well, I think it's the other way round. I think it's them who don't understand. None of them do. And that's why they keep going round and round in circles.

Perhaps it was the fact that he had so often played games with his imagination in this place before, perhaps it was because he wanted to help his parents so much, perhaps it was because in this derelict and neglected garden the old and the new touched that Neil was able to step outside the usual bounds of time and space. I can't be sure *why* it happened, but *that* it happened is certainly beyond any doubt.

As he was still thinking the whole problem through, he was clutching hold of one side of the iron archway and spinning round, passing through the curved entrance time and again, his head thrown back, and calling out:

'Why? WHY? *WHY*??'

The faster he whirled, the more blurred the trees looked, the more luminous the sky seemed. He had the feeling that if he could go JUST THAT LITTLE BIT FASTER, his feet would leave the ground and he would be able to fly. The 'whys' he was shouting into the air became mere sounds, like the screeching of the gulls overhead:

'Whaaaa-eeee!!!'

And without any warning, he heard an answer.

'There are, naturally, any number of more than adequate responses to this somewhat vague query, though I understand that the standard reply is "because".'

Lost in his spinning as he was, the sound of a voice speaking so clearly, and so close to his ear, had a devastating effect on Neil. If, like you, he had been sitting reading a book, the voice might have made him jump. But whirling round the archway made this impossible. Instead, his left hand released its grip on the pole and he was launched headfirst into the air, like a human cannon-ball.

He just had time to think 'I'm flying!' for a split second before smashing into the small, hard object which halted his trajectory, broke his fall and knocked him temporarily unconscious.

Chapter 2

Inside the Thought Domain

The first thing Neil saw as he started to come round was a tall, gaunt figure wearing clothes like those his grandfather had on in all the old family photos. There was a huge, baggy suit with wide lapels, trouser turn-ups and a tapered waistcoat with mother-of-pearl buttons. His tie was striped and matched the handkerchief peeking out of his top pocket. His shoes were heavy brown brogues.

'So good to have you with us, my boy,' he said. 'Thought for a horrible moment that I'd scared the life out of you. Completely,' he added.

Neil smiled nervously.

'Welcome to the Thought Domain. I am the Great Methodical, but you can call me sir, if you find it easier.'

'Pardon?' said Neil, looking round in bewilderment. He could hardly take it all in. The old garden, the trees, the shrubs, the archway: everything familiar which had been there only a moment before had vanished. And in its place? The main characteristic which struck Neil was the sheer immensity of wherever he now was. To one side was a black wall stretching away over the horizon. To the other was a towering silver edifice. And in this enormous barren landscape, with the exception of himself, the old man standing in front of him appeared to be the only form of life there. Below him the ground was arid and brown; the endless expanse of sky above was pale grey. To Neil it all looked like a weird cross between a lunar landscape and a high-tech sports complex.

I must be dreaming, Neil thought to himself.

'Dreaming?' said the Great Methodical, evidently reading his thoughts. 'Oh no. You're as much here as . . . as . . .' He seemed at a loss for words. 'As I am,' he said, with a theatrical flourish.

The more concrete the Great Methodical assured him it all was, the more agitated Neil felt himself becoming. How could he just 'lose' the park and find himself in this . . . this . . . Panic was beginning to take a hold of him.

'Where am I?' he said.

'I've already answered that one,' said the Great Methodical, slightly more sharply. 'You really must learn to pay attention a little better. Perhaps if you have a look at our map it'll help you,' he said, rooting through his pockets. 'Though, to be honest, I think you ought to get up first. You're really not doing poor Shambles any good at all lying on him like that.'

Neil looked down and saw, to his horror, that beneath him was a small and extremely bony man lying in the dust. His face was white, his strands of red hair dishevelled, his clothes dirty and torn at the elbows and knees.

'I am *so* sorry,' said Neil. 'I didn't see you there. I . . .'

'So it would seem,' said Shambles huffily.

'Manners,' said the Great Methodical absent-mindedly to Shambles as he unfolded a large map on the ground.

'You see,' said the Great Methodical, pointing into the distance. 'There are the Plains of Thought.'

Neil looked, but apart from the wall he couldn't see anything other than grey nothingness. All that space with so little in it, it seemed a real waste.

'Look!' said Neil. 'I know that you keep telling me that this is the Thought Domain, but where is it? What is it? And what am I doing here?' His voice betrayed his nervousness.

'Calm down, calm down,' said the Great Methodical

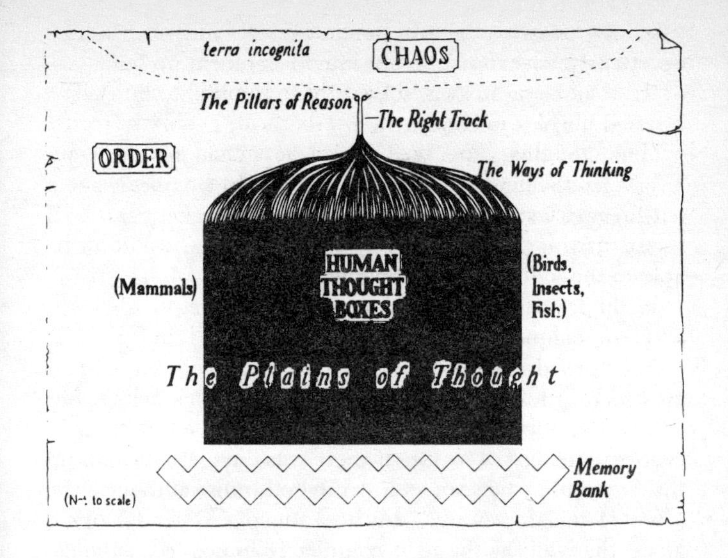

kindly. 'There's absolutely nothing to worry about. This is,' he said, 'another dimension, if you like. The place where thoughts go.'

'Another dimension,' said Neil quietly.

'In a manner of speaking,' said the Great Methodical.

'Well, what am *I* doing here?' he shouted, fear getting the upper hand once again.

'Ssh. It's all all right,' continued the Great Methodical. 'I'll come to that in due course. The wall there is the edge of the Plains of Thought. It is the outer extreme of the Thought Boxes. You can't actually see them from here, but they look like this grid pattern on the map,' he explained.

'But what *are* Thought Boxes.' persisted Neil, interest in his situation slowly taking over from the blind panic he had felt initially.

'They are extremely important,' said the Great Methodical. 'Indeed, the very reason for my being here. They are where thoughts are kept. Now I'd like you to listen very carefully to what I am going to tell you,' he added pompously, 'because I do not intend to repeat myself.'

'It's like being back at school,' thought Neil to himself as he tried his best to concentrate.

'Thought Boxes are, as I said, where thoughts are kept. Everyone alive in the world has a Thought Box here, like a left-luggage locker, where their thoughts are kept safe and sound. If you didn't have a Thought Box, you wouldn't be able to think at all, now would you?'

Without waiting for an answer, he continued:

'Here, behind us, is the Memory Bank.'

Neil turned round to look at the largest building he had ever seen in his life. He had seen big buildings before, but this was on a completely different scale from anything he'd ever experienced. The top, if there was one, was so high up that it couldn't be seen as it drifted off indistinctly into the mists of the upper areas of the atmosphere. And looking along the wall, he found it completely impossible to make out the end of the building either, as it zig-zagged its way towards the horizon. And as the land was flat, it must have been a very, very long distance away indeed. The wall facing Neil was made of a dull silver material, with narrow strips of darkened glass forming vertical lines which pointed up to the clouds.

'Master Edifice for Mental Order: Retention and Yielding, MEMORY in other words,' explained the Great Methodical.

'But what is it?' asked Neil.

'It is the place where a miniaturized copy of each and every thought ever conceived is logged and filed,' he said.

The fact was almost too much for Neil to take in. Every single thought!

'What?' he said, 'Since the beginning of time?'

'No,' said the Great Methodical, 'not that long ago, but since *Homo sapiens sapiens* first walked on the earth, hunting, living in caves, doing whatever men did then. Of course,' he added, 'there were dinosaurs before them, but quite frankly they never got round to doing much thinking. Big bodies, but brains the size of walnuts. No, it wasn't worth preserving their thoughts.'

Neil's head was spinning.

'So,' said the Great Methodical, in his matter-of-fact way, 'everyone's thoughts are kept in Thought Boxes while the people are alive, then they are copied and stored in the Memory Bank.'

'And what happens to the thoughts themselves?' asked Neil.

'Oh, what a bright boy you are,' said the Great Methodical, 'I really must congratulate myself on choosing such a clever chap to come and help us.'

The Great Methodical pointed to the area to the north of the map called Chaos.

'That is where the old thoughts go. They don't like being tied down, you see, so as soon as the person has no further use for them, they go to Chaos, which is like a heaven for thoughts. No one has any control over them there; they are free to do what they like.'

'You make it sound as if thoughts were real things,' said Neil.

'But they are, they are!' exclaimed the Great Methodical. 'Everything which is thought of in your world exists here as a real and tangible object.'

'Incredible,' said Neil. 'Even the things *I've* thought of?'

'Of course,' he replied. 'Somewhere out there is your own Thought Box. Some of your thoughts will already have been stored in the Memory Bank by now, and one day everything you have thought of will be set free and will enter Chaos. It's all so wonderfully, wonderfully systematic,' he added, his eyes shining proudly.

And yet at Neil watched him, he saw the old man's face sadden, as if he was remembering something unpleasant.

'Right, well, if you haven't any more questions about the map, I would propose the following,' said the Great Methodical. 'One, a look around the Memory Bank. Two, a short explanation of the contents of the Thought Boxes. And three, if you are still interested in helping us out, and I hope you will be, then I'll outline the task we'd like you to carry out.'

'Fine,' said Neil. It all seemed a bit too much, like being back in school being told what to do. But on the other hand, he was too inquisitive about everything now to turn his back on the opportunity to have all his questions about the Thought Domain answered.

The Great Methodical obviously read the different motives Neil had for agreeing to his suggestion, but he decided to ignore them.

'Admirable, my boy,' he said. 'I can tell it's going to be a pleasure working with you.'

They walked towards one of the massive entrances of the Memory Bank. Above it, in luminous green computer letters, passed the sentence: THOUGHT FOR THE DAY. YOU CAN LEAD A MAN TO THOUGHTS BUT YOU CAN'T MAKE HIM THINK.

'That's not quite right, is it?' said Neil, puzzled.

'As right as it'll ever be,' said the Great Methodical. 'We like to inspire our workforce with a selection of the thoughts from mankind.'

The metal panel door slid open to let them enter.

If possible, it was even more incredible inside the building than outside. The cavernous expanse of pure space gaping above him took Neil's breath away. Countless thousands of lights gleamed and flashed – crimson, emerald, yellow, magenta, blue and white – bars and circles lower down, a shimmering constellation in the upper reaches above him. Illuminated signposts pointed in various directions to the different departments: Animals; Architecture; Arts; Blueprints; Brainwaves . . . Small electric cars were being driven along narrow-gauge tracks. A bustling army of little men and women were hurrying from place to place, pushing trolleys, heads down, clip-boards under their arms.

'This is absolutely fantastic,' said Neil. 'Amazing!!'

He remembered a programme he had seen on the inside of a beehive. There was that same humming activity vibrating throughout the entire complex.

'It is simply incredible,' said Neil in awe. 'But there's something I don't quite understand.'

'Fire away,' said the Great Methodical.

'Well, if man was living in caves when you started collecting all the thoughts, how could you have a place like this, so modern and everything?'

'Another excellently perceptive question, my boy,' said the Great Methodical. 'You see, it is like this. Obviously, to store all the thoughts of so many people, we needed a bright, convenient, well-lit place. It wouldn't have been any use storing all that valuable information in caves, would it? So we "thought" of this place. We can think of anything here and have exactly what we want, whether it's technically possible or not.'

It seemed like the best of all possible worlds to Neil.

'And so it is,' said the Great Methodical, reading his thoughts again. 'At least it was until the human population began getting so uncontrollably enormous. That's half the trouble with everything these days. Do you realize that of all the men and women who have ever lived, half of them are alive now? It's staggering. In 1850, when that herb garden we found you in was built, there were just over a thousand million people on earth. There are more people than that in China now. In 1900 there were one and a half thousand million, in 1930 over two thousand million, in 1960 over three thousand million and at this moment the earth is trying to support five and a half thousand million people. Even as I speak more are being born. Every single second! Can you begin to imagine the amount of work it takes to store and record the thoughts of all those people? I'm understaffed and horribly, horribly overworked.'

Neil looked at the frail-looking old man in front of him,

with his grey-white skin and deep bags under his eyes – even the bags had bags!

'It's all getting to be too much,' he continued wearily, 'and I haven't had a holiday for over six thousand years. Everyone needs a break now and then. Don't you agree, Neil?'

Neil nodded enthusiastically.

'Yes, sir,' he said.

It's really not surprising he looks such a wreck, thought Neil to himself, and then, remembering that his thoughts could be read, felt immediately guilty.

'It doesn't matter,' said the Great Methodical. 'You're right. Sometimes I look in the mirror and I think, Methodical, you're overdoing it. Give up. Hand in your notice. But who to? I *am* the boss.' He shrugged and laughed bitterly.

'Could I look round a bit, sir?' said Neil, trying to change the subject.

'Of course, of course,' said the Great Methodical. 'Showing a keen interest in it all is just what we were hoping for,' he added. 'Where would you like to start?'

'I don't know,' said Neil. 'Wouldn't it be all right for me just to wander around on my own?'

'My dear boy, I hardly think you know what you are asking,' said the Great Methodical. 'The complex is nearly a hundred and twenty miles long, and, on the last count, over two hundred storeys high.'

'So I can't, then,' said Neil, slightly disappointed.

'When anyone here has to go from one office to another, he has to fill out a form in triplicate – that's three times,' he explained. 'He has to say which department he is going to and when he expects to arrive. If, for any reason, he is over half an hour late, we send out search parties.'

Neil laughed: 'Okay,' he said. 'You win.'

'Better that I win than you get lost,' said the Great Methodical.

'What shall we look at, then?' said Neil.

'What interests have you got?' he asked.

Neil thought for a moment. 'Well,' he said, 'I like . . .', but before he could get the word out, the Great Methodical had exclaimed:

'Music! Of course, a splendid place to commence.'

They climbed into a small car, something like the bumper cars you get at fairgrounds, pressed a button on the dashboard and immediately they sped off. All Neil could say was 'WOW!!' as they raced along the corridors. They turned left, they turned right, they went straight ahead, they went into glass tubes which turned into lifts and whisked them up to different levels at a speed which left Neil's stomach on the ground-floor. He realized with a shock that the reason he had been able to see so far up was that all the floors were made of crystal.

A neon display announced their arrival in the Music Department, and a spindly woman with wavy hair and bright red lips approached the car as the Great Methodical applied the brakes.

'Aah, Tone,' he said. 'Glad you're here.'

'Great Methodical, sir, I'm always happy to be of any assistance to your wonderful eminence,' she said, smiling grotesquely and wringing her hands together.

'Neil,' said the Great Methodical, 'allow me to introduce Miss Dorothea Tone, supervisor in charge of the Music Department.'

'Neil, Neil, Neil,' she trilled. 'Such a pretty name, a delightful name. And what can I do for you?'

'If you could just show him around a little,' said the Great Methodical.

'Your wish is my command, sir,' she said, smiling again. 'Come, young man.'

Neil climbed out of the car and followed her.

'Half an hour should suffice,' called out the Great Methodical.

'Half an hour it shall be,' said Dorothea Tone. 'Now, Neil, what type of music interests you in particular?

Baroque, Gregorian Chant, Indian Classical Sitar, Punk? You name it, it's all here.'

'All of it?'

'All of it.'

'Have you got that one that goes: "bom bom bom bom"?'

'Beethoven's Fifth? Most certainly.'

They walked down a long corridor to a sub-section of the department, Eighteenth–Nineteenth Century: German, and typed in the request on the digital display unit at the end of the row. Halfway down the glass shelf a light went on and the whole area was filled with the sound of the famous striking chords in all their symphonic splendour.

'Cor!' was all Neil said.

'Impressed?' said Dorothea Tone. 'Played as it was always meant to be played: straight from Beethoven's imagination. And if you look, you can follow the musical score.'

And there, as Neil peered at the lighted screen, he could see the notes coming up one after another after another.

'Gosh!' said Neil.

'Next?' said Miss Dorothea Tone.

'Have you got anything more modern? Danny and the Spacemen?' he said, thinking of the most obscure group he knew.

'American, are they?' asked Dorothea Tone.

'English,' said Neil.

They stepped on a section of moving floor and sped along to the department which dealt with Twentieth-Century Pop: English.

'Now, type in whatever it is you want to hear,' she instructed.

Neil did so, and a second later the room was full of the driving beat of the bass and drums, with the vocals singing over:

Well, I will, but you won't,
And I do, but you don't,
So come on come on come on, yeah, yeah . . .

'You're sure that was what you wanted to hear?' said Miss Dorothea Tone, raising one eyebrow.

'Yeah,' said Neil. 'Great, isn't it?'

'If you like that sort of thing, I suppose,' she said and sniffed. 'Why don't we just try one at random?' she suggested.

'Okay,' said Neil.

'Close your eyes, then,' she said.

Neil did as he was told and the moving floor whisked them off to another corner of the department. A minute later they stopped next to a glass panel.

'Press the query button,' said Dorothea Tone.

Suddenly the air was resounding with the melodies of tinkling bells, sounding like pieces of glass jangling in a soft breeze, accompanied by the irregular beat of a tom-tom drum and the occasional high-pitched singing of a woman.

'Guess what it is,' said Dorothea Tone.

'Japanese?' said Neil.

'Not bad,' said Dorothea Tone. 'Okinawan, actually. And century?'

Neil shrugged. 'Nineteenth?'

'Let's have a look.'

He pressed the query button for a second time. THIRTEENTH CENTURY flashed up on the screen.

'Still, not bad for a first attempt,' said Dorothea Tone consolingly. 'Oh, good grief,' she said. 'Is that the time? We must be getting back.'

'And not before time!' said the Great Methodical as they arrived. 'We've got a great deal to get done, you know. No time to waste at all. I'm surprised at you, Tone,' he said.

'I do apologize ever so profusely, sir,' grovelled Miss Dorothea Tone. 'It really wasn't my fault,' she said. 'It was his,' she added, pointing at Neil.

'It wasn't,' said Neil.

'Oh, don't you worry about her,' said the Great Methodical to Neil under his breath. 'She never was able to bear up under the strain of all the responsibility she has. Needs to find scapegoats, you see.' Then, turning to Miss Dorothea Tone herself, he said loudly: 'Thank you so much for sparing some of your precious time to show my young friend around.'

'Yes, thanks a lot,' added Neil, nodding keenly.

'It was nothing. Nothing at all,' she replied, beaming widely. 'And do come back again.'

Neil couldn't help wondering how many other people he would meet in the Thought Domain would be so two-faced.

'Now, is there anything else you'd like to see?' asked the Great Methodical.

'Oh yes!' said Neil.

He was interested in the race to get into space between the Russians and the Americans, and in the Aeronautics Department (Space Travel): Twentieth Century he saw the blueprints for Yuri Gagarin's first spaceship. He saw the thoughts of John Glenn as he sat in his capsule looking down on the blue and green earth from his first orbiting of the world. 'That's one small step for a man; one giant step for mankind,' he heard Neil Armstrong saying as he stepped down on to the surface of the moon.

And they looked in the literature departments and picked out novels and poems, published and unpublished, written and just thought about, in numerous languages from all over the world; it seemed to Neil that everyone everywhere had tried to write a poem at some time or other, even if it was only a little verse for the inside of a Valentine card.

And they looked at paintings, sculptures, car designs, inventions, machines, dreams, holograms, cities, mystery plays, ships, trips and magical tricks, and despite all this they still managed to see only a tiny fraction of the million, billion, zillion thoughts stored there in the Memory Bank.

'Everything has to be cross-referenced, so you can find it by the type of thought, the person who thought it, the time it was thought and the place it was thought in. And this is further complicated by the number of languages spoken on earth. You speak English, Neil, a major language, but there are so many others. In India, including dialects, there are over a thousand languages, so the whole process is . . .'

Apparently exhausted by the guided tour, the Great Methodical suddenly sat down on the floor and held his bony, grey head in his bony, grey hands. He groaned slightly.

'Are you all right?' said Neil, concerned.

The old man, suddenly looking *just* like someone who had gone six thousand years without a holiday, continued to stare blankly at the floor, mumbling words Neil couldn't decipher.

'Pedi, Sotho, Chwana, Thonga, Nyanja, Bemba, Kikuyu . . .'

'Sir,' said Neil more anxiously, shaking the Great Methodical's shoulders.

'Languages, languages,' he said. 'I bet you didn't know there were so many.'

'I certainly didn't,' said Neil, thinking of school, where they were trying to teach him French and German. Even those two extra ones seemed far too much like hard work.

'Sometimes it all becomes that little bit too overwhelming,' said the Great Methodical, getting up off the floor and dusting himself down. They climbed back into the little car and aimed towards a distant sign marked EXIT.

Outside again, and the silver panel of the massive building slid silently shut. Neil looked up and was surprised to see that the thought for the day had changed. In place of the previous saying the green lights were now spelling out: A PLACE FOR EVERY THINK AND EVERY THINK IN ITS PLACE. The Great Methodical caught Neil looking at it questioningly.

'Not all thoughts are necessarily grammatical,' he said.

'That wasn't what I was thinking,' said Neil. He paused. 'How long were we in the Memory Bank?'

'Haven't a clue, my boy,' he said. 'Why?'

'Well, if there's a new thought for the day, it must be a new day, and I haven't been to sleep or anything, have I?'

'Time is as time does!' he said cryptically. 'It doesn't seem to do the same things here,' he explained, 'as it does in your world.'

'What do you mean?' said Neil.

'Well, you must have noticed how time sometimes goes slow, like in the middle of a geography lesson, and other times it whizzes past, like during the holidays. Well, it's the same here. But we don't measure it. If a lot of time went past while you were in the Memory Bank, you must have been enjoying yourself. Now, let's have a little light refreshment,' said the Great Methodical.

Immediately, the little bony man who'd broken his fall earlier appeared with a tray balanced on his upturned hand and offered Neil a glass of green liquid and a slice of cake.

'Sit yourself down,' said the Great Methodical, and Neil looked round to see a small table with two chairs behind him. He was fairly sure that they hadn't been there a moment before, but then he was becoming used to the unusual happenings here in the Thought Domain.

'So, we can cross number one off our list. Guided tour of the Memory Bank completed. Were you satisfied?'

'Yes,' said Neil. 'Though . . .'

'Well?' said the Great Methodical.

'I just wonder why you bother,' said Neil. 'I mean, I can see the point of keeping Beethoven and all the famous people on your files, but to keep *every* person's thoughts there, isn't that a bit unnecessary?'

'Aah, Neil, but who can say what is important and what is not? Who can tell who will become famous? How can we know which particular thought is going to have an influence on the future?'

Neil nodded slowly.

'You see, Neil, if we start choosing between one thought and another, it means we are influencing the thoughts themselves. And that we are not allowed to do.'

'Then what's the point of storing them at all, if you can't influence anything?' said Neil.

'Another excellent question,' said the Great Methodical, 'and one which almost brings us to the reason you were sent for. You see,' he continued, his face turning serious and sad, 'mankind is going through a great many problems at the moment, and,' he added ominously, 'not all the fault lies with him alone.'

Neil felt the hairs on the back of his neck tingle.

'But let's go and look at the way thoughts are contained here before we get on to such serious matters,' he said. 'Finish your drink, Neil, and we'll go and inspect the Thought Boxes.'

They were artificial constructions made of tall squares of black Perspex, and as Neil and the Great Methodical approached them, Neil could hear a quiet and indistinct mumble coming from them. The Great Methodical put his hand on Neil's shoulder and guided him to a set of stairs at the end of the Thought Boxes which led them up to the top of the five-metre-high wall.

The view across the top of the five thousand million boxes was impressive only because of the number. The sight repeated itself time after time as the boxes receded into the distance and vanished over the horizon as a smooth black surface. Neil followed the Great Methodical around the criss-cross patterns of paths which interlocked at the top of the boxes. The view above the Thought Boxes might not have been very exciting, but what they enclosed was to take Neil's breath away.

Looking down he saw the most complicated writhing of moving objects he had ever seen. It was as though a room had been filled with people performing a strange dance, but on looking closer he saw that all the objects in the room were dancing too, and when he looked closer still he saw that a lot of the things in the room were quite bizarre. From apples to dismembered heads, from curtains to chrysanthemums, from bicycles to beer bottles, they were all taking part in the same curious modern ballet. Twisting and turning, milling and mumbling, jockeying for prime positions down there in their boxes.

The tops of the Perspex walls were about three metres across and all together they formed a regular criss-cross pattern of roadways. The width of the roads was just enough to allow two of the little cars that Neil had seen in the Memory Bank to pass one another comfortably. There were plenty of them, all being driven by the same small people, to and fro along the interlocking series of roads.

'What are they doing?' asked Neil.

'General maintenance,' said the Great Methodical. 'Let me explain. These boxes are where all the thoughts of living people are kept, and there were, let me see, 5,531,986,287 of them at the last count. Because of the increase of population, it means that new ones are being erected the whole time. As you can see, the boxes are all a standard size of one hundred and twenty-five cubic metres, which is deemed sufficient space for the average person to store his thoughts in. As a child . . .' He turned to Neil and said sharply:

'I *do* hope that you're paying attention!'

'Yes, I am,' said Neil, realizing for the umpteenth time that he couldn't get away with letting his mind wander in the Thought Domain.

'Where was I? Ah, yes. As a child learns, his box gradually fills up with all the thoughts he has. Because the box is empty to start with, it is easier to take in new thoughts – that's why babies are so quick to learn. As the child gets older, there is more competition amongst the thoughts and the learning process slows down accordingly. By the time the child reaches adulthood, the box is almost full, and it is at this point that the choosing process takes over. The individual learns to discriminate. All the thoughts constantly battle with one another for an important place in the box. As the person is obviously taking in new thoughts the whole time it gets to a situation where the box is overfilled, and that is why the little workers are needed. They constantly weed out the weak, useless thoughts which get pushed to the top of the box and remove them to make room for new thoughts.'

'And what happens to them?' asked Neil. He was trying ever so hard to concentrate, but being bombarded with so much new and weird information was proving a bit tiring.

'The old thoughts?' said the Great Methodical. 'They are recorded and stored in the Memory Bank. Firstly, because all thoughts must be recorded for the future of mankind, and secondly, because sometimes the person needs to use a thought which has already gone. In this case we make a copy from our records and place it back in the box to assist the person's memory of some old thought. After the thoughts have been recorded, the workers take them to the edge of the Plains of Thought. Do you remember on the map?'

'Yes,' said Neil. 'To the Ways of Thinking.'

'Precisely,' said the Great Methodical. 'Where they make their own way to the Right Track and through into Chaos, away from all the ordered demands we make of them here. They are free.'

'It's odd knowing that every time I think of something I am somehow putting it in prison,' said Neil.

'Indeed,' said the Great Methodical. 'Every thought is born in chains.'

Neil looked down into several of the boxes full of the active thoughts.

'This one must belong to a baby,' he said, pointing to a practically empty box containing thoughts of milk, unformed faces, vague sounds.

'Correct,' said the Great Methodical. 'And this one to a youngster,' he said, nodding to a half-filled box of school books, footballs, song-lyrics and music papers.

'But I can still see the early thoughts as well,' said Neil.

'Yes,' said the Great Methodical, 'but they are right on the surface and extremely unimportant. Look, they are hardly moving.'

Pulling Neil from the boxes, the Great Methodical led him back to the stairs. Once again, Neil sensed the great sadness from deep within the old man and was filled with a sense of foreboding. He knew that he hadn't been brought to the Thought Domain merely for a holiday, and began worrying about what surprises, what dangers, what horrors might be lying in wait for him. And perhaps more important still, he wondered how long it would all take. He thought of his mum and dad sitting worrying about their missing son. If only he could just let them know that he was okay and would be back as soon as he could.

'Come, Neil,' said the Great Methodical. 'Now you have seen the entire operation, it is time to tell you why I brought you here. You must listen very carefully to my tale, and at the end, you will have to tell me whether or not you are prepared to help us.'

Neil nodded. 'Go on then,' he said seriously.

'Well, as you can see,' started the Great Methodical, 'for this place to work well, everything has to be completely well-ordered and systematic. In a word, methodical.' He smiled. 'And for centuries it was like that. But,' he said, and took in a deep breath, 'something has gone wrong. Something has gone disastrously wrong, and if the error isn't corrected soon, then the whole of mankind is in a serious danger of extinction.'

'Extinction?' said Neil. 'What, you mean like dinosaurs, and mammoths, and dodos?'

'Exactly,' said the Great Methodical. 'Man could end up as dead as the proverbial dodo.'

'What happened, then?' asked Neil.

'It happened in Chaos,' said the Great Methodical. 'The door between Order and Chaos was designed to be one-way only. Thoughts would be freed from Order and allowed to go to Chaos, but were never allowed to return. Something went amiss, though, and a particularly unpleasant thought became very powerful in Chaos, very powerful indeed. It was so powerful that it forced its way back into the Order region of the Thought Domain and spread its evil designs here. It grew and grew, becoming more and more dangerous, feeding off the fear it inspired. It took the form of an emormous evil bird which destroyed everything which came near it.'

Neil felt his skin prickling with fear; felt tremors of nervousness going up and down his spine.

'It made a series of attacks on us,' continued the Great Methodical, 'influencing all the thoughts here. For several centuries it was a wicked but nevertheless controllable force. Then, earlier this century, it made its most serious attack of all. For a while we all feared that the end of the world would take place. Its insane ideas spread down to the human level via the polluted Thought Boxes and the world was taken to the brink of destruction through the Second World War. We knew it was the evil Gander's work, together with its battalions of wicked geese, because of the effect they had on humans. Men and women started marching like geese. They lost their individuality. Goose-stepping gaggles of soldiers spreading their evil all over the world. Germany, Italy, Japan – the ideas took on most strongly there at first. A whole system based on fear and destruction. And people knew when the danger was approaching, because their skin was covered in clammy goose-pimples, in anticipation of the encroaching horror.'

Neil stood there, mouth open, knees knocking. It all sounded so immense. How could *he* do anything?

'We were lucky then,' said the Great Methodical. 'We banished the Gander from the Thought Domain and its influence in man's thoughts subsided. We hoped we had destroyed it completely, but recently we discovered that it had merely retreated to the farthest corners of the Domain to try a new course of action. And this is proving even more effective. It could prove even more deadly.'

'How?' asked Neil in a shocked whisper.

'Well, the Gander and its cohorts are spreading fear among the thoughts which should withdraw from Order and go to Chaos. It is the Gander's method to sow the seeds of irrational fear everywhere it goes. And it is working. The thoughts no longer wish to enter Chaos because they are afraid. And now the Ways of Thinking are completely blocked, the Right Track is packed solid with immovable thoughts and, because of this, when the Thought Boxes become full there is nowhere for the old, useless thoughts to go. So they have to remain.'

The Great Methodical took a deep breath.

'And so,' he said, 'there is no room for new thoughts, no room at all, and people have stopped thinking. Only the same tired, old thoughts remain, going round and round and round in their heads.'

Neil felt as though someone had struck him on the back of his neck, so shocking was the sound of these words which described perfectly how he had spoken about his parents.

'And intuitively, you knew this to be the case,' said the Great Methodical. 'Am I right?'

Neil nodded in silence.

'It was for this reason alone that we were able to bring you here.'

'But what can we do about it?' said Neil.

'Someone,' said the Great Methodical slowly, 'must go and remove fear from the Pillars of Reason and Chaos so that men and women all over the world can start thinking again. And that someone must be a human, as no one from the Thought Domain can enter Chaos and come back again, and must be a child, as by the time adulthood has been reached it is already too late.'

'And that someone is me?' said Neil, and gulped nervously.

'After long and painstaking analysis,' said the Great Methodical, 'we reached the conclusion that you would indeed be the best-suited person.'

'Will it be dangerous?' asked Neil timidly.

'Yes,' said the Great Methodical. 'I cannot tell a lie. It

will be dangerous. But having said that, if no one goes, it will mean the end of mankind.'

Neil sat down on the ground. He thought of his mum and dad. He thought of Miss Beale. He thought of all his friends' mums and dads. He thought of all the information stored over the centuries in the Memory Bank. He thought of how he had wanted to do something about it all. He thought of the possible danger. He thought of everything nice that had ever happened to him.

'I've decided,' said Neil seriously. 'I will go. And I'll do my best to destroy the Gander.'

'Well done, my boy,' said the Great Methodical. 'I knew you wouldn't let us down. Well done, brave chap!'

Chapter 3

Setting Off on the Quest

'Well, Neil,' said the Great Methodical, 'the time has nearly come for you to start on your long and difficult journey.'

Neil shuddered as eager anticipation mixed with nervousness. He felt so small and insignificant whenever he thought of the enormity of the task ahead. And yet he so wanted to succeed that he was sure that everything would work out all right. If only he didn't have to go all on his own, though.

'But you don't,' said the Great Methodical, responding to his unspoken fears and wishes.

'I don't?' said Neil.

'While it is true that it is up to you alone to carry out the final task of removing irrational fear from the Thought Domain, you will not be totally without help.'

'Great,' said Neil. 'It'll be much better travelling with someone.'

'Precisely,' said the Great Methodical, taking a large silver whistle out of his back pocket. The long, piercing, high-pitched sound it made when he blew it forced Neil to cover his ears with his hands. The whistle was obviously a rallying call as, immediately, a long row of girls appeared in front of them. They all stood there, legs astride, hands behind their backs, looking at Neil expectantly.

'Right,' said the Great Methodical. 'Choose the one who

you think would be best suited to the journey you have to face.'

Neil looked at them all again and suddenly burst out laughing. 'But they're all the same,' he said.

'Ah no,' said the Great Methodical. 'There you are mistaken. Each and every one of our workers in the Thought Domain is completely different, with individual strengths and weaknesses, each with his or her own idiosyncracies, each with his or her own distinctive personality. So take your time to get to know them and then make your choice.'

Neil looked back and forward along the row of girls, and the longer he took the more individual they seemed to be. This one's left eyebrow arched more than the others, that one's mouth turned down in a somewhat more miserable expression than the rest. He felt he was beginning to see through the superficial similarities of bobbed hair and bright blue dungarees to the real person inside. Some of them waited placidly as he walked up and down the line, like a general inspecting his troops, while others began to shuffle their feet irritatedly. He looked them up and down, searching for any giveaway clue as to which of them would make the best companion.

'Ask them some questions?' suggested the Great Methodical.

'Okay,' said Neil. But what questions? He needed someone dependable, but they all looked dependable. He needed someone who wouldn't panic in the face of danger, but none of them looked as if they would. Most importantly, he needed someone who he could get on well with.

'How old are you?' he asked one.

'Three thousand, two hundred and twenty-one years, five months and sixteen days old,' came the prompt, and extremely surprising, reply.

'How old?' said Neil. The girl in front of him looked about twelve or thirteen.

'Three thousand, two hundred and twenty-one years,

five months and sixteen days old,' she repeated in the same flat monotone.

'Our workers are designed not to age,' said the Great Methodical. 'Indeed, nothing in the Thought Domain can really age. Including yourself, my boy,' he added. 'Anyway, no time for more explanations. We must get on. Are you ready to make a decision yet?'

'Well, definitely not her,' said Neil about the girl (if girl was the right word for someone so old) who had just spoken. 'Far too precise.'

'How old are you?' he asked another.

'About three thousand years old,' she answered.

'That's more like it,' said Neil. 'Would you like to come with me on the adventure?'

'If you like,' said the girl. 'I'm not really that bothered.'

'Too indifferent,' thought Neil. 'And what about you?' he said to a third girl.

'Me? Are you talking to me?' she responded, blushing a deep crimson. 'I . . . I . . . I . . .'

'Too timid,' he thought, and passed further along the line.

'Why should I take you with me?' Neil asked yet another.

'You need someone to boss around,' came the reply.

'And why should I take you?' he asked another.

'You need someone to boss *you* around,' she said.

'And what about you?' he asked the next in line.

'Sometimes, it's just nice to have a good friend with you,' she said.

It was the best reply Neil had received so far. He made a note of which one she was, but didn't want to choose immediately.

'Why do you want to go and defeat the evil Gander?' he asked the next girl.

'I feel it is my duty to go to the farthest reaches of the Thought Domain to seek out and eradicate anything which might endanger the safety and smooth-running of the system which operates here and which I feel is the most workably worthwhile way of . . .'

'Thank you,' said Neil, cutting her short. 'Gasbag,' he thought. 'And you?' he said to the next one.

'There comes a time in every person's life when he or she has to stand up and be counted, to refuse to simply sit by and let injustice follow injustice in this world, where all too often it is a case of survival of the fittest and devil take the hindmost, even when the . . .'

'Next?' said Neil.

'I like fighting,' she replied simply.

'And you?' said Neil, returning to the one he had liked before. The girl beckoned and as Neil got to her, she whispered in his ear:

'Eye Owe Tea Why
Eye Why
See Why Tea.'

'Is this some kind of riddle?' said Neil. 'What's all this about "eyes" and "teas"? What does it all mean?'

The girl just smiled at him.

'Come on,' said Neil. 'Tell me what it means.'

'I'll only tell you if you choose yours truly,' she said, and winked.

'You mean you,' said Neil. He laughed and turned round to look at the Great Methodical. But he wasn't giving anything away: his face remained motionless as he waited for Neil to make up his own mind.

'Okay,' said Neil. 'I'll take you.'

From behind him he heard the Great Methodical applauding.

'Bravo, Neil, an excellent choice. Shipshape will help you as much as she can, I am sure, and will undoubtedly also be good company. You see what I meant about them all being different. First impressions can be so deceptive.' The girl called Shipshape walked forward and held out her hand.

'Pleased to meet you,' she said and shook hands with Neil.

'Same here,' he said. He was always a bit embarrassed shaking hands with people and also he was still itching to find out what the answer to the riddle was.

'Eye Owe Tea Why
Eye Why
See Why Tea,' he repeated. 'Well, what does it all mean?' he blurted out.

Both Shipshape and the Great Methodical burst out laughing.

'She's already told you, Neil,' said the Great Methodical. '*I*'ll *O*nly *T*ell *Y*ou *I*f *Y*ou *C*hoose *Y*ours *T*ruly, and that, as you so rightly pointed out, was me,' said Shipshape, laughing. In fact, everyone was laughing, including the others in the line who Neil hadn't picked.

'I was tricked,' said Neil. 'Still, I'm sure that I'll get on with anyone who could pull a fast one like that,' he added.

Suddenly Neil noticed that at the back of the crowd of laughing faces there was one person who was not joining in the fun. It was the little man he'd landed on when he had first entered the Thought Domain, shuffling around disconsolately on his own.

'Who is he?' asked Neil, pointing out the sad figure.

'I told you before,' said the Great Methodical.

'Yes, I remember that he's called Shambles,' said Neil, 'but I mean who *is* he? He looks so different from everyone else here and really out of place.'

'True,' said the Great Methodical. 'He is the last remaining example of a discontinued line. They proved far less reliable than the model Shipshape belongs to.'

'During the problems with the Gander,' said Shipshape, 'they started working for the other side.'

'It was Shambles, in the end, who alerted us to what was going on,' continued the Great Methodical, 'and because of his loyalty, his life was spared when the others were all banished to Chaos.'

'He must be very lonely,' said Neil. 'He looks really miserable.'

'He is, poor old fellow,' said the Great Methodical. 'He never really got over the whole tragedy.'

'Could I ask a favour?' asked Neil. 'Do you think Shambles could come along with us?'

'Oh no!' interrupted Shipshape. 'That whole range was always slow and inefficient, and Shambles is a particularly mediocre example. What use could he possibly have?'

'I don't know,' said Neil, 'but I just have the feeling that he might be useful at some stage, just because he does think so differently. And he won't be in the way, will he?'

To Neil's surprise, the Great Methodical seemed to agree with him.

'Always useful to get a second opinion,' he said, 'and invaluable to get a third.'

On being summoned, Shambles came slouching over to them. His name was completely appropriate. He looked a complete mess, although, as Neil guiltily remembered, part of the fault lay with him. He had after all been responsible for the ragged tears at the elbows and knees of his clothes. He was pale and thin with long greasy hair and a pinched nervous expression around his eyes and mouth. If a fight between Shipshape and Shambles should ever occur, Neil didn't think much of Shambles's chances.

'Shambles,' said the Great Methodical. 'Young Neil has asked whether it would be possible for you to accompany him on his epic journey to destroy the wicked one. Will you accept his offer?'

Shambles half shrugged, half nodded, and his mouth twisted slightly downwards on one side.

'Was that yes or no?' asked the Great Methodical.

'Sort of yes, if you're really sure you want me,' said Shambles in his whiny voice.

'Sort of yes!' exclaimed Shipshape. 'What sort of answer is that meant to be?'

'Yes, yes, yes. I would like to go. Is that better?' said Shambles directly to Shipshape.

'It'll do,' said Shipshape. 'But you could have said that in the first place.'

'Listen,' said Neil, feeling it was high time he said something. 'If we're going to succeed with our quest, we're all going to have to work together. I chose you both and I would like to travel with you both, but if you're just going to argue, then I'd rather go on my own.'

Neil surprised himself with his words; he'd never before been in a position where he had to tell people what to do. It had always been the other way around. He stared sternly at the two of them as they shuffled their feet sheepishly and wouldn't meet his gaze.

'Well done, Neil, my lad,' said the Great Methodical. 'I can see that the three of you are going to make a great team. Now I want you all to shake hands with one another.'

Shambles and Shipshape shook hands with one another, and then both turned to shake hands with Neil. And Neil realized that he didn't feel embarrassed about it any more.

'Good,' said the Great Methodical. 'Now, you'll need a few more things for your trip, so, let me see,' he said, rummaging through his many pockets. 'Now, where are we?' After much searching, he came up with a miniaturized version of the map of the Thought Domain together with a compass, both of which he handed to Neil. Next he gave him what looked like a bar of toffee.

'Oh, great!' said Neil.

'Now, this is no ordinary toffee,' said the Great Methodical. 'It is Food for Thought. You should nibble a little of it if you are running short of ideas. But on no account should you consume too much of the sweetmeat,' he added pompously, 'as this could lead to a brainstorm.'

Then, out of his inside pocket he took a small furry animal. It was a silver-grey colour with tiny black eyes and a little stubby tail.

'Aaah,' said Neil.

'Ugh!' said Shambles. 'A rat.'

'It's not a rat,' said Neil. 'Rats have long scaly tails.'

'Well, what is it, then?' demanded Shambles.

'It's an Inkling,' said the Great Methodical, 'and though you think it looks weak and useless now, there may well come a time when this little Inkling will get you out of a very nasty scrape, so guard it well. Here you are, Neil.'

'Thanks,' said Neil, stroking the tiny animal and listening to it purr like a kitten. 'Inkling, Inkling,' he whispered into its pink ears.

'And this,' said the Great Methodical, 'this is perhaps the most important thing you must take with you, so guard it very carefully.'

Neil put the Inkling away and held out his hand. The Great Methodical placed a small, hard, brown object in his palm.

'That is the Seed of an Idea,' said the Great Methodical. 'The type of idea which grows from it will depend on you, so use it wisely.'

'I'll try,' said Neil, wrapping the tiny seed up carefully in his handkerchief and putting it into his blazer pocket.

'How many more things have we got to carry?' complained Shambles.

'That seed's really going to weigh us down, isn't it?' said Shipshape sarcastically.

'It all adds up,' said Shambles peevishly. 'And anyway, it's not just the weight. We'll need our hands free if we're going to stand a chance of defeating the evil Gander, won't we?'

'True, true, true,' said the Great Methodical, attempting to smooth over the situation. 'Here,' he said, retrieving a small canvas bag from somewhere inside his jacket. 'Put all your bits and bobs in this, Neil.'

'Now, there's just one more thing,' he continued as Neil swung the strap of the satchel over his neck. 'None of us knows precisely what lies in Chaos, but you must remember that nothing there is rational, and what is more . . .'

'Hang on a minute,' said Shambles. 'I thought that anything or anybody that went into Chaos couldn't come out again. You surely don't expect us to sacrifice ourselves, do you?'

'I was *not* talking to you,' said the Great Methodical angrily. 'I'm getting somewhat tired of your constant interruptions, Shambles!'

'Hear! Hear!' agreed Shipshape.

'I realize that *you* couldn't return. I was directing my comments to Neil, who, as a human child, *can* return.'

Neil watched enviously as pure relief spread all over Shambles's face.

'I don't expect anyone to sacrifice themselves,' continued the Great Methodical, noticing the worry in Neil's eyes and thoughts. 'You'll be fine,' he said, patting Neil on the back. 'You'll simply need a key to get out again. That much is perhaps obvious, but more I cannot say. Until you're *sure* you have it though, Neil, don't go in! As I was saying,' he continued, 'as Chaos is so unpredictable, there is little I can give you to combat the effects, except this.' He gave Neil a small glass disc. 'It will help to keep things in proper perspective,' he explained.

'Is that it?' said Shambles.

'I think so,' said the Great Methodical. 'Just remember these three things: SEEING ISN'T BELIEVING; NOTHING IS WHAT IT SEEMS; and IF YOU THINK SOMETHING IS DANGEROUS, IT WILL BE!'

The three of them nodded, although none of them really knew what the Great Methodical was trying to say.

'And so, dear friends,' said the Great Methodical, 'I think that is just about all I have to say. It remains for me only to bid you all farewell and to wish you all the success in the world.'

It was an emotional moment, and as they all climbed into the little car, Neil noticed that he wasn't the only one with tears in his eyes. Shambles sat in the driver's seat and set off as Neil and Shipshape turned to wave to the others, who were all eagerly calling out encouraging things like 'good luck' and 'come back safe and sound' and 'see you soon!'

Neil wondered just how soon they would all meet up again, if at all. But at least the adventure had got underway. He felt in such high spirits that he couldn't contain himself any more, and as the Great Methodical and the others got smaller and smaller, he let out a loud whoop of excitement.

'Off at last!' he shouted.

'Yeah, at last,' said Shambles. 'Away from the tedium of working for the Great Big Boring Old Windbag!' he added, pushing his foot down on the accelerator.

'Don't you like him, then?' said Neil.

'It's not a case of liking,' added Shipshape. 'It's just that everything here is so dull! That's why I was so glad that you picked me. *Anything* for a change!'

'Order, Order, Order!' said Shambles. 'It's not surprising that the Gander had such a massive and swift impact. At least it offered something different.'

'What did the Gander actually do, then?' asked Neil.

'Not much,' said Shambles. 'It just suggested that things could be much better if we changed the way men and women thought, so we popped some of the Gander's thoughts in their Thought Boxes. By the time we realized it was a trick and life was getting even worse, the consequences in the world had become enormous.'

'A world war,' said Shipshape.

'So all the negative thoughts had to be weeded out of the Thought Boxes and banished,' said Shambles.

'But the trouble is, you can never destroy a thought once it has been conceived,' said Shipshape, 'and so all the trouble has started up again.'

'And it's still boring here,' said Shambles, 'so the same thing will probably happen all over again.'

'Yeah. Shambles is right, I'm afraid,' said Shipshape. 'It *is* dull here. It's because the Great Methodical wants to be able to keep a check on everything the whole time, so it's all got to be as simple and uncluttered as possible.'

Neil looked around at the expanse of nothingness: simply mile after mile of Thought Boxes disappearing into the distance. Even the sky, if you could call it that, was uninteresting – just a dull, grey, endless area with no colour, no clouds, no sun.

'You could do with some trees and hills, and maybe a couple of lakes, and some birds,' said Neil.

'It would be a start,' said Shambles. 'It's time the Great Methodical realized that too much order isn't good for anyone!'

Neil thought about what Shambles had just said, and it began to occur to him that if he was going to be able to destroy the evil Gander for ever, it would only be possible if some changes came to the Thought Domain itself. Order can never be imposed against its will. Without those changes, the Domain would be open to attacks from Chaos time and time again.

'But I'm jumping the gun a little,' he warned himself. 'First, we've got to get rid of the immediate danger, and that means destroying the Gander once and for all!'

Chapter 4
Thoughtless Accidents

The knowledge that something had at last got underway was enough to raise the spirits of the three occupants of the car. Shipshape started to sing a song she was making up as she went along, and as the others learnt the words they joined in. Even the Inkling let out an occasional squeak from inside Neil's satchel.

Oh, Oh, Oh, evil Gander beware,
We're coming to cook your goose.
We'll pluck your feathers out one by one
And stick your head through a noose.
With a parry and a thrust and a sharp back-hander,
What's sauce for the goose is sauce for the Gander.

Oh, Oh, Oh, wicked Gander watch out!
We've heard enough of your lies.
We'll pull your gizzard inside out
And turn you into game pies.
With a parry and a thrust and a sharp back-hander,
What's sauce for the goose is sauce for the Gander.

As they repeated their battle-song over and over, the singing became louder and more raucous. Neil imagined himself as the little avenger who would destroy the big baddy, just as in all the stories he had read and all the films he had seen. He was David coming to slay the giant Goliath armed only with a sling. He was St George riding a great white steed, dressed in shining armour and carrying only a small shield and tiny sword as he rode into valiant battle with the monstrous fire-breathing dragon. He was young Jack who climbed to the top of the magic beanstalks to rid the world of the man-eating ogre who lived there. He could hardly wait to find out what form his own opponent would take as, full of confidence and curiosity, he sped on towards his unknown destiny.

'Hello there!' came a voice, and Neil looked round to see a small car travelling parallel to them, five Thought Boxes away.

'Hello!' called Shipshape. 'What are you up to, Sheera?'

'The usual,' she called back. 'We can't all go off on quests, you know. Some of us still have to shift the old thoughts away from their boxes.'

'I thought that everything was already blocked up,' said Neil to Shambles.

'Well, the Ways of Thinking are blocked now,' he said, 'but the Thought Box area is still largely clear, so we're still moving the thoughts as near to Chaos as we can. Although, to be honest, we know that after they have been dumped off, most of them just stay put, too frightened to complete their journey.'

'Good luck to you all,' called Sheera as she stopped to weed out some of the superfluous thoughts of an overflowing Thought Box.

'See you soon!' called Shipshape. 'I hope,' she added under her breath.

'Hey,' said Neil. 'That's not the attitude. Of course we'll be back soon.'

'Such enthusiasm and faith,' said Shambles. 'I remember I was young once.'

'You old fogey,' laughed Shipshape. 'You were never young.'

Neil looked at the pair of them. He liked both Shipshape

and Shambles, even though they were so different. Shipshape was a little taller than Neil, though slimmer. Her eyes were blue and smiley; her hair was thick and fair. It was her voice that Neil particularly liked: it was soft and clear and sounded as though she was just about to laugh the whole time. Full of energy, even as they were driving along, Shipshape was drumming out the beat of their song on the dashboard the whole time.

Shambles couldn't have been much more of an opposite. He was thin and nervy, his fingers constantly fiddling with imaginary threads of cotton and picking at specks of dirt even while driving. His green eyes darted around as though he was convinced something was about to leap out at him at any moment. Unlike Shipshape he seemed continuously anxious. Neil could only hope that their differences wouldn't lead to any difficulties. Hopefully Shipshape's enthusiasm and spontaneity coupled with Shambles's caution and logic would lead to a good balance.

And on they drove. On and on and on, through the monotonous order of the countless rows of Thought Boxes.

'It makes you wonder what they've got to think about,' said Shipshape. 'All those millions of people, each with their own private thoughts.'

'And I suppose that a lot of those thoughts must repeat each other,' said Neil.

'You're right there,' said Shambles. 'Quite a boring lot you are, on the whole. Half of the world spends its time thinking about how to get hold of what it hasn't got, and the other half spends its time thinking about keeping what it has got. Pathetic.'

'That's not a very nice thing to say,' said Shipshape.

'Well, a lot of people aren't very nice.' said Shambles. 'Or rather, their thoughts aren't. I suppose that they're all I'm qualified to talk about.'

'You mean that people are greedy?' asked Neil, trying to make sense of Shambles's criticism.

'Put it this way,' said Shambles. 'Sometimes I feel very

tempted to take some of the thoughts of the hungry people in the world and put them into the Thought Boxes of all those who think about nothing other than making more and more money.'

'But we're not allowed to do that, of course,' said Shipshape.

'No,' said Shambles bitterly. 'It wouldn't do for rich people to have to think about what it's like being poor.'

Neil thought of what his mother used to say when he left food on his plate: 'Think of all the poor children in the world who can't afford a nice meal and be grateful for the food in front of you!' And he told Shambles what she'd say.

'Well, I suppose it's a start,' said Shambles, 'but I don't think you really understand what I'm saying. I'll show you,' he said, slowing the car down.

'No!' said Shipshape. 'We haven't got time to stop and go sightseeing.'

'It won't take a minute,' said Shambles.

'That's not the point,' persisted Shipshape. 'We've got a job to do and we ought to get it completed as soon as possible and . . .'

'Listen,' said Shambles calmly. 'You're forgetting how powerful the evil Gander has shown itself to be. Neil *must* understand just how rigidly fixed people's thoughts are, so that he knows what he's up against.'

'Well, perhaps you're right,' said Shipshape reluctantly. 'But let's make the stop as quick as possible. Okay?'

'Okay,' said Shambles.

Neil looked at Shipshape. He had the feeling that she wasn't just concerned with the time but was also trying to protect him from something. But Neil wanted to find out as much as he could about the way people think. He didn't want to be 'protected' from grown-ups' answers any more.

They all climbed out of the car and looked down into some of the adjacent boxes. The sprawling mass of thoughts all jockeying for position fascinated Neil.

'I can hardly believe that this is all going on inside me as well,' said Neil to Shipshape.

'It does look a bit chaotic,' agreed Shipshape.

'Hey, come over here, you two,' called Shambles. 'This is a pretty good example,' he said.

Neil looked down into the half-filled box.

'What do you think?' asked Shambles.

Neil remembered the Thought Boxes that the Great Methodical had shown him.

'Well,' he said. 'It must belong to a boy or girl.'

'Why do you think that?' asked Shambles.

'Because it's only half full,' said Neil. 'The person can't have had time to fill the box up yet.'

'Look more carefully,' said Shambles.

Neil was still keen to discover everything there was to know about the Thought Domain, but something about Shambles's voice made him wary. He knelt down and looked into the box. The thoughts weren't as active as others he'd seen. Most of them were of food, but not the sort of food he was used to. There were no pork chops, no fish and chips, no roast beef and Yorkshire pudding followed by apple pie and custard. Instead, he saw a small portion of rice steaming in a wooden bowl. He caught sight of a copper urn filled with water. He saw thoughts of bundles of firewood. He saw a small but brightly shining thought of an emerald green paddy-field with rice swaying in the wind and an ox ploughing the earth. He saw a smaller drab thought of a child with twisted legs lying in a wooden cot. And there were other thoughts that Neil was unable to identify; songs sung in a language he didn't recognize.

'What does it all mean?' asked Neil.

'You can tell a lot from a person's thoughts,' said Shambles. 'For a start, we know that this person is poor, because the main thought is food, but, as you can see, only of a little rice. Not a very good diet.'

'And can you tell where the person is from?' asked Neil.

'Yes,' said Shambles. 'Listen to the little thought of a song. Can you hear it?'

Neil listened carefully to the slow and repetitive tune, but he couldn't make out the words at all.

'The singing is in Nepalese,' said Shipshape. 'I think,' she added.

'That's right,' said Shambles. 'And do you know where Nepal is, Neil?'

Neil shook his head.

'What's the highest mountain in the world?' asked Shambles, out of the blue.

'Mount Everest,' said Neil promptly. 'Twenty-nine thousand and twenty-eight feet high and first climbed by Sir Edmund Hillary and Sherpa Tenzing Norgay on 29 May 1953.'

Shipshape smiled and patted Neil on the back.

'Well done!' she said.

'That's certainly well and truly fixed in your Thought Box,' said Shambles. 'Well, Mount Everest is on the northern border of Nepal.'

'Oh,' said Neil.

'It's odd how limited our knowledge can be, isn't it?' said Shambles. And Neil had to agree. He looked down into the Thought Box again. There was something he didn't really understand.

'Why isn't there a picture of Mount Everest in with all those thoughts,' he asked, 'if it's in their country?'

'Because it isn't important for that person,' said Shambles. 'Because the person hasn't got time to fill his or her head with facts about highest mountains and men who had the time and money to climb them!'

'But it *is* important, isn't it?' said Neil, feeling rather confused. At school everyone seemed to think that highest mountains, longest rivers, dates of battles and the names of kings and queens were the most important things in the world to know. 'What is important, then?' asked Neil.

'To this person,' said Shambles, 'and I should think it is a woman, the essentials are important.'

'Why's that pot essential, then?' he asked, pointing at the thought of the copper urn.

'It's for water,' said Shambles. 'In Nepal very few people have tap-water in their houses.'

'What do they do, then?' asked Neil, who was hardly able to believe that any house wouldn't have taps with hot and cold water.

'Every day,' said Shambles patiently, 'the women of the families take their pots and walk miles to a well to draw water, and then, with the heavy pot balanced against their hips, they walk the same number of miles back.'

He'd never thought about it before, but for the first time it occurred to Neil that he was quite lucky having a bathroom full of as much water as he needed.

'Of course,' continued Shambles, 'they only have to do this in the dry months. In the winter they can take the snow and melt it. But to do that they have to make a fire first, and that,' he added, 'is why the thought of the firewood is there. Unfortunately, they seldom live near woods and so once again it takes hours to collect enough to last a whole day. It has to go a long way, as it's used for warming their houses, cooking their food and melting the snow.'

'So they don't have electricity or gas?' said Neil.

'No, Neil, they don't,' said Shambles.

Neil hesitated for a moment. He was curious about the woman's thoughts and keen to find out more, but almost frightened of asking any more questions. It was all so strangely different.

'And the thought of the small child there?' he said quietly.

'You see the legs,' said Shambles. 'He's suffering from rickets.'

'What are they?' said Neil.

'*It*'s a disease which affects the bones if people don't get enough Vitamin D,' explained Shambles. 'And you get Vitamin D from food like egg-yolks and cod-liver oil, but not from rice.'

'But look at the bright green field there,' said Neil. 'Why don't they sell some of the extra rice and buy other food with the money?'

Neil noticed that Shipshape had turned away sadly. She had been looking more and more miserable as Shambles had been explaining and Neil wondered if something he had said had upset her.

'What do you notice about that particular thought?' asked Shambles.

'It's really bright and clear and sparkling,' said Neil, 'especially compared with all the others.'

'The reason it's so bright,' said Shambles, 'is that it isn't true. The everyday thoughts of food, warmth, water, caring for her sick son are all drab and colourless. Only the one thought stands out, and that's because it isn't a part of her life. It is a wishful hope. She cannot give up the notion that one day the barren patch of land she owns will suddenly yield a rich crop of rice that will solve all her problems. But at this moment it is still nothing more than a dream twinkling to her from a never-never future.'

Neil had the feeling he was going to cry.

'It's not fair,' he said, feeling all hot and angry, trying to swallow back the painful lump in the back of his throat. 'It's just not fair.'

'True,' said Shambles. 'It isn't fair, an accident of birth, but it's the way over half the people of the world have to live.'

And then Neil did start to cry. He tried to wipe them away, but the big, warm, wet tears flowed round his fingers and down his burning cheeks.

'Are you, happy now?' said Shipshape to Shambles angrily. 'Is that what you wanted?' She put her arms round Neil and gave him a big hug. 'Come on, Neil,' she said, 'take my hankie and blow your nose.'

'I didn't know,' said Neil.

'Hey,' said Shipshape, gently lifting a teardrop off Neil's chin, 'you're leaking!'

'I just didn't know,' Neil repeated.

'That's why I'd like to take some of those thoughts,' said Shambles, 'and show them to the well-off people. But I didn't mean to upset you like that,' he added quietly.

'It's not your fault,' said Neil. 'I'm glad you showed me. There's no hope of any change before I get all the thoughts moving again, is there?'

'There certainly isn't,' said Shambles.

'Well, we'd better get a move on, then,' said Shipshape. 'Come on, chop-chop, back to the car and let's get going again. We've spent more than enough time here.'

As they walked back to the car, Neil looked down into every Thought Box he passed. Some were as empty and desperate as the Nepalese woman's had been. Some were full of books, pieces of music and famous paintings. Some were full of nonsense like thoughts of faster cars, bigger stereo systems and always more money: pounds, dollars, yen, marks, francs . . . And some, Neil noticed with a shock, were full of the dazzlingly bright thoughts, so brilliant that he had to look away: heads full of nothing but dreams.

'I think I'd better drive for a while,' said Shipshape when they got to the car.

'Why?' asked Shambles.

'We're behind schedule,' said Shipshape.

'Oh, I see, and you don't think I drive fast enough,' said Shambles.

'Well, I did think of getting out and walking,' said Shipshape. 'It might have been a bit faster.'

'More haste, less speed,' said Shambles. 'You'd have us crash.'

'All I'm saying is that I was a little surprised when that snail went racing past us!' said Shipshape.

'You're an idiot,' said Shambles. 'Do you know that? A real idiot!'

'But at least I'm not a slow idiot!' said Shipshape.

'Stop it, both of you,' shouted Neil crossly. 'As you can't decide, I'll toss a coin. Heads or tails?' he called.

'HEADS!' shouted Shipshape and Shambles together.

'Heads or tails?' Neil called out again.

'TAILS!' they both yelled.

'This is hopeless,' said Neil. 'Third time lucky. Heads or tails?'

'TAILS!' they called in unison.

'Good grief!' said Neil. 'Decide which one of you is going to call.'

'How do we do that?' asked Shipshape.

'Let's toss for it,' said Shambles.

'NO!' said Neil, 'Shambles, *you* are heads; Shipshape, *you* are tails.'

He spun the coin into the air, caught it on his upturned palm and slapped it down on the back of his other hand.

'Heads,' he said. 'Right, Shambles continues to drive. And Shipshape can take over after the next stop.'

Shambles was driving, a little faster perhaps, but certainly not racing. Shipshape was demonstrating her irritation by strumming her fingers on the side of the car and sighing noisily. Neil was wondering whether he hadn't been a bit *too* bossy, when suddenly everything and everyone was thrown into complete confusion. There was a blur of movement in front of the car, followed by a dull thud and a little whimpering cry. Shambles slammed on the brakes and sent the car spinning round and round, desperately near the edges of the Thought Boxes.

'Mustn't drop into a Thought Box!' thought Neil, clutching hold of his seat.

Shipshape was shouting, 'You idiot, you blithering imbecile, you crazy, dimwitted heap of brainless slurry!' to no one in particular.

And Neil was thinking: 'Stop. Stop! STOP!' He wished that everything would stop: the car spinning, Shipshape shouting, the wheels skidding. And then, as suddenly as it had all begun, his wish came true and the car, Shipshape, the wheels all came to a halt.

'What on earth . . . ?' said Shipshape.

Neil opened his eyes cautiously and peered around him. The first thing he saw was Shambles slumped over the steering wheel. His heart missed a beat.

'Shambles!' he shrieked, tugging at his shoulders.

'He's all right,' said Shipshape. 'Aren't you?'

'Eenghmmmphh,' was all Shambles could answer as he leant back in his seat.

'Did you bang your head?' asked Neil.

'No,' said Shambles. 'It wasn't my head I hit.'

'No! It was me!' came a whiny voice from behind the car.

All three of the occupants leapt out of their car and ran to the back to inspect just what had spoken. There, lying on the ground with its wing twisted round, was a large white bird.

Neil, Shambles and Shipshape all looked at one another. Then they looked back at the bird. Then back at each other. Neil wondered whether they'd hit one of the evil Gander's cohorts, or perhaps even – but no, they couldn't have had such incredible luck. This couldn't actually be the Gander itself, could it? Wounded and vulnerable because of a chance road accident?

'What are you dolts gawping at?' snapped the bird.

'You don't think this could be one of the Gander's wicked geese, do you?' Neil whispered to Shipshape.

The bird evidently had good ears.

'Of course I'm not a goose, you fools!' it screamed. 'I'm a duck. A duck! And thanks to your ridiculous carelessness whilst in charge of a motor vehicle, a lame duck at that.'

It tried to stand up, wobbled pathetically and fell down again.

'You sure you're not a goose?' said Shambles, looking suspiciously at the bird. 'You look too big to be a duck to me.'

'Listen!' said the duck and let out a bellowing QUACK. 'Ever heard a goose making a noise like that?'

'Geese hiss,' said Neil to Shambles.

'Hiss,' Shambles instructed the bird.

'Hiss?' said the duck. 'What do you think I am? A gas leak?'

'Stop playing for time,' said Shambles. 'Hiss.'

The bird tried its best, but all three of them had to admit that the noise it produced was more of a quack than a hiss.

'Okay,' said Shambles. 'So you're a duck. But what were you doing in the middle of the road like that? I might have killed you.'

'You might have killed us, more importantly!' said Shipshape.

The duck lowered its voice. 'That might have been better, compared with the alternative,' it said mysteriously.

'Explain yourself, duck,' said Shipshape.

'There was . . .' began the duck, and shuddered at the memory. 'There was so much . . . horror. It was . . . all the most terrifying things you could ever imagine, suddenly there . . . threatening to destroy us . . .'

Neil felt cold shivers running up and down his spine. He could sense panic creeping up on him.

'What do you mean?' he said.

The duck turned to him. 'How should I explain?' It paused. 'What's the most frightened you've ever been?'

Neil thought back. Once, he had been in the park and an enormous Alsatian had come rushing towards him with its mouth snarling, saliva dripping from its razor-sharp teeth. Or even more frightening was the time when he'd been on the balcony when the window had accidentally closed. He had tried to climb along the ledge when suddenly fear had grabbed him and he couldn't move. The ground below him dropped thousands of feet away. He was so dizzy that he couldn't look down, and he couldn't move and he couldn't close his eyes. His legs turned to jelly and he just kept thinking, please let this be over. No, there was another time. Even more terrifying.

'I was in a room,' he said, 'a strange room in a big hotel. It was the first day of our holidays and I couldn't sleep properly. I was so excited. I finally fell asleep and had this horrible nightmare. The whole of my class went on this school trip, but it was all just a trick and this massive evil person threw us all into a giant furnace. I could see the flames flickering, and it got hotter and hotter. And then I screamed and screamed. There wasn't a fire at all. It was just the sun coming through the leaves. But in that dream, that was the most frightened I've ever been.'

'Well,' said the duck slowly. 'It was just like that, only much, much, *much* worse. We had to get away from the screaming terror which seemed to be inside us, but there was no escape!'

'*There* you are!' came a voice.

'Sheera,' said Shipshape. 'We meet again.'

'What a day,' said Sheera. 'It takes such a long time to collect your thoughts when they've taken fright.'

'What happened?' asked Shipshape.

'It was partly my own fault,' said Sheera. 'I should have taken more notice of the tell-tale signs. I felt goose-pimples all down my arms but put them down to the chilly wind. I should have realized that they were because of the nearness of the Gander or its wicked geese.'

Neil paid careful attention. It was the nearest to an encounter he'd had with the evil one so far.

'Are they still around somewhere?' he asked, looking over his shoulder nervously.

'No,' said Sheera. 'You'd certainly know if they were. The Gander and its geese never stay long in one place. They don't need to,' she added. 'They threw everything into turmoil and then retreat.'

'And so much terror can be caused in a split second!' said Neil, and swallowed anxiously.

'I'm worried,' said Shambles.

'You're always worried,' said Shipshape.

'I mean it,' said Shambles. 'This is the furthest into the Thought Domain that the wicked Gander has ever dared to come. We're less than a day away from the Memory Bank, which means that an attack could happen any time now. If they get to the Memory Bank, everything that men and women have ever thought will be lost for ever. This is all much, much more serious than I thought. Come on, we haven't got a minute to lose.'

Sheera picked up the thought of the duck and placed it back in her cart.

'If you're not successful,' said Sheera, 'this could well be the last trip to the Ways of Thinking I'll ever make.'

'We'll do our best!' said Neil.

'You're a very brave boy,' said the duck. 'And I've got one very important piece of advice for you,' it shouted out as Sheera started to drive away. 'NEVER TAKE ANYTHING FOR GRANTED!!'

'I wonder what that means?' said Neil.

'No time for wondering now,' said Shipshape. 'With the danger so imminent, we really must get a move on . . .'

'Before it's all too late!' said Shambles sombrely.

Chapter 5

Problems with the Foggiest Idea

A long time had passed since the duck had shouted its words of parting advice as Sheera had driven away, but Neil, Shipshape and Shambles were still standing on the road by their car. They hadn't run out of petrol. They hadn't got a flat tyre. In fact, the accident hadn't damaged the car at all. It was in perfect working order and only waiting for the ignition key to be turned. Similarly, its three intrepid occupants, and even the Inkling, were ready and raring to go. Yet none of them made a move.

'It's all *your* fault,' said Shambles to Neil.

'Your blaming him like that isn't going to help us much,' said Shipshape. 'And anyway, if you hadn't overreacted to that duck you wouldn't have lost control of the car.'

'Lost control!' exclaimed Shambles indignantly. 'It was a miracle that I managed to keep the car on the road at all.'

'You've got to take some of the blame, all the same,' persisted Shipshape. 'You should have seen the duck earlier.'

'Absolute rubbish!' shouted Shambles, who was getting more and more irate. 'If he'd used his brain we wouldn't be in the mess we're in now.'

'You're *so* pig-headed!' said Shipshape, also beginning to raise her voice.

'Well, it's true. It's a fact. And that's that!' said Shambles.

Neil remained silent. He couldn't bring himself to say anything because he agreed with Shambles. He thought it *was* his fault.

What had happened was this. When Shambles slammed the brakes on, two things occurred. The car went into an almost uncontrollable spin and the Inkling, in its panic, bit into the nearest object it could find. On their own, neither event would have been that important, but happening together the result was disastrous. By the time the car had come to a standstill, none of them knew which way it was facing, and as the expanse of Thought Boxes looked the same in every direction, they got no clues from looking around them. This shouldn't have been a problem, but when they came to use the compass they found that it was this that the Inkling had sunk its teeth into. The outer casing was buckled, the needle bent. In short, the compass had been made totally useless. It was a one in a million chance that such a sequence of events should take place, but take place it had, and now they were all well and truly stuck.

'If only I hadn't put them both in my satchel,' said Neil quietly.

'Yes, if only,' said Shambles sarcastically.

'Well, it's happened now,' said Shipshape comfortingly. 'It was unfortunate, but it's not the end of the world.'

'It could be!' said Shambles. 'Or had you forgotten why we're here?'

'What a stupid thing to say!' shouted Neil, finally losing his temper with Shambles's smug replies. 'Do you really think I could forget that?'

'Who knows?' said Shambles.

'Look!' said Neil. 'I've said it was my fault, what more do you want? *You're* the brainy one. *You* get us out of here.'

Shambles fell silent and turned away sulkily.

'And please don't start sulking. It doesn't help!' said

Neil, a comment guaranteed to make Shambles sulk all the more.

Neil felt out of his depth. He didn't want to argue with anyone. He just wanted to get the quest over with so that he could go home. Everything had suddenly become very big and he felt like a very small boy indeed. His shoulders were simply not wide enough for the amount of responsibility which had been heaped upon them. Why had he been chosen anyway? Surely there were others who could have carried out the task much better.

'I've failed. I've failed,' he muttered miserably under his breath. And he fought back the waves of panic which kept threatening to overwhelm him completely.

'I just refuse to believe that we're done for,' said Shipshape in her typically optimistic way. 'What about the Inkling? The Great Methodical said it would be invaluable. Perhaps he meant in this sort of situation.'

Influenced by Shipshape's contagious enthusiasm, Neil took the sleeping Inkling out of his satchel and prodded it. But apart from a little high-pitched squeak it made no sound.

'Be nicer to it,' suggested Shipshape.

So Neil stroked it under its chin and listened carefully, but the little animal only purred and then went back to sleep again.

'Stupid, useless rodent!' said Shambles. 'The Great Methodical must have meant valueless, not invaluable!'

They looked at the map again. Their destination was to the north of the Thought Domain, but looking around there was no way they could work out which way north was. It all looked the same.

'If only there was a sun here,' said Neil, as it occurred to him once again how characterless it all was. 'Travellers lost in the desert can find their way by following the sun. Or the stars. But then, it never seems to get dark here.'

'How can it?' said Shipshape. 'Someone somewhere on

earth is always thinking, so it's a constant operation here to keep all those thoughts in order.'

'Oh,' said Neil, and wondered when he'd have the chance to get any sleep. But he didn't ask. Shambles already thought he was stupid. He didn't want him to think he was lazy as well.

And so they stood there, looking around them hopelessly, wondering what on earth they could do. Neil looked at Shipshape and Shambles, but couldn't begin to guess what was going on inside their heads. For himself, he kept thinking of possible ways out of their predicament, but every path led to a dead-end. And the more hopeless the situation seemed to be, the more difficult it became for Neil to control his rising panic.

'Stay calm. Breathe deeply and count to ten,' he instructed himself. 'One – two – three – what on earth are we going to do? No compass, a useless map. This is absolutely . . . four – five – I've failed! It's all my fault! Six – seven – eight – don't panic, don't panic, it'll be all right . . .' But the trouble was that Neil simply didn't believe his own thoughts. It wasn't all right at all. In fact, it had all gone wrong. Terribly wrong.

'Let's go through the options open to us,' said Shipshape.

'What's the point?' said Neil miserably.

'Stop it!' said Shipshape. 'It's bad enough having to put up with Shambles sulking all the time. If you start as well, I'm going home.'

'And which direction might home be in?' said Shambles. 'If we knew that, we would know which direction the Pillars of Reason and Chaos were in.'

'Now, the first option, as I see it, is as follows,' said Shipshape, ignoring Shambles. 'We could wait here until someone on routine Thought Box patrol comes past, but that could be too long a wait. We could split up and take three of the four possible roads, but not only could we all miss the right one, but alone we would be too weak against the wicked Gander anyway, so that's out too.'

In the end they decided to abandon the logical methods of solving the problem and gave themselves up to luck. After all, it couldn't make things any worse. And maybe, just maybe, introducing a little random luck into the ordered life of the Thought Domain might just work.

What they did was to label the roads A, B, C and D. Then they all took a piece of paper and wrote on it the road they thought they should take. Then they compared results. The first time Neil had written C, Shambles A and Shipshape D. The second time Neil wrote C, Shambles D and Shipshape B. The third time Neil wrote A, Shambles wrote B and Shipshape wrote D. And so it went on. Sometimes two of them got the same letter, but they had already decided that it would have to be a unanimous decision before they would take the road. It wasn't until the eighty-seventh attempt (Shambles had been counting!) that they all wrote the same letter down, and so it was the road marked D that they finally took.

Although they were possibly taking the wrong road, all three of them felt instantly happier the moment they got moving again. With Shambles and Neil happily agreeing about the ways the Great Methodical should relax his rules in the Thought Domain and Shipshape sitting at the wheel singing a nonsense song about the thoughts of sheep counting humans in an effort to fall asleep, the atmosphere was altogether better.

One more man jumped through the hoop,
One more woman looped the loop,
Down the rope and round the pulley,
Woolly bully, woolly bully.

Babes are born and sheep are shorn,
I'll never get to sleep till dawn,
People are hairy, sheep are woolly,
Woolly bully, woolly bully.

Zzzzzzzzzzzzzzzz!!

'Do you know what?' said Neil, looking puzzled.

'What?' said Shambles.

'I think that Shipshape's song must be actually making me fall asleep,' he said.

'She doesn't sing *that* well,' said Shambles. 'It sounds more like a sea-shanty than a lullaby.'

'Well, my eyes seem to be going all funny,' said Neil, squinting into the distance.

'It definitely doesn't seem to be as clear as it was,' Shipshape agreed.

'You must need glasses,' said Shambles. 'I always knew that *your* model of Thought Domain helper must have faults. Efficient, but half-blind,' he added.

But there really was something happening. Neil wasn't falling asleep and Shipshape didn't need glasses. Whereas the view had been clear and crisp right down to the horizon only a few moments earlier, it was now distinctly fuzzy. The Thought Boxes were disappearing into a haze which was rapidly approaching the car.

'What is it?' said Neil. 'I didn't think you had weather here.'

'We don't,' said Shipshape and Shambles simultaneously. The next instant, the car and its three hapless occupants were enveloped by a thick and swirling fog.

'Well, what's this then?' spluttered Neil as the fog coiled into his nostrils and filled his mouth.

'Oh no!' said Shambles.

'Surely we couldn't be that unlucky,' said Shipshape.

'What *is* it?' asked Neil, feeling apprehensive.

'I have the horrible feeling . . .' began Shipshape.

'. . . though we could be wrong . . .' continued Shambles.

'. . . but that's very unlikely . . .' said Shipshape.

'. . . that . . .' they said together.

'YES?' said Neil.

'It's the foggiest idea.'

The words sounded familiar to Neil, but somehow not quite right.

'What's that?' he asked.

'What does your mother say when you ask her one of your difficult questions?' asked Shambles.

'"Get on with your breakfast", usually,' said Neil.

'When you're not eating breakfast, then,' said Shambles impatiently.

'"Ask me later",' he suggested.

'Oh, Neil,' said Shambles, sounding irritated. 'When she's got time and no excuse not to answer, what does she say if you ask her a *really* complicated question like . . . like . . .'

'Like "How high is the sky?"' said Shipshape helpfully.

It suddenly clicked! 'She'd say, "I haven't the foggiest idea",' he said slowly.

'And haven't you ever wondered what the foggiest idea might be?' asked Shambles.

''Coz now you know,' said Shipshape. 'We're right in the middle of the foggiest idea now.'

'And if we're not careful, in a great deal of trouble too,' said Shambles seriously.

'But what IS it exactly?' said Neil. He'd always thought it was just a stupid expression, without a proper meaning.

'It's extremely bad news,' said Shipshape, drawing the car to a halt.

By now the fog was so thick that Neil could barely see either of his companions, although they were still sitting right next to him. Driving was completely out of the question, as there was too much of a danger of driving over the side of a Thought Box and into some poor unsuspecting person's thoughts.

'The foggiest idea isn't in fact one idea at all,' explained Shipshape. 'It's a collection of all the confused notions, half-baked theories, ill-conceived plans and flimsy excuses put together.'

'Why aren't they all packed off to Chaos like the rest?' asked Neil.

'It just isn't possible,' said Shambles. 'They're all so

insubstantial that when we try to load them on to carts, they simply fall apart and drift away as fine particles in the air. Gradually, over the centuries, they have formed themselves into this suffocating fog which drifts aimlessly around the entire Domain.'

'Luckily,' said Shipshape, 'it doesn't affect human thought much, although sometimes its presence helps people to understand something intuitively, to grasp a concept quite new to them, that sort of thing.'

'So when people haven't even got *that* tiny idea, they say they haven't even got the foggiest idea,' said Neil.

'Exactly that,' said Shipshape. 'And at this moment, I wish *we* didn't. It's extremely treacherous stuff.'

'If only we hadn't taken this particular road,' said Shambles.

'Oh, don't start all that,' said Neil. 'It's not worth it.'

'Sorry,' said Shambles sheepishly. 'I'm just feeling a bit nervous.'

'Can't we just wait until it passes over?' asked Neil.

'Trouble is,' said Shipshape, 'it's notoriously unpredictable. We could be stuck here for ever.'

'Well, we can't drive,' said Shambles. 'That's definitely out. Far too dangerous.'

'Then the only alternative is to go on foot,' said Shipshape.

'Is that a good idea?' said Neil doubtfully. He was remembering all the warnings he had seen on television telling drivers not to leave their vehicles if they got stuck in bad weather.

'We haven't got any option really,' said Shipshape.

'But we might get lost,' said Neil.

'We are lost,' said Shambles.

'I mean, we might lose each other,' said Neil. 'And if it *does* clear, then we might not be able to find the car again.'

'We need to leave some kind of a trail,' said Shipshape.

'But what?' said Neil. Once again the characterlessness of the Thought Domain was hindering their progress. There were no pebbles they could leave to mark the way; no clumps of grass they could knot; no sticks they could make arrows with.

'Ooh, I think I might have a piece of chalk,' said Shambles, searching through his pockets.

'Found it?' said Shipshape.

'Hang on a m . . . oh, I've just remembered,' he said. 'I lent it to someone in the Memory Bank.'

'Typical,' said Shipshape. 'Any more bright suggestions?'

'Stop bickering!' said Neil. 'I've got an idea.'

It was a peculiar feeling to be standing with eyes open and yet unable to see anything. Neil turned his head to where Shipshape's voice had come from.

'What are you wearing?' he asked.

'T-shirt and dungarees,' said Shipshape.

'Oh yes,' said Neil. 'And you, Shambles?'

'Shirt, trousers and jumper,' said Shambles. 'And they're all torn, I might add,' he said, 'thanks to you.'

'The jumper's ruined, is it?' said Neil.

'Totally,' said Shambles. 'All the wool is coming undone at the elbows.'

'Mmm. That's what I thought,' said Neil. 'Well, in that case, you won't mind us using it, will you?' Shipshape caught on immediately. 'Brilliant idea, Neil. We could unravel it and tie each other to the wool so we won't get lost.'

'Yeah, and I thought we could tie one end to the bumper of the car, so that if it does clear soon, we'll be able to trace our footsteps back.'

'My jumper,' said Shambles.

'Come on,' said Shipshape, 'we all have to make sacrifices.'

'And you *did* say that it was ruined,' said Neil.

'And it isn't cold anyway,' said Shipshape.

'I suppose you won't believe me if I say it's got sentimental value?' said Shambles.

'No,' said Shipshape and Neil together.

'And I suppose I haven't got much choice, have I?' said Shambles.

'No!!' said the other two again.

Shambles reluctantly pulled the jumper off and held it out. Groping around in the fog, Shipshape finally found it and took it.

'Just the job,' she said, pulling at one of the frayed threads of the jumper. Having unpicked the first row, the wool unravelled easily and Shipshape wound it round her hand into a neat little ball.

Neil was still dubious about the whole plan. Abandoning the car seemed a stupid idea to him, but if they were right about the fog remaining, then there wasn't much else they could do. It was so boring stuck in the thick, grey fog that, this being the Thought Domain, time would pass accordingly slowly, and they couldn't afford to waste a precious moment more than was absolutely necessary. Not being able to see made the danger seem even more imminent. Neil suddenly had a horrible and terrifying thought. What if the Gander had somehow gained control over the foggiest idea, and was trying to trap them at that very moment? Perhaps it wasn't such a bad idea to try and get away after all.

Shipshape tied one end of the ball of wool to the bumper of the car and then looped it round their right wrists, linking all three of them together so that none could wander away. They set off into the impenetrable fog. Neil was at the front, Shambles in the middle and Shipshape brought up the rear, slowly releasing the wool as she went.

'Bye bye, jumper,' said Shambles sadly.

And they walked and walked and walked. Keeping to the one straight roadway, they didn't deviate from their chosen path. On they trudged through the oppressive density of the fog. None of them were singing now. Even thinking was too difficult in the swirling confusion of half-ideas. Neil kept trying to concentrate on the task ahead, but time and again he found his mind wandering. Something vague would occur to him but would disappear if he tried to focus his attention on it. He would think he partly remembered what he wasn't even sure he had ever known. It was all too confusing.

Gradually he started to wonder what he was doing, walking blindly along this narrow road tied to a piece of wool. And then he would remember Shipshape or Shambles and his thoughts would come together. But only for a moment. And then his mind would wander off again. It was as though the thick, confusing fog had coiled its way right into his brain, filling his head with its bewildering nothingness.

'Hey! You're going the wrong way, Neil!' came a voice from behind him.

He must have turned off without realizing it and, apart from the voice, he noticed the wool cutting into his wrist.

'Sorry,' said Neil, unsure of himself.

'Are you okay?' asked Shipshape.

'I think so,' said Neil.

They kept walking, and the pain in his wrist was all he could think about. It was like a Chinese burn, and with every swing of his arm, the wool rubbed at it more.

'Stupid stuff,' he thought to himself as he slipped it off.

'Hey, Neil! What are you doing now?' came the voice from behind him again. But this time it didn't mean anything at all to him as he stumbled off into the white fog.

It was so weird not being able to see. If he held his hand to his face, it became just visible about three inches away from his eyes. And he couldn't taste anything. The fog in his mouth had taken away any remainder of his last meal and replaced it with its own blandness. He pinched his arm and it didn't hurt at all. The fog was wrapped around him like a thick but cold blanket, isolating him from everything which he half-remembered should still be there. Occasionally he heard a sound like someone calling, but most of the time it was silent. The fog had stopped his ears up. He shouted into the fog:

'Aaaayeeeee!! Waaaaaayeeeeeeee!!!'

But the noise was dead. He strained to hear an echo, but there was nothing.

Louder, he shouted: 'Eeeeeeeyaaaaaaaa!!!'

But still there was no sound of an echo.

And he had the feeling that he had always been standing in the fog. And he always would be. And, after all, it wasn't that bad. It could go on for ever and ever for all he cared.

Meanwhile, and true to form, Shipshape and Shambles were arguing again. This time it was over whose fault it had been that they had lost Neil. The fact that they couldn't see each other seemed to make their words all the more harsh.

'If you hadn't spun the car in the first place, we might have avoided the fog,' said Shipshape.

'If you hadn't been so keen to go on foot, we might still all be together,' retorted Shambles.

'If you'd taken better care of him, he wouldn't have got lost. After all, you were next to him, you dolt!' said Shipshape.

'And if you'd tied the wool round his wrist a bit better, he wouldn't have been able to slip it off,' said Shambles angrily.

'Eeeeeeeyaaaaii!' came a distant cry.

'What on earth is that?' said Shambles.

'Aaaaaayoooooooeee!' came the sound again.

'There it is again!' said Shambles.

'It must be Neil,' said Shipshape.

'Do you think he's in any trouble?' said Shambles.

'I don't know,' said Shipshape. 'Let's follow the noise and find out.'

Holding on to one another so that they wouldn't end up totally on their own, Shipshape and Shambles followed the strange yowling sound. Ages passed before they saw a shadowy figure a little way in front of them.

'There he is!' said Shambles.

'Thank heavens for that!' said Shipshape, running towards him.

By this time, Neil was completely lost. Try as he might he could not find his echo. It was a shame, but the further he had walked, the less it seemed to matter. All of a sudden, he heard a voice behind him:

'Neil,' it said.

But for Neil himself, the word didn't mean anything. He had forgotten his own name.

'Thank goodness we found you,' said a second voice.

'Thought we'd lost you for good,' said the first one.

The fog was gradually beginning to clear and Neil looked at the two strangers. One was a tall girl with bobbed hair, the other a thin and red-haired man.

'We'll have to act quickly,' said the thin one. 'He can hardly recognize us.'

Neil noticed that they seemed nervous about something, but didn't know what. He didn't react as the taller one took his satchel away from him and rummaged through it.

'There it is.'

'How much should we give him?'

'Just try one square to start with.'

Neil watched motionless as they took the toffee-like slab and snapped off a portion. He didn't resist as they slipped it into his mouth. On tasting the sweet creaminess, he started chewing automatically. The taste was delicious; it seemed to fill his whole body, making him tingle from head to toe. Surely nothing he had ever eaten had ever tasted so fantastic. He chewed greedily and swallowed the sticky lump.

'Who am I?' said the thin man.

'Search me!' said Neil. He looked through the clearing fog at the man. There was definitely something familiar about that thin red hair and the pained expression on his face, but no name would come.

'One more square?' suggested the girl.

'Okay.'

This time Neil took the square himself and closed his eyes in pleasure as the delectable taste pumped its way round his entire body again. When he opened his eyes he saw Shipshape and Shambles standing in front of him, looking anxious.

'Hello?' they said tentatively.

'Hello!' said Neil.

'Who are we?' asked Shambles.

'Pardon?' said Neil.

'What are our names?' asked Shipshape, slowly and clearly.

'Shipshape and Shambles, of course,' said Neil.

They both grinned.

'Welcome back, Neil,' they said. 'Welcome back.'

Neil looked around. He felt a twinge of pain around his wrist. Where had the piece of wool gone? The last thing he remembered was walking along the road tied to the other two, and now . . .

'What happened?' he asked.

'You lost your senses,' said Shambles. 'It's very common the first time someone is confronted by the foggiest idea.'

'It's so confusing that you even forget who you are,' said Shipshape. 'It's as if you stop existing.'

'It was lucky I didn't get too far, then,' said Neil.

'Didn't get too far?' exclaimed Shipshape and Shambles together.

'We've been following you for what seems like days,' said Shipshape.

'How did you manage that, then,' asked Neil, 'with the fog and everything?'

'That was easy,' said Shipshape. 'Luckily, you kept calling out.'

'It sounded almost like howling,' said Shambles.

Neil had a vague memory. 'I think I was trying to find my echo,' he said.

'Well, it's just as well,' said Shipshape. 'Otherwise, we *would* have lost you.'

'And how did you bring back my memory?' he asked.

'It wasn't exactly your memory which had gone,' explained Shambles. 'More your understanding. Because your senses had gone, your brain was being starved, so quite simply we fed it.'

'With Food for Thought,' said Shipshape.

'Oh, that toffee the Great Methodical gave me,' said Neil.

'Precisely,' said Shambles.

'It was delicious,' said Neil. 'Shall we finish it up?'

'You've had enough,' said Shambles.

'If you have too much,' said Shipshape, 'your senses overload and get all jumbled up. You start hearing smells, seeing noises. It's far too chaotic, not at all to be advised.'

By this time, the fog had almost completely cleared. Only a few last wisps remained. As they were able to see more and more of their surroundings, it became clear that they had wandered right away from the human Thought Boxes and into something far less organized.

'Where are we now?' asked Neil, looking round at the apparent chaos of debris.

'Way off course, I'm afraid,' said Shipshape. 'We're right in the outer limits of the Thought Domain.'

Neil took a closer look at the area around him. There was a rough grid pattern, as with the human Thought Boxes, but the boxes here were shallow and overflowing, and there had been little attempt to keep the thoughts separate from one another. In the immediate vicinity was almost nothing but bones.

It was all quite spooky, like the leftover remnants after a massive bloody battle. The thousands upon thousands of dead bodies had been reduced to skeletons which were lying every-which-way across the ground. A more careful look revealed that the bones were all legs and ribs, and probably of animals, not humans.

'What *is* this place?' said Neil. 'It's horrible. Like a big cemetery where they've forgotten to bury the bodies.'

Shipshape laughed. 'Nothing so gruesome,' she said. 'This is the area for dogs' thoughts.'

'So we're in the animals' part of the Thought Domain,' said Neil.

He was amazed. He'd often sat watching friends' dogs and cats and wondered whether they could think at all. Sometimes it seemed as though they could. Sometimes his next-door-neighbour's dog seemed to be having nightmares. If its dreams were full of dead bones, it was hardly surprising!

On the whole, though, Neil was disappointed with the dogs. They seemed so intelligent and yet their heads were full of just one thing. His dad had always said that a dog was a man's best friend, but it seemed as though the only friends the dogs had were bones and more bones.

'You can see why it doesn't particularly matter if their thoughts are kept separate, can't you?' said Shambles.

'Look,' said Shipshape. 'There's a thought of a cat.'

'And there's a couple of tins of dog-food. And a stick.' said Neil.

'But by and large, they're pretty single-minded,' said Shambles.

'Perhaps if their thoughts were all kept separate, they'd remember where they'd buried their bones,' said Neil.

'Perhaps,' said Shambles. 'Come on then, we'd better get going.'

'Which way do we go now?' asked Neil.

'Up this way,' said Shipshape, pointing to the grey human Thought Box area way over in the distance. She gave Neil back his satchel and the three of them headed off.

They hadn't gone too far, picking their way through the mass of bones, when it became clear that they had wandered into some other animals' area. The bones thinned out and disappeared and Neil heard the sound of the most beautiful music he had ever heard. The actual boxes were empty and the music swooped and swirled around all of them. It was a wonderful sound, composed of haunting and echoing combinations of pure pipe-like notes: now low and trembling, now soaring up and harmonizing with a second note, now chattering in a descending scale of tones. Neil stopped and listened with his eyes closed, and the music washed over him in wave after wave of liquid melody which never repeated itself.

'Come on, Neil,' said Shipshape softly, leading him away.

'It's so lovely,' said Neil, spellbound.

'But let's move anyway,' said Shambles.

'Is listening to it dangerous, then?' asked Neil, suddenly feeling shivers running down his back and wondering if it was one more trick of the wicked Gander.

'No,' said Shambles. 'It's not dangerous, but it's certainly bewitching, and we've already lost so much valuable time that it might already be too late. The forces of evil are getting stronger by the minute!'

'What is the music, then?' asked Neil as they walked away.

'It's the sound of the dolphins,' said Shipshape.

'Dolphins!' said Neil.

They had always been his favourite animals, with their smiley faces and chattering voices. He didn't know that they could sing so beautifully too.

'They compose their songs below the surface in the oceans' depths,' explained Shambles. 'They tell each other legends and fables and epic poems through their own special musical language. Stories of ancient cities with schools of dolphins battling against the sharks, manta rays and giant squids. Tales of adventure, daring, friendship and love. And more recently, tragic songs about being hunted by men with harpoons.'

'I wish people didn't kill them,' said Neil simply. Since coming to the Thought Domain he had discovered a lot of things that he wished people didn't do.

'Still, they are helped by the way they think,' said

Shipshape. 'Because their songs are not trapped within individual boxes, what one dolphin sings, they all hear, so if one dolphin finds danger in a certain place none of the others will ever return there.'

'Like telepathy, you mean?' said Neil.

'That's right,' said Shambles.

'Good luck,' whispered Neil to the dolphins as Shipshape led him away.

They walked on, past the thoughts of gorillas, past the thoughts of chimpanzees. Gradually, the boxes were becoming more similar to human ones. Over to their left were some absolutely gigantic boxes, far larger than those of humans, and because of their size, none of them were totally full.

'What do they belong to?' asked Neil.

'Guess!' said Shipshape.

'Well, they're so big; elephants, I suppose,' said Neil.

'Exactly right,' said Shipshape, 'and it's because they're so big that it's true that an elephant never forgets.

Somewhere in that enormous box is every thought the elephant has ever had.'

'Nearly there,' said Shambles, peering into the distance.

Neil looked over and saw that he was right. The regular order of the human Thought Boxes could be seen just ahead of them. But seeing the rigidly divided thoughts of men and women made Neil think back to the dolphins.

It must be so strange to be able to know what other people are thinking without saying anything, he thought. You wouldn't need any telephones or satellites any more. Just think the message to someone! And he pictured the dolphins swimming freely, living their lives under the waves.

'It must be nice to be a dolphin!' he thought.

Chapter 6
Under Attack

Their quest was certainly proving to be far less straightforward than Neil had anticipated. There seemed to be so many pitfalls and stumbling blocks in the Thought Domain that he wondered if he would *ever* reach the gateway to Chaos. Still, they all felt relieved to be back among the human Thought Boxes once again. Neil felt particularly happy that his wandering off into the fog hadn't resulted in complete disaster.

'We still don't know which way to go, though,' said Shambles. 'This is really getting quite ridiculous. If we've just come from the area left of the human Thought Boxes, then we need to turn left again now. But if we were on the right, then we need to turn right. But how can we possibly tell which side we were on?'

'Easy,' said Neil. 'We were on the left.'

Both Shipshape and Shambles stared at him disbelievingly.

'How do you know that?' said Shambles.

'I just do,' said Neil. 'Trust me. We need to go along here.'

They both followed him, but Neil could sense they were itching to know how he was so sure which direction to go in.

'Come on then!' said Shipshape finally. 'You can't keep us in suspense any more. How did you know?'

'As I said, it's easy. We were in the area for dogs, dolphins and elephants, weren't we?' he said pulling the map out of his satchel. 'Well then, we must have been in this bit marked "mammals" on the left.'

'Brilliant,' said Shipshape. 'I didn't even know what mammals meant. Did you, Shambles?'

'I think I might have heard the word somewhere,' he said evasively.

'He's jealous because you knew something he didn't,' whispered Shipshape and laughed.

'I learnt the word at school,' explained Neil bashfully.

'Well, it's a lucky thing you did,' said Shipshape.

Neil couldn't help wondering if some of the other problems they had had to face might have been avoided if he had paid attention to more of his lessons at school. That was the trouble, you never knew what was going to be useful at a later date.

Now they knew where their destination lay, they marched on purposefully in that direction, trying to make up for some of the lost time. Without a car, though, this was going to be very difficult. Not only is it slower getting somewhere on foot rather than by car, but they also soon discovered that they couldn't help noticing all sorts of interesting things as they passed by the Thought Boxes, things which they simply wouldn't have seen had they still been whizzing along in their car.

'Do come along!' insisted Shipshape for the umpteenth time as Neil paused to look down into a Thought Box.

'Coming,' he said.

Neil knew that they were behind in their schedule and he knew the danger of wasting any more time, but nevertheless his curiosity always got the better of him. It was so fascinating here in the Thought Domain. How was he expected to ignore all the strange, new sights surrounding him?

'What now?' shouted Shambles, as Neil stopped yet again.

'This one's really odd!' said Neil. 'It's going all bright.'

'It's probably just a thought of the sun or something,' said Shipshape. 'Come on, Neil.'

'"All bright", you say,' said Shambles. 'I think I know what that is.'

'What?' said Neil.

'Come along. *Both* of you!' said Shipshape.

But in the same way that Neil could not resist the temptation of discovering something new, so Shambles could not bottle up any knowledge he had. He knew what the bright light meant and so he went over to Neil to explain.

'I don't know if you've ever heard of meditation?' he said.

'You mean like sitting cross-legged and concentrating on something?' said Neil.

'Well, that sort of thing,' said Shambles. 'Although you don't have to be cross-legged to do it,' he added with a smile.

A couple of the boys in Neil's class did karate and they'd told him how they had to do mental exercises as well as the movement routines. They'd said that they had to sit and concentrate on the thought of a candle or a special word, but it hadn't made much sense to him.

'The person here must be very good at meditating indeed,' said Shambles. 'See how bright the light is becoming.'

Neil looked down into the Thought Box. Inside, he saw the thoughts all coming to a standstill one by one. They curled up into small motionless balls round the sides of the box and appeared to go to sleep. As they retreated, a large space was left in the centre where a pale light was gradually growing in intensity. At first, it had been like the soft glow of a full moon behind the clouds, but as Neil watched the light became increasingly dazzling. He had to squint to prevent the blinding light hurting his eyes. He looked back towards the other thoughts, but they had become completely invisible now beside this one pulsating silver ball of light.

'Do you know what?' said Shambles.

'What?' said Neil.

'People who get to be experts at meditation can do all sorts of fantastic tricks,' said Shambles.

'What sort of tricks?' asked Neil.

'Levitation, making themselves invisible, flying,' said Shambles. 'You name it, they can do it!'

Neil thought enviously about someone being able to fly. He'd always wanted to. Sometimes he'd dreamt that he could: it started off as a swimming dream and it got faster and faster until he left the water and soared off skywards. He decided there and then that as soon as he got back home *he* would start meditating, so that he too could learn to fly.

'The only problem,' said Shambles, 'is that to achieve the purest white light, you have to give up all your wants, so if you *want* to fly, then that want will prevent you from ever doing it.'

'There's always a catch,' said Neil, wondering if it would somehow be possible to *pretend* not to want to fly. Probably not, he thought sulkily.

'Come along, you two,' said Shipshape. 'Shambles, what on earth do you think you're doing filling the boy's head with such nonsense?'

'It's not nonsense,' said Shambles.

'If I could fly, I'd have a better chance against the Gander,' said Neil.

'Forget flying,' said Shipshape irritably, 'and get a move on!'

They walked on in silence. Shipshape was setting the pace and the other two were attempting to keep up with her. Neil couldn't resist looking down into the Thought Boxes as they passed by. Some of the things he saw were so strange that he could hardly believe anyone could have such thoughts. It frightened him a little to see what was there, hidden from view behind what were probably pleasant enough faces. He knew he would never again feel the same sitting on a bus watching the blank expressions of the other passengers, knowing what at least some of them must be thinking of.

'Is it my imagination,' said Shambles, 'or does it keep getting colder?'

'I noticed it as well,' said Shipshape. 'Look, my arms are all covered in goose-pimples.'

'So are mine,' said Neil. And he realized that he had been feeling distinctly uneasy for the previous little while.

'You know what it must be?' said Shipshape, in her hushed and ominous way. 'The nearby presence of the wicked Gander itself.'

Neil shivered nervously. The dangerous part of their mission was getting nearer all the time.

'It must have gone,' said Shipshape, inspecting her arm again.

'Does this mean we're very near?' said Neil.

'Not at all,' said Shipshape. 'The Gander has become so powerful that its effects can be detected from enormous distances. And goose-pimples is the most minor of symptoms anyway. You see, the problem is,' she continued, 'although there are . . .'

She suddenly became aware that she was walking alone and talking to herself. She turned round and saw that Shambles and Neil had stopped some way back and were peering down into yet another Thought Box.

'This is getting absolutely ridiculous!' she yelled. 'Don't you two realize the importance of what we're trying to get done?'

'Of course,' shouted Neil. 'But this won't take a moment.'

'If I didn't know you better, I'd say that the pair of you had been influenced by the Gander itself!' she shouted angrily, marching over to them. 'What is so interesting in this particular Thought Box?'

It was a normal Box and inside the thoughts were the usual mixture of chaotic ideas all jockeying for position. But one thing was different. Everything in this particular box was bathed in a soft green colour.

'It looks really pretty,' said Neil.

'It might look pretty, but that little thing,' Shambles said, pointing to a small green angular thought, 'is colouring all the other thoughts.'

'What is it, then?' asked Neil.

'Envy!' said Shambles.

'Envy?' repeated Neil, and shuddered as the small venom-green thought turned round. It was glowing like the face of a luminous watch.

'Of course,' said Shambles, 'all men and women have emotions, they're essential. But sometimes one gets out of control, and all the thoughts of the person are coloured by the imbalance.'

'So green isn't the only colour?' said Neil.

'Oh no,' said Shipshape, joining in the explanation. 'There are lots of others. Red, for example.'

'Which makes you angry,' explained Shambles.

'And blue,' said Shipshape.

'Which colours all your thoughts with sadness,' said Shambles.

'Yellow,' said Shipshape.

'Which makes the thoughts timid and anxious and makes the person act like a coward,' said Shambles.

'And brown,' said Shipshape.

'Which makes people fed up, dissatisfied, bored.'

'Aren't there any nice emotions?' asked Neil.

'Oh yes,' said Shipshape. 'Have you heard of the expression seeing the world through rose-coloured spectacles?'

'Yes,' said Neil, remembering that his mother said it sometimes. 'It's seeing everything beautiful and happy, like when someone falls in love,' he added with a grimace.

'That's right,' said Shipshape. 'Well, from up here, it looks like a chubby little round thought, glowing pink.'

'But even the nice ones are dangerous,' said Shambles, 'because it still means that there is an imbalance in the person's thoughts.'

'How do you get rid of the unpleasant emotions, then?' said Neil.

'Oh, you don't get rid of them,' said Shambles. 'All emotions are necessary, but they have to be balanced. If there is an equal amount of all of them, then the Thought Box remains uncoloured.'

'Why aren't there lots of different colours, then?' said Neil.

'Hmmm. How to explain,' said Shambles.

'Look,' said Shipshape, 'you know about rainbows, don't you? How all the colours of the spectrum come from white light.'

'Yes,' said Neil, desperately trying to remember all the work he'd done in physics lessons with prisms and light.

'Well, it's similar,' said Shipshape. 'Like when you draw all the colours of the rainbow on a disc and spin it. All the colours disappear and you get a white card. It's the same. If all the emotions are balanced, then there is no colouring and the person is able to think clearly. And NOW,' said Shipshape sternly, 'could we please get moving again. We can't afford to make any more stops.'

They continued walking and Neil thought again of his own Thought Box. He imagined how blue it must have looked the day his dog died and how red it must have become when Miss Beale was getting at him in the dreaded geography lesson that morning. That morning, he thought with a sudden jolt. It all seemed so far away, in time and distance. Miles and miles and years and years away.

Once again, they all shuddered involuntarily as the presence of the evil Gander made itself felt. The number of times he felt the goose-pimples rising on his arms was increasing. They must be getting nearer their goal.

'Look!' shouted Shambles.

'Where? Where?' said Shipshape, and threw herself to

the ground to escape whatever danger must be near. 'Get down, Neil,' she whispered and pulled him down next to her.

Neil felt his heart beating frantically as his mind imagined all kinds of terrors which might be there waiting for him when he opened his eyes again.

'What are you both doing?' asked Shambles, turning round and seeing Neil and Shipshape huddled together on the ground.

'Didn't you see something?' said Shipshape, still whispering.

'Yes,' said Shambles.

'Well, get down then,' instructed Shipshape.

'Why?' said Shambles.

Shipshape looked at him curiously. Neil opened his eyes and looked too.

'What *did* you see?' asked Shipshape slowly, her eyes narrowing.

'Erm,' said Shambles a little nervously. 'That.' He pointed down into a Thought Box.

'Not another thought,' said Shipshape. 'What on earth is the matter with you? I thought you'd seen the Gander itself, the way you shouted.'

'Well, not quite,' said Shambles sheepishly, 'but it *is* interesting.'

'Oh, good grief!' said Shipshape. 'What is it this time? It'd better be worth scaring me half to death.'

'Come over here and have a look, Neil,' said Shambles. 'Quick!'

Neil picked himself up and ran over to where Shambles was standing. He looked down, but what he saw made little sense to him. It was a bit like watching a boxing-match. The two contenders, though, looked far from normal. In the far corner was a round plump, monkey-like creature with bright red cheeks and piercing blue eyes. On the near side was a thin, angular imp with hollow blue cheeks and sly eyes the colour of pea-soup. They were slowly circling one another, not allowing their unblinking stares to wander from each other for an instant. All around them the other thoughts were cheering and jeering, whooping and booing, shouting with joy and howling with dismay as first one and then the other got the upper hand.

'What's all this about?' asked Neil.

'The one on the right is Yes,' said Shambles, pointing to the plumper of the two. 'And the other one is No. They're trying to make a decision.'

'How do you mean?' said Neil.

'Exactly what I say,' said Shambles. 'Whoever owns that Thought Box has a decision to make, has to decide whether to say yes or no to something, and so Yes and No are battling to decide.'

Neil stood there with his mouth open. 'You mean,' he said at last, 'that every time I choose something, then a real fight has to go on inside my Thought Box?'

'Precisely that,' said Shambles.

'More and more and more and more odd!' said Neil in bewilderment.

He continued watching the two figures performing their curious game of evasion, skirting round one another for ages before suddenly kicking out, punching or lunging forward to take the other in a winning wrestler's hold.

'Fantastic,' said Neil. 'Do you know what the decision is about?' he asked.

'Yup,' said Shambles. 'Look over there at the back. See that misty-looking thought?'

Neil looked and saw the faint outline of a book.

'It has to meet all the other thoughts first,' Shambles explained, 'to see if it's compatible. The ones that like it cheer for Yes, so it has to try to appeal to as many of the other thoughts as possible.'

'It sounds as though they like it,' said Neil, as the hoorays drowned out the boos when Yes got the upper hand.

‘It’s a complicated business,’ said Shambles, ‘and sometimes the decision-making can go on for ages.’

‘What’ll happen to the thought if No wins?’ asked Neil.

‘Oh, it’ll just disappear,’ said Shambles. ‘But if Yes wins, it’ll become a fully-fledged thought.’

As Neil continued to look, the other thoughts went up to the wispy book to inspect it. They sniffed at it, poked it and prodded it, asked it questions and deliberated over its cover. The fight kept going.

Suddenly it was all over.

No had turned its head for the briefest of moments to look at the crowd. It must have been disturbed by so many of the thoughts chanting ‘Yes, Yes, Yes, Yes.’ And in that instant the competition was decided. Yes leapt on to the shoulders of No, got it in a headlock and brought the two of them toppling down to the floor. As they landed, Yes kept its advantage, twisted No’s angular arms back in a full-Nelson and tied them together. Then it brought up the legs and knotted them up with the rest. The defeated No lay there in the centre of the cheering thoughts while Yes went over to welcome the newly accepted book to the Thought Box.

‘At this point, the person will have bought the book, or taken it out of the library, or borrowed it,’ explained Shambles. ‘The decision has been made, and as you can see, the decision was *yes*.’

‘And that always has to take place?’ said Neil.

‘It has to,’ said Shambles. ‘It’s no good having one thought in your head which doesn’t fit with all the others, is it?’

While Neil and Shambles had been observing the Yes–No contest, Shipshape had gone for a short walk. She had felt too ill at ease to stand there idly. The attacks of goose-pimples were getting worse and worse, and she could feel the hairs on the back of her neck standing up. This always meant impending trouble.

‘Keep on stopping like that . . . quite ridiculous . . . what on earth is the matter with them?' she mumbled to herself irritatedly. She turned around and saw the two of them still peering down into the Thought Box. 'Absolutely crazy . . . totally irresponsible . . .' she continued.

She had half a mind to leave the two of them and to go off and sort out the wicked Gander on her own. But on further reflection, she knew that there must have been a very good reason for the Great Methodical recruiting the little boy from 'the other side'.

'Hey! Shipshape, Shipshape!' called a voice from behind her. She turned round to see one of the other workers rushing towards her.

'Shiner,' said Shipshape. 'What brings you here?'

'They . . . they . . .' she began, but it was hopeless. The girl was far too out of breath to speak.

'Take your time,' said Shipshape.

Shiner bent over double and breathed slowly. Gradually, the bright maroon face turned back to a more healthy colour. She straightened up.

'They know you're here!' said Shiner.

'Who do?' said Shipshape.

'The Gander and the hordes of geese who work with it,' she said. 'They know that you, Shambles and the boy are out to destroy the Gander and they are trying to get to you before you reach the Pillars of Reason.'

'But how do you know?' asked Shipshape.

'All the thoughts are talking about it,' explained Shiner. 'They refuse to move now. The entire system of the Ways of Thinking is getting blocked. It's becoming chaotic, and,' she added, 'I must say, it wasn't easy finding you. You're way behind schedule, you know?'

'Don't I just know it?' said Shipshape, exasperated. 'But look,' she said, pointing into the distance where Shambles and Neil were still intently inspecting the Thought Box where the decision was being made.

'You'll have to make them get a move on,' said Shiner.

'There really isn't a moment to waste now. The situation is almost totally out of control.'

'So I wasn't imagining the goose-pimples,' said Shipshape.

'Oh no,' said Shiner. 'There have been patrols of geese out looking for you for ages now. They must have come really close to you at times.'

'I knew it,' said Shipshape. 'Okay, Shiner. Well, thanks for the information, and all I can say is that I'll do my best.'

'Fine,' said Shiner, 'Well, I've got to report back to the Great Methodical now, so I'll wish you good luck.'

'Thanks,' said Shipshape. 'I'm sure we'll need it.'

She turned and ran back to where Shambles and Neil were standing.

'Have you finished?' asked Shipshape. 'We *must* get going, I've just met Shiner and she says the Gander knows we're here, patrols of geese are out looking for us *and* we're way behind schedule.'

'Okay, okay, keep your hair on,' said Shambles.

'Be quiet, Shambles,' said Neil. 'This is serious, isn't it?'

'I'm afraid it is,' said Shipshape.

'Right,' said Neil, feeling angry with himself for all the dilly-dallying. They obviously couldn't spare the time to inspect each and every interesting phenomenon in the Thought Boxes. 'Come on then!'

They headed off towards their goal with their faces serious, their legs marching as fast as they would take them and their minds fixed on the job ahead. On and on they went, silent and determined. Occasionally they would all sense the prickly nervousness as one of the Gander's patrols came near to them, but the geese passed by without seeing the three lone adventurers.

A considerable amount of time passed before anyone spoke again. In the end it was Shipshape who broke the silence.

'Would either of you mind if I sang?' she asked.

'No. Go ahead,' said Neil, glad that the heavy atmosphere had been lightened at last.

Soon they were all joining in this latest of Shipshape's impromptu songs. It was a counting song, set to the tune of *On the First Day of Christmas*. The melody brought all sorts of memories flooding back to Neil and he wondered if he would be at home for Christmas this year. And whether he would get any presents!

We're coming to get you,
You might as well give in,
You wicked Goosy Gander.

We're coming to get you,
You might as well give in, with your
Two White Lies,
You wicked Goosy Gander.

We're coming to get you,
You might as well give in, with your
Three Big Fibs,
Two White Lies,
You wicked Goosey Gander.

And so it went on, up till the twelfth verse, which they all sang over and over again.

We're coming to get you,
You might as well give in, with your
Twelve Taradiddles,
Eleven Wily Whoppers,
Ten Tricky Dickies,
Nine Roger Dodgers,
Eight Cheating Cowboys,
Seven Vicious Rumours,
Six Sneaky Swindles,
Five False Friends,
Four Tall Stories,

Three Big Fibs,
Two White Lies,
You Wicked Goosy Gander!

'DUCK!!' screamed Shambles suddenly.

All three of them immediately dropped to the ground. As Neil nervously looked up he saw a giant goose pulling out of a dive that would have knocked them all for six had the powerful wings or savage beak made contact.

'That's some goose,' said Shambles.

'I thought you said it was a duck,' said Shipshape, grinning.

'Ha, ha,' said Shambles sarcastically.

'I don't think this is the time for jokes,' said Neil, shakily picking himself up off the ground. 'We've got to get out of here somehow.'

The goose which had attacked them was now circling round and round overhead, screeching an echoing wail to alert all the other geese in the area. And they certainly weren't taking their time. Even as Neil was looking up at the sky he saw that the call of the patrol goose was having the desired effect. From various parts of the horizon he could see dots materializing. With shocking speed they grew to the size of large, vicious birds preparing to dive-bomb.

'Run!' shouted Neil.

Fear and urgency helped him to run faster than ever before. He raced along the tiny road in his vain attempt to escape the birds. But legs are slower than wings. It was an attempt doomed to failure.

He glanced hurriedly over his shoulder to see if Shipshape and Shambles were following him. But to his dismay he saw that they were both running in different directions. A massive white bird was aiming at each of them. Twisting his head round a little further, he saw that one had its sights on him too. He collapsed down on the ground just in the nick of time and lay there shaking as the bird skimmed over his hair and flew off with a disgruntled squawk to prepare for the next attack.

He got back to his feet and set off again. Faster, faster, as fast as he could possibly run. But it couldn't possibly be *quite* fast enough, and as Neil realized that the birds would be bound to catch him he felt his legs suddenly grow leaden.

Stealing another look, he saw to his horror that there were now four of them all aimed at him. There was nowhere to run to. There was nowhere to hide. There was only one alternative to being smashed down to the ground by the birds and it was this alternative that he took. Without a moment to spare, he took a flying leap off the path and down into the nearest Thought Box. As he jumped, he looked round and saw Shipshape and Shambles doing exactly the same thing.

'What do I do now?' he asked himself nervously. The immediate danger had passed, but looking up and seeing the geese circling overhead, he wondered how they were ever going to get out of their predicament. It all seemed totally hopeless.

Chapter 7

Shipshape and Shambles Get Boxed In

Shambles's Story: Obsession

'Geronimo!' yelled Shambles as he leapt into the box and out of the reach of the attacking birds.

With the immediate danger over, he looked around him at the other occupants of the Thought Box. He remained disdainfully unimpressed. A fairly rag-bag assortment, he thought to himself with a sniff.

He sat down over by the wall and contemplated his situation, weighing up the pros and cons of a) trying to continue the quest on his own, b) locating the others and c) waiting for the geese to give up and fly away. He looked up at the sky. One lone goose was up there, circling round and round. It was moving so slowly that, silhouetted against the sky, it was almost impossible to tell whether it was a goose or a hawk.

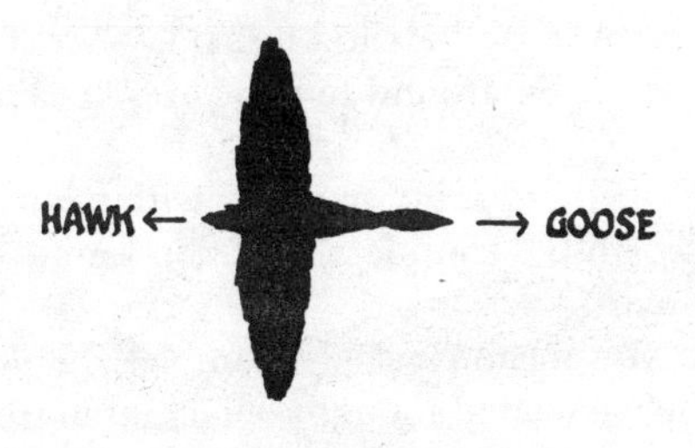

'It's funny,' he mused to himself. 'If I were a mouse, I'd be terrified of seeing a hawk, but as Shambles, I'm scared of its being a goose. And if it remained motionless, I wouldn't know whether to be afraid or not!'

He looked up again and smiled smugly.

'I bet the other two wouldn't have made such an observation that it's only the direction they fly in that makes geese geese and hawks hawks. And if they couldn't see exactly what's what, then they wouldn't know when to be on the look-out for danger!'

But then, of the three companions, it was Shambles who considered himself the intellectual. After all, he looked like an intellectual, didn't he? He was pale and pasty, with greasy, lank hair; intellectuals didn't concern themselves with outward appearances. He was thin and weedy; intellectuals preferred to develop the mind rather than the muscles. He was witty and clever, although the dolts he was surrounded with (nice though they were) were not even bright enough to recognize his mental superiority.

The problem was his lack of practicality. To be blunt, Shambles was practically useless. That is, useless at all practical things. He had to concede that Shipshape, for all her reckless enthusiasm, was far better at getting out of tricky situations. And now, stuck in someone's Thought Box, separated from the others and being watched by one of the enemy geese, he missed Shipshape's practical mind, which would be sure to come up with the best solution to the situation.

'Hi!' said a rather thin thought.

Shambles looked up. 'Hello,' he said.

'Haven't seen you around here before,' it said. 'You new here?'

'I just dropped in,' said Shambles with a laugh.

'Hardly worth the trouble, if you don't mind me saying,' said the thought.

'What do you mean?' asked Shambles. He looked more closely at the emaciated thought of a child in front of him.

'Well, I can't see you lasting long,' it said simply. 'You'll get swallowed up like all the rest.'

'Swallowed up!' said Shambles, suddenly feeling somewhat alarmed. 'What by?' he asked, wondering if there was a thought of a man-eating tiger lurking in a dark corner of the Thought Box.

'By that lot,' said the thought, pointing.

Shambles looked over. He had already noticed the pile of odd-looking shapes and taken in the fact that there seemed to be an uncommonly large number of edible thoughts, but he hadn't really bothered to inspect them all that carefully. Looking now, it became clear. The Thought Box was dominated by a massive heap of food. He made out cream eclairs, jam doughnuts, scoops and scoops of multi-coloured ice-cream dripping with chocolate and raspberry sauce and topped with nuts and vermicelli, thick sandwiches of peanut butter and honey, slices of Black Forest gâteau, cream cakes and lemon meringue pies, marshmallows and truffles, nougats and fondants. And that was just a start!

'That looks like a problem to me,' said Shambles.

'You can say that again,' said the thought.

'And where do *you* fit into this box full of goodies?' asked Shambles suspiciously. 'Why are you so thin when there's so much for you to get your teeth into?'

'Can't you see how my skin shines?' said the thought. 'I am little more than a dream.'

'A dream?' repeated Shambles.

'A dream of how she would like to look,' explained the thought.

Shambles looked hard at the adolescent. He couldn't even tell if it was a boy or a girl. He didn't understand what the thought had said.

'What does he or she really look like, then?' he asked.

'It is a she,' said the thought, 'but to be honest, I'm none too sure what she looks like.'

'Why not?' persisted Shambles.

'Because her real body keeps changing!' the thought said

simply. 'I am the ideal: this bony boy-like figure of a girl. But as for the real body, it keeps going from being immensely fat to incredibly thin. I just can't keep track at all.'

'An obsession,' said Shambles fearfully.

'Exactly,' said the waif-like thought. 'She is totally obsessed with food, but terrified of getting fat. She can't think of anything else.'

'Locked up with an obsession,' said Shambles. Even as he was watching the pile of food it was growing larger. A dozen Viennese whirls and a torrent of pistachio ice-cream appeared, swiftly followed by a cascade of sugared almonds. He looked up at the steep sides of the walls and wondered nervously whether he'd be able to scale them in an emergency. And at the rate the pile of food was expanding, an emergency seemed increasingly likely.

'Is she from a poor country?' asked Shambles naïvely.

'No,' said the thought. 'You'd think so, wouldn't you? But no, she's from a wealthy family in a wealthy country. But there are so many pressures on her to stay thin, that she'd rather starve herself to death than put on an ounce of weight.'

'It sounds crazy,' said Shambles.

'It's a disorder,' said the thought, nodding. 'They call it anorexia.'

'And it looks as though it's got to a fairly bad stage,' said Shambles, noticing the mountain of food beginning to quiver as a rockfall of apple dumplings rolled downwards.

Apart from the wobbling mass of food there were still one or two other thoughts in the Box, but these were small and weedy. They huddled together near the walls anxiously. Shambles wondered what had happened to all the other thoughts that must have been there before the obsession had taken over. And as he was watching he had his answer.

A small white dog was standing over by the far corner wagging its tail unenthusiastically and sniffing at a ginger brown guinea-pig. Neither animal noticed as the food slid over towards them. Suddenly, a wobbling portion of strawberry blancmange enveloped them both. The guinea-pig disappeared at once, but Shambles got one last glimpse of the wide-eyed horror of the dog as it too was swallowed up. The girl would never be able to think of the dog or the guinea-pig again. They had been erased by the dominant thought in her head: food.

Shambles knew that the situation was dangerous.

'I could be next,' he said to the thought.

'True,' it said. 'I'll remain, because she needs to maintain this image of ideal slimness. But all other thoughts are superfluous.'

'I am superfluous!' thought Shambles in alarm.

In all his time in the Thought Domain, Shambles had seen many obsessions. He had seen the thoughts of those obsessed with guns, which had wiped out any other thought; with violence which had beaten all the other thoughts into submission; with a loved one whose face would be imprinted on every other thought. But never, never had he seen anything so apparently harmless take on such horrifying dimensions.

The mound of food was still growing. Second by second, the feast of gourmet delights was multiplying. A stream of confectioner's custard ran down the left side of the mount, where a dozen or more sponges had just appeared. Peach melbas and profiteroles, glacé cherries and jelly babies appeared out of nowhere.

A couple more demoralized thoughts were engulfed. Even a thought of a battered old teddy-bear could not avoid the multi-coloured edible mountain. From Shambles's experience, the thoughts of teddy-bears were generally the most resistant: people almost never forgot them. Things certainly were just about as bad as they could get.

'How am I going to get out of here?' he shouted.

The goose was still in the sky above him. Compared with the horrors he was having to face inside the Thought Box, the confrontation with a mere goose would be a pushover. But how to get out?

'What would you suggest . . .' he started to say to the waif-like thought before realizing that it was no longer beside him. He turned back, only to find that the amorphous heap of comestibles had advanced on him. He was cut off, trapped in a corner and about to be swallowed up himself.

'Help!! HELP!!!' he screamed frantically. But he knew that the cry for assistance was pointless.

'Remain calm and take everything step by step by step,' he instructed himself. But how on earth could anyone remain calm when faced with imminent suffocation by a massive slab of bread pudding?

His exits were all barred and still the pile grew, threatening to occupy every last square millimetre of the Thought Box. He stared upwards, hypnotized by the colours of a massive Knickerbocker Glory as it spiralled down from the top, deep rivers of raspberry and vanilla sauce pouring down towards him like lava from an ice-cream volcano. At the last possible instant, just before the sticky goo struck, he leapt on to a wafer and, balancing as best he could, surfed away temporarily out of danger.

As he rounded the curve, an avalanche of lemon sherbert came tumbling down on him. He leapt from the wafer and then hopped gingerly from marshmallow to marshmallow floating in chocolate sauce, as if crossing a river by stepping-stones. A giant plain-chocolate biscuit offered him a temporary island and a chance to get his breath back. He looked round to see the marshmallows disappearing beneath a mixture of sherbert and whipped cream. The digestive biscuit started to wobble and tilt, causing Shambles to crouch down and clutch on to the sides for all his worth. But it was hopeless. He was forced to abandon biscuit and leap for the safety of a passing Swiss roll. Standing on the spiralled cake made it start to rotate and Shambles had to walk to stay upright. Faster and faster the

Swiss roll turned, faster and faster Shambles ran, terrified of falling into the swirling, treacly mass below him.

The entire Thought Box was by now full of food. The obsession had taken complete control. Even the little waif-like thought was nowhere to be seen; no space left even for dreams.

The only good thing about the present situation was that he found the increase of food was slowly raising him up. Floating on his precarious rafts of wafers and rusks, he was gradually being lifted towards the top of the perpendicular walls.

'If I can just avoid falling,' he said encouragingly to himself.

Some after-dinner chocolate mint-creams came spinning down the slope offering more stepping-stones, albeit slippery ones. Shambles used a long thin chocolate finger-biscuit as a balancing pole.

'Mustn't fall! Mustn't fall!' he urged himself. So near to the top now, and yet if he did slip, it would all be over in a moment.

A sudden stream of coffee fudge sauce caught him unawares and swept him over to the far wall on a spinning macaroon. Shambles closed his eyes, held his breath and waited for the inevitable impact. As it smashed into the wall, the macaroon split into two and Shambles was stuck with one leg on one half and one leg on the other. Divided, the two halves of the broken biscuit seemed intent on getting as far away from each other as possible, and they dragged Shambles's legs with them. He felt himself being forced to do the splits.

'This is awful. AWFUL!!' he yelled.

He had no alternative but to try jumping to safety and, summoning all his remaining strength, he leapt for the top of the wall, which was still about three feet above his head.

Although the macaroon pieces threatened to give way under his feet as he jumped, he somehow just about managed to hook his finger tips over the top of the Thought Box.

'If only I was stronger,' thought Shambles miserably to himself as his weak and aching arms threatened to give way. 'Come on, come on!' he encouraged himself.

In the end, it was the feeling of the swirling mass of creams and juices round his feet which fired him with just enough panic to allow his arms to lift him.

'I refuse to be drowned in a trough of condensed milk!' he yelled and gave a final heave. A last volley of cream puffs bounced off his back as he levered his arms over the edge and dragged himself out of the box full of the treacherous food which had almost consumed him.

'Thank heavens for that!' he said, as he realized he was safe. And with that he fainted.

Shipshape's Story: The Madman

Shipshape was running as fast and low as she could to escape the attacking goose. With her head twisted round to keep an eye on the goose swooping down on her, she prepared to hit the ground just before it made contact. Hopefully, the goose wouldn't be able to pull out of the dive in time and would crashland. What Shipshape had not considered was the possibility of a dual attack. And this was a mistake, for a couple of seconds before the goose she was watching hit her, she was walloped on the side of her head by the wing of the second goose. The impact flung her into the air, head over heels in a perfect somersault, which threw her down into the nearest Thought Box, where she was deposited unconscious on top of the unsuspecting thoughts inside.

'What is it?'

'Is it a bird? Is it a plane?'

'Do you think it's a meteorite?'

'It might be dangerous. Let's tie it up.'

Words were filtering through Shipshape's head as she started to come round. She felt hands on her body, feeling, testing, prodding her. She shook them off angrily.

'Careful, it could be violent.'

'It might bite.'

She opened her eyes to see that there were thoughts all around her, all over her, all staring at her with a mixture of surprise and hostility. Again she kicked the intruders away and closed her eyes.

'It *does* seem vicious,' said a thought.

'Any thought of a rope around here?' asked another.

Shipshape pulled her unwilling eyelids open again and looked around her properly.

'Get off me!' she yelled, 'and you can put that rope away. I'm *not* dangerous.'

'Prove it! Prove it! Prove it!' shouted a short, fat, round thought, bouncing up and down on Shipshape's knee.

'Scram!' said Shipshape, and kicked the ball-shaped thought to the far end of the box.

'Temper, temper!' said a paper-thin thought dressed in white.

'Well, how would you feel, suddenly surrounded by hostile and aggressive strangers?' asked Shipshape.

'And how would you feel if you'd just been flattened by some flying alien?' retorted the thought.

'Hmmm,' said Shipshape, seeing that they had reasonable grounds for complaint. 'Sorry about that,' she said, 'but it really wasn't my fault.'

'Are you really sorry?' asked a tall, thin thought with a head like a ball-point pen.

'Yes,' said Shipshape. 'I am really well and truly sorry.'

The biro-thought turned and waltzed away with the paper-thin thought, and when the latter returned the words APOLOGY GRACIOUSLY ACCEPTED were written upon it. All the thoughts formed a circle around Shipshape (except for those underneath which looked up at her) and they all bowed together.

'Welcome to the thoughts of Emperor Ferdinand of Loopitania!' they all announced as one.

'An emperor,' thought Shipshape. 'Landed on my feet here all right, even though I really landed on my back!'

She smiled to the assembled thoughts and turned round to curtsy to them all, each and every one.

The Thought Box was bathed in a pale pink light which made the thoughts surrounding her positively glow with joy. Shipshape thought that she had never been in such a friendly and happy atmosphere before in her life.

'Wouldn't you care for a seat?' a small, furry thought asked her.

'Cigarette? Drink? A little snack?' offered another.

'No, really,' said Shipshape. 'I can't stay that long. I'm just waiting for the coast to clear before taking my leave of you all.'

She looked up at the sky.

'You see, I had to escape that vicious bird,' she explained, pointing to the circling goose.

'Ah, the geese,' said a brown and blue thought. 'But you mustn't get so distraught all because of a silly old bird. And in any case, we want you to stay here with us. For ever!' it added, and grinned so widely that Shipshape couldn't help feeling a twinge of unease. But this she dismissed a moment later, angry with herself that this open display of warmth and friendship should make her feel anything but happy. The life of an emperor was certainly to be recommended if it led to such a stable set of thoughts.

Had Shambles been there, he would have realized at once that the pink tinge to the Thought Box indicated an imbalance in the emotional stability. He would have been suspicious. He would not have trusted the jolly, rosy faces so unquestioningly. But Shipshape was not Shambles. She was the practical half of the team who took things at their face value. Confronted with the over-friendliness of the thoughts, she was prepared to simply accept their hospitality. It was only when one of the thoughts rushed up to her and sank its razor-sharp teeth into her forearm that she began to suspect that all was not what it seemed to be.

'Aaaargh Ooowww!!!' she yelled and tried to shake the attacking animal off.

The offending fanged thing was small, blue, furry and smelt of burnt fat. Its eyes were bloodshot, its teeth yellowed and now, as Shipshape looked down, dripping with blood. *Her* blood. She screamed again, tugging at the revolting creature, which simply bit in all the harder and scratched at her T-shirt with sharp, curved claws.

'Help me!' called Shipshape to the others. She looked round for someone or something to come to her aid, but to her horror she saw that the faces which had been so friendly a moment ago were now all contorted with rage. And they were shouting at *her*! Jeering, taunting, hideous faces cheered on the ragged little creature to even worse feats of savagery.

While Shambles probably wouldn't have got into such a tricky situation, Shipshape, who was by far the stronger of the two, was in a much better position to get out of it. She grabbed the furry beast by its scrawny neck with her free hand and squeezed as tight as she possibly could. The vile little creature screeched in pain and as it did so unclenched its clamped jaws. Having gained the advantage, Shipshape took hold of the animal by its leg and slung it at the wall. The crowd of onlookers cheered and jeered in equal numbers.

'What's going on here?' demanded Shipshape. 'First you're all friendly and want me to stay for ever and the next minute I'm being attacked.'

'And the next minute I'm being attacked,' repeated a big, fat thought tauntingly. 'You sound like a real dingbat,' it said. 'I don't think I like you at all. Wanna fight?'

'Yeah, come on, you weed,' shouted another.

Soon they were all chanting one word: 'Kill, kill, kill, KILL!'

Shipshape looked from one angry red face to the next. It

suddenly dawned on her that the colour of the Thought Box had subtly shifted from pink to red. The emotion had shifted with it, changing from friendliness to anger. She realized the awful danger she was in.

'Come on then. Hit me. Hit me, then,' said the big thought, bouncing around on light feet, jabbing out at Shipshape's jaw. 'Come on, you coward!'

'Do you always go round hitting girls?' asked Shipshape.

'What's that got to do with it?' said a voice behind her. 'Girls, boys, they can all fight.'

Shipshape felt small hard hands at her back forcing her on to the angry thought in front of her that seemed so intent on a scrap. With no option, she mustered all her strength and threw as powerful a left hook as she could manage. It caught the big, fat thought's gloating face. A straight right to the nose landed an instant later. The bully toppled over and immediately burst into tears.

The light in the Thought Box turned yellow.

'Oh, please don't hit me again. Please, please. Please don't,' whined the thought. It crawled towards Shipshape and lay grovelling at her feet. 'Don't, don't don't!' it whimpered in a cowardly way.

It occurred to Shipshape that this emperor, if the person *was* in fact an emperor, and this she was beginning to doubt, was far from being mentally stable. Whoever this person was, he or she was definitely not quite right in the head at all. Even as Shipshape was considering the change from anger to cowardice as the colour in the Thought Box had changed from red to yellow, it changed once again, this time to a poisonous shade of green that could only signify jealousy.

A thin, slinky thought of a woman dressed in a tight, green, satin dress approached her.

'You've been eyeing up my boyfriend, haven't you?' she challenged. 'You keep your disgusting thoughts and intentions off him.'

'What boyfriend?' said Shipshape.

'And don't come the I'm-so-innocent-butter-wouldn't-melt-in-my-mouth with me!' shrieked the woman. 'You can't pull the wool over my eyes. I WAS NOT born yesterday!'

And with that she slapped Shipshape hard across the face. Her dark red nails scratched her cheeks and when Shipshape put her hand to her face she saw that the woman in the green dress had drawn blood.

'Let that be a lesson to you!' she screamed.

For the first time ever, Shipshape felt afraid. She couldn't handle the sudden shifts and changes of mood. She didn't know how to react in the face of such irrational behaviour.

'Okay, okay,' said Shipshape, realizing that there was no point whatsoever in trying to talk rationally to the woman. 'If I upset you, then I am sorry,' she added.

'Well, just make sure you remember,' said the woman. 'I'm letting you off lightly this time, but you won't be so lucky next time. I can promise you that!' And she flashed her wicked red nails in front of Shipshape's eyes.

'And you!' she yelled at another thought. 'I saw you touch him. Do that again and you're mincemeat.'

Shipshape turned away.

'How on earth do I get out of here!' she said to herself.

'Talking to yourself?' said a voice from behind her. 'First sign of madness,' he said. 'Well, actually, no it isn't,' he corrected himself.

Shipshape asked him what the first sign was.

'The first sign,' said the thought, a small chubby boy with a shock of vertical fair hair, 'is looking for hairs on your palms. The second is finding them. Talking to yourself is actually the seventh sign of madness. Do you want to hear what the third, fourth and sixth signs are?'

'What about the fifth?' asked Shipshape.

'There isn't a fifth reason,' said the boy sullenly.

'Why not?' asked Shipshape.

'There just isn't,' he said. 'And what's it to you anyway?'

'Nothing. Just wondered,' said Shipshape.

'Anyway, the third sign of madness is looking like you and the fourth sign is talking like you and . . .'

'You're making them up as you go along,' said Shipshape.

'Don't interrupt. It's very rude,' said the boy.

'And the sixth sign is being called Shipshape.'

'How did you know my name?' said Shipshape, shocked.

'Pardon?' said the boy nonchalantly.

'How did you know my name was Shipshape?'

'Was?' said the boy. 'You mean it isn't any more?'

'Yes, it is!' said Shipshape. 'How did you know my name *is* Shipshape?'

'Is it?' asked the boy with theatrical amazement. 'Well, well, well. What a surprise and what a coincidence! Shipshape, eh? Well then, you must be mad! The sixth sign and all that.'

Shipshape found herself growing increasingly angry. She shook the insolent boy by the shoulders, but the light in the Box had turned to brown and the boy merely sat down on the ground and ignored her.

'I'm so fed up!' he complained.

The light flashed to blue.

'I'm so depressed.'

'We all are. Oh, woe, woe, woe is us! It's all so awful, so miserable, so depressing, so drab, so, so, so, so sad!' echoed all the other thoughts in the Thought Box, and a general wailing moan filled the air.

Blue. Brown. Blue. Brown. The colour in the Thought Box alternated between the two shades, and as it did so the thoughts chanted:

'We're so miserable. We're so bored. We're so miserable. We're so bored!'

Suddenly the light turned to a dazzling shade of orange. The thoughts instantly became animated and friendly again. Shipshape knew that she had to act quickly to use their temporary good mood to escape from the Thought Box. The chubby boy who a moment before had been surly and uncooperative was suddenly polite, helpful and sociable.

'Is there any way I might be of assistance?' he asked.

'I would very much like to get out of this Thought Box,' said Shipshape.

'Well, that shouldn't prove too much of a difficulty,' said the boy.

'But the top of the wall is too high up,' said Shipshape, 'and there don't seem to be any thoughts of ladders around.'

'Then we must improvise,' said the boy with a smile. He looked round the Thought Box for a moment. Then something seemed to occur to him and he turned back to Shipshape.

'Why do you want to leave this wonderful place, anyway?' he asked.

'I've got a lot to do,' said Shipshape.

'No, that's no use as a reason,' said the boy. 'Try again. Why do you want to leave?'

'I've got to destroy the evil Gander,' explained Shipshape.

'Possibly commendable in itself, but still not a good enough answer.'

'Well, what is a good answer?' asked Shipshape irritably.

'One that gets you out of here,' said the boy simply. 'Now, think carefully and try once more. Why do you want to leave?'

Shipshape thought and thought, but she simply had no idea what the boy wanted her to say. Once again she wished that Shambles had been there. He was much better at these riddles and games. She looked at the boy watching her expectantly, but couldn't think of any appropriate answer. She shrugged.

'Oh, I don't know,' she said. 'It's high time I left, that's all.'

At once she felt herself floating up into the air. She

looked giddily down at the mêlée of thoughts below her, still bathed in their orange glow.

'Bravo!' said the boy encouragingly. 'And once again before you start to sink.'

'I really must fly!' said Shipshape, latching on to the idea. She found that she could fly around the box as well as any bird. But she wasn't getting any nearer the top.

'Come on, hurry up,' called the boy.

'I want to live the high life, to take high tea and hire taxis on the high street at high noon!'

She rose up inch by inch with every key word.

'Wonderful!' shouted the boy from below her.

'I shall raise Cain to get out of here. I shall raise the wind.'

The colour was still orange, but Shipshape knew it couldn't last for much longer, and she knew she had to get out before it changed again. As she ran out of words she felt herself descending.

'I must come up with something else,' she cried desperately, and the words she'd unconsciously used did the trick. She rose a little further.

'What's up?' she yelled. 'I'm up to date, up and about, up up and away!'

Again her mind went blank.

'Just a couple of feet to go,' she called down to the boy.

'Everyone's got a couple of feet to go,' he called back.

'A couple of feet left.'

'You mean a couple of left feet?'

'No! I mean I CANNOT GET OUT!' she shouted.

'You need a hand, never mind about the feet.'

Shipshape felt herself sinking back down to the thoughts below.

'This is hopeless,' she yelled. 'I think I'm going out of my mind.'

'Going out of your mind?' said the boy. 'Wrong again. You're going out of *our* mind. Bye bye.'

And suddenly Shipshape found herself back on the path

next to the lunatic's Thought Box. She looked back inside. The colour had changed again. There was a dull brown glow tinting all the thoughts. The boy was sitting there on the floor with his legs crossed staring dejectedly at a small heap of sand. Time after time, he would pick up some of the soft grains and let them trickle slowly down on to the ground. Shipshape knew that it would be impossible ever to guess what he was seeing in those grains. She knew she was watching the irrational mind of the madman at work. His emotions had remained unchecked and wild like a small child's, while becoming as dangerous and strong as any adult's. It was a terrifying combination and Shipshape could feel only relief that she had come out more or less unscathed.

Catching a movement out of the corner of her eye, she turned to see that this was no time to relax. Shambles was lying motionless on the path and the goose which had been circling in the sky had landed and was just about to fly off with him. Shipshape leapt to her feet. She would have to act as fast as lightning!

Chapter 8
Neil Gets Lost in his Own Thoughts

There had been six geese aiming to get Neil when he had jumped into the Thought Box. That was more than were after Shipshape and Shambles put together. The evil Gander had evidently singled him out as the most important of the three companions. Luckily, Neil did not realize this. If he had, he would have been far more worried about his own safety.

'Wheeee!!' he had cried out as he had launched himself into mid-air. At that moment, his only concern was to escape from the geese. A micro-mini-instant later, however, he had completely forgotten the geese, forgotten his two friends, forgotten the Thought Domain and the reason why he was there!

Unlike Shipshape and Shambles, who had felt bewildered and disorientated on landing inside the strange Thought Boxes, Neil was immediately overwhelmed with the most wonderful feeling of having arrived home. Everything felt cosy and familiar and he wandered around happily amongst all the thoughts there.

'Hiya! Hello!' he said, as he recognized more and more of the thoughts.

The reason that the contents of this one particular Thought Box all seemed so familiar was hardly surprising. Of course, the odds against his doing it were staggering. At least 5,531,987,287 to 1 against. But Neil had achieved the almost impossible and done just that. He had landed in his own Thought Box.

In front of him stood Miss Beale; but it wasn't the Miss Beale who taught him geography every day, it was his thought of her. She was taller than the original, with a thin, ugly mouth and bad breath.

'Morning, Miss Beale,' he said, and as it was all inside his thoughts he added what he'd always wanted to say to the real one: 'you smelly old goat!'

'Neil Davies! You insolent little wretch, how dare you?' replied the thought of Miss Beale.

'Oh pipe down, pie-face!' said Neil.

'You can go straight to the headmistress's office,' she ordered.

'And you can go and jump in the lake!' shouted Neil, enjoying himself. 'And make sure it's full of piranhas!'

'You horrible boy!' said Miss Beale.

'You ugly old bag!' said Neil.

'You naughty, naughty, naughty boy!' she said.

'You warty, warty, warty toad!' said Neil.

'How dare you!' she screeched.

'I dare,' he said, turning away. He was getting a bit tired of the situation. Once you were in the position to insult someone you'd always wanted to insult, it soon became pretty boring. He walked away from the ranting teacher and, passing friends and enemies from the playground, he came to his mother and father.

'Mum! Dad!' he said to the two of them.

The two thoughts of his parents answered him and Neil was filled with that curious mixture of feelings. He knew he loved them a lot and that they loved him. But at the same time they were the ones who always stopped him doing the things he wanted to do and made him do the things he didn't. Neil wanted to question the two thoughts confronting him now about all the things he found so confusing. But he couldn't. He had to keep reminding himself that they were not his *real* parents. They were only *his own* thoughts about them.

The thought of his father stretched out his strong arms to Neil, who automatically grabbed hold of the hands and walked up the front of his body, turning over and landing back down on his feet. It was something he had done years and years earlier.

'Again, again!' he insisted excitedly.

'Bedtime now, Neil,' came the inevitable response that made him sulk.

When he looked back up again, he saw that both his mum and dad had grown taller and younger. The thought of his mother was wearing a pair of glasses which she had broken years before. Neil felt confused. But the promise of an aeroplane ride from his dad dispelled all the questions and worries.

Wandering along past the succession of thoughts, Neil felt more and more at ease. Everything seemed to be getting clearer and simpler. He pulled off the furry little seedpods of lupins and stroked them down his cheek and over his lips. He picked up the memory of a small, baby sparrow and held its warm, feathery body to his face.

'What's that you've got there, Nibs?' said a voice from behind him. He turned and saw his young mother towering over him. Nibs was the nickname he'd had when he was very small. He thought he had forgotten the name, but there it was again. Nibs. Nobs. Nabs. He giggled, and then remembered the little bird again.

'He can't fly, mummy,' said Neil.

'Well, let's try and help him,' said his mother, and they took the fledgling into an old familiar kitchen with red and white squared lino and a silver stove. With painstaking care, the tiny bird was fed a mush of bread, milk and chicken paste with an eye dropper and a matchstick.

There was snow in the garden and Neil was out there with daddy, who was about a hundred times bigger than Neil would ever be. All wrapped up in woollen mittens and scarves, with bright red wellies on his feet, Neil was helping as the big man pushed and pushed a giant snowball around the grass. As it rolled, it got bigger and bigger. And that was magic. Then they made another snowball and put it on the first one. And then with pieces of coal and a big straw-hat, the snow suddenly became a snowman. And that was even better magic.

In the corner of the room was a big tree covered with lights. One bulb was the shape of Father Christmas, one was of a pineapple and one was a lantern. And there were red, green and purple glass balls which made your nose look enormous and your eyes and mouth look tiny when you got up close to them. And the presents were all wrapped with pretty paper.

A pillow-case was lying there on the bed. All lumpy and full of toys and games, like ludo and a plastic tr . . . tr . . . trumpone, and shouldiers with red and black uniforms, and a Winnie-the-Pooh book that daddy would have to read at bedtime.

'It's the sea,' said mummy, as he looked down from her mountainous shoulders to the swirling foaming water around her ankles. She lifted him down and the water was cold. Not like bathtime. And it moved. When he rubbed his eyes they stung. He ran out of the water, but looking back it was all wavy, so he waved to it and ran back into the salty waves again.

'Where's your bucket?' called daddy.

'There!' said Neil pointing.

'Fetch it for daddy,' said mummy, and Neil went toddling over with the little metal spade.

His daddy made him a boat out of the sand, a boat with a seat and sides which the sea couldn't wash away. And he sat in the boat with his spade as a paddle and rowed across the world.

'Neil! Neil!'

Crawling round the carpet, the big, soft, red and brown carpet. The blue budgie was whistling and talking to him. Over by the door, leaning against a table-leg, was teddy.

'Neil! Neil!' came the distant cry again.

Who was it calling? It didn't sound like mummy or daddy.

Teddy was soft and smelt of warm eiderdowns and milk. He looked at Neil through his one orange-brown eye. Neil held the other eye in his hand. He swivelled round and sat down on the carpet, legs out straight, thumb reassuringly in mouth, teddy on lap, waving his velvety paws, stroking Neil's nose.

'Neil! Up here, Neil!' came the voices again.

'Whaa??' said Neil, shaking teddy.

Neil was lying in a large, black pram watching the coloured shapes suspended above him. Sometimes giant faces appeared. Sometimes someone tickled him and said coo-chee-coo-chee-coo!

Then there was a rope hanging down. A rope with a loop on the end and the same strange voice shouting his name: 'Neil! NEIL!!'

He was about to roll over and go back to sleep when something happened. He felt a strange tickling in his ear, as if whiskers were poking their way around inside. And as he concentrated on the feeling, he heard an odd little whisper. He couldn't quite make out the words and he wasn't sure what he was meant to do. But he had the weirdest idea that it had something to do with the rope. And the whispering and tickling continued, trying to tell him something . . . Something to do with the rope, with the loop . . .

He was lying on his back on a large towel, gurgling. The rope was still there.

'Neil! Neil! NEIL!!' He heard the sound of the voices again.

Slowly, he stretched out his hands and held on to the loop of the rope. The instant he did so he was lurched off the towel and found himself dangling in mid-air. It was like being pulled up the side of a cliff and he hung on for dear life. Higher and higher and higher and . . .

'Shipshape! Shambles!' he said, recognizing his two friends at the top of the Thought Box 'Hello.'

'Neil!' they both cried out in unison. 'Are we glad to see you!' They both gave him a huge hug.

'Hey, what's up!' said Neil, noticing that his friends' reaction to seeing him again seemed a little extreme.

'Good grief!' said Shambles. 'You know what, Neil? I sometimes don't know whether you're an asset or a liability.'

'A what or a what?' said Neil.

'What he means is,' said Shipshape, 'we seem to spend half our time trying to rescue you.'

'Rescue me!' said Neil, astonished. 'What from?'

'He doesn't even remember,' said Shipshape.

'Of course he doesn't,' said Shambles. 'He couldn't. It's all locked up where it belongs again.'

'What are you two going on about?' said Neil. 'And what's this?' he added, noticing the length of rope he was still holding.

'That,' said Shambles, 'was your lifeline. You'd have been lost for ever without it.'

Neil realized that something extremely dangerous had taken place, something which he had erased from his memory completely. And so as they continued their walk northwards towards the Ways of Thinking he kept quiet and listened carefully to all they had to tell him. He laughed at the thought of Shambles almost drowning in a Thought Box full of syrups and creams. He congratulated Shipshape on the mental gymnastics she had gone through to get herself out of the madman's thoughts. And all the while he could hardly wait to hear what horrors he himself had been hoisted away from.

'So,' he said, 'Shambles was lying there unconscious, exhausted by his battle with the biscuits.' He couldn't help sniggering.

'It was no laughing matter,' said Shambles indignantly.

'Sorry,' said Neil, trying to wipe away his smile. 'And Shipshape was tired out from her meeting with the Emperor of Loopitania. So what happened next?'

'Well might you ask,' said Shipshape. 'Well might you ask. I got out, so drained that I could hardly stand up, and what did I see? Shambles, unconscious, lying there, just about to be carried off by the biggest goose you've ever seen. I daresay he would have been taken to the evil Gander's nest and served up as a little titbit.'

'What did you do, then?' asked Neil, his eyes wide.

'The only thing I could do,' said Shipshape, her eyes blazing fiercely. 'I leapt up and, with no thought to my own personal safety, I rushed valiantly over to the monstrous feathered fiend and grabbed hold of its thick, muscled neck. The struggle which ensued was awe-inspiring as we rolled wrestling, tussling, round and round, over and over the ground. Once I thought it was all over: the savage beast got on top of me and I watched in horror as its cable-like neck reared back ready to strike. The razor-sharp beak would have killed me in an instant. But maintaining clarity of mind in the face of almost indomitable odds, I skilfully . . .'

'And modestly,' said Shambles quietly, so that only Neil could hear.

'Succeeded in twisting out of reach in a move so stunningly deft . . .'

'And modest,' whispered Shambles.

'As to defy belief.'

Neil and Shambles exchanged little secret smiles. Despite

her obvious embroidery of the story, they knew that Shipshape had saved them both and let her indulge herself.

'So I was on top,' she continued 'I'd got the demonic brute on its back and was anxious not to allow it to release its pinioned wings. What do you think I did next, Neil?'

'You stabbed it through the heart,' Neil suggested.

'But I had no knife, no dagger, no sword,' said Shipshape dramatically.

'You hit it with a rock or something?' he said.

'I looked around,' said Shipshape, 'but there were neither rocks, nor branches, nor clubs, nor anything else I might have used to knock the winged devil senseless.'

'Well, you couldn't have poisoned it, and you couldn't have suffocated it, or drowned it . . . I give in,' said Neil.

'Aha!' said Shipshape triumphantly. 'You give in. And so did the goose. Though almost dropping from the effort, I managed to keep cool, calm and collected . . .'

'And modest,' whispered Shambles, not quite quietly enough.

'Shut up, you ungrateful little man,' said Shipshape imperiously.

'Well, that put me in *my* place,' said Shambles. 'A thousand apologies, your ladyship.'

'As I was saying,' Shipshape continued. 'Cool, calm and collected as I was, I slipped off the belt from round my dungarees and, with a sleight of hand which any magician would have been proud of, I looped it round the beast's neck and twisted it as tight as a tourniquet. Its eyes went red. The neck strained. The wings tensed. Just as I was beginning to fear that I would have to release my grip, that the struggling bird was too much for me, its body went limp. And I knew the fight was over. The goose was dead.'

'Phew!' exclaimed Neil. He almost felt he'd done the fighting himself. 'Well done, Shipshape. Well done!!'

'Yes,' said Shambles. 'If it hadn't been for you, I wouldn't be here now.'

'If it hadn't been for me, none of us would be here now,' said Shipshape. 'And that includes you, Neil.'

'Well, as I said before, well done!' said Neil. 'You've rescued the whole quest from disaster.'

Neil started thinking. He wondered whether he would have been as lucky if he had been in Shipshape's position. He wondered if he would have been as cunning and clever as she had been. Not for the first time, he had to ask himself why the Great Methodical had chosen him of all people to save mankind.

'Ahem!'

After all, it wasn't as though he was particularly big, or strong, or even brave.

'AAHEMM!!'

Neil was suddenly conscious of Shipshape clearing her throat. She was obviously after some attention.

'Are you all right?' said Neil.

'I . . . er . . . just wondered whether you'd like to hear the end of my story, that was all,' she said, trying, and failing, to sound nonchalant. 'Or perhaps you've got bored with it?'

'No, no,' said Neil, feeling instantly guilty and flustered. 'Sorry. I thought you'd finished.'

'Finished?' said Shipshape. 'Can you believe the boy?' she said to Shambles. 'He thinks I've finished and I've hardly even begun!'

'Well, there's no need to exaggerate,' said Shambles. He turned to Neil. 'There are two remaining problems. One: how to dispose of the dead body. And two: how to find you.'

Neil thought back as hard as he could, but it was no use. He simply could not remember anything at all about where he'd been.

The three companions continued walking towards their goal. Shipshape was at the front, striding purposefully forward, recounting her tale, while the other two followed slightly behind, listening attentively.

'So,' said Shipshape, 'Shambles had by now regained consciousness, and first and foremost, we had to get rid of the dead goose. And that was no easy matter, I can assure you.'

'Why couldn't you just have shoved it into any old Thought Box?' said Neil.

'Strictly prohibited,' said Shipshape. 'Depositing anything in a Thought Box is the most highly punishable offence here in the Thought Domain.'

'But no one would have minded about one dead goose, surely,' said Neil.

'Dead or alive, the evil of the wicked Gander's cohorts is so powerful,' said Shambles seriously, 'that it was too much of a risk to take.'

'So what *did* you do?' asked Neil, who hadn't noticed any trace of a dead goose lying around.

'Well, we couldn't let it affect the mind of a human being,' said Shambles.

'And we were too far away from the animals' thoughts,' said Shipshape.

'And we couldn't leave it out in the open.'

'And we couldn't bury it.'

'And the thought of cooking it and eating it was positively disgusting,' said Shambles, with a grimace.

'Never know what we might have picked up,' added Shipshape.

'*So*,' said Neil again, slightly irritated by the games they were playing with him. 'What did you actually DO?'

Shipshape stopped in mid-stride and turned towards him.

'It never does to hurry a good story,' she said.

Seeing the frustrated expression on Neil's face they both laughed.

'Let's put him out of his misery,' said Shambles. 'As we couldn't put the goose into the head of a *living* person . . .' said Shambles slowly.

'You had to find a dead person,' said Neil, interrupting excitedly.

'You've guessed it,' said Shipshape.

Shambles explained how every time someone on earth dies, the light in their Thought Box goes out and the thoughts inside stop moving about. They wait there in the darkness until the regular patrols of the area come across the extinguished light. Then the Thought Domain worker loads the old thoughts on to a truck and takes them to the road which leads to Chaos.

'It was the first real stroke of luck we had the whole time,' said Shipshape. 'We moved out in concentric squares, walking until we found a full box with no light. On the third square out we found exactly what we needed.'

'In fact,' said Shambles, 'we actually saw the light going out. I rushed over and watched as the thoughts came to a halt, one by one.'

'It was quite an emotional moment,' said Shipshape.

'True,' said Shambles. 'Thinking of that life coming to an end.'

'But also very useful,' said Shipshape, as practical as ever. 'We dragged the goose over and, my word, it was heavy! And then "thud!", it dropped down into the box below.'

'It can't do any harm there,' said Shambles.

'And even if anyone does discover it, they'll think it was just one of the person's thoughts. Anything else would be impossible to prove.'

'What can I say?' said Neil, full of admiration for their resourcefulness. 'Well done *again*! Both of you!'

The story had been long, but their journey was longer. Occasionally Neil would think that the light was beginning to fade, that the night was approaching. But it was no more than an optical illusion, the effect of his eyes tiring at the sight of the millions and millions of Thought Boxes stretching away all round him.

There really should be some sort of relief here, he thought

to himself. Birds, trees, sun, mountains on the horizon, that sort of thing.

And as he looked around at the immensity of the Thought Domain it occurred to him that somewhere in the middle of all this classified order was a tiny area which belonged, in a way, to him. His own Thought Box.

'I wonder what it looks like?' he said, thinking aloud.

'What's that?' said Shambles.

'My Thought Box,' said Neil.

And before Shambles had even noticed Shipshape's frantic attempts to make him be quiet, he answered.

'Oh, it was much like all the others.'

Neil stopped.

'What do you mean?' he said.

'He meant it *would* be like all the others,' Shipshape interrupted.

'But he said *was*,' said Neil. He turned round and looked back at the grey expanse behind him. He knew that he would never find the box again.

'Why?' he shouted angrily. 'Why wouldn't you let me see it? Why didn't you tell me?'

'Neil!' said Shipshape crossly. 'Just quieten down and listen for a moment. You weren't just near your Thought Box, you were actually *in* it. You'd jumped into the middle of your own thoughts and it was the most dangerous place in the Thought Domain for you to be.'

'But why?' asked Neil, sure that Shipshape was trying to fool him. 'How could my own thoughts hurt me?'

'Because,' said Shipshape slowly, 'you get into a vicious circle of regressive memory.'

'What does that mean?' said Neil, unconvinced.

'It means that each thought you confront triggers off a previous thought, and mentally you get younger and younger and younger. You lose the ability to write, to walk, to talk and, finally, even to think, which is a contradiction in itself, as there you are, amongst your own thoughts. The illogicality of it all would destroy you and fix you mentally at a time before you started thinking.'

Neil only half understood.

'I still don't think it's fair,' he said sulkily. 'All those things I could have learnt about myself and I can't remember a single thought. The whole episode might just as well never have happened.'

'And it's a great pity it did,' said Shipshape.

'But what would have been the harm of just looking down at my thoughts?' said Neil. 'To see what was going on. You could have let me do that, couldn't you?'

'No, not even that,' said Shipshape.

'Why not?' said Neil.

'Every scientist will tell you,' said Shambles, 'that the watching of an experiment affects the result. Watching anything affects the thing being watched. Can you imagine how catastrophic it would be if you looked down at your thoughts, reacted, watched the reaction, reacted further, watched that further reaction, *ad infinitum*? It would make you lose your mind. Literally.'

'You were in a great deal of danger,' said Shipshape. 'And the only thing we could do was to get you away as quickly as possible.'

Neil still only half understood. But he *was* convinced that his two friends had had his best interests at heart, and his anger and disappointment gradually subsided.

'I'm sorry,' he said finally. 'I was just disappointed, that's all.'

'That's okay,' said Shipshape.

'Quite understandable,' said Shambles.

'So how did you get me out?' said Neil. 'Was it difficult?'

'It most certainly was,' said Shipshape. 'You were very nearly a goner.'

'I was?' said Neil.

'You see,' said Shambles, 'it took us ages and ages to find you . . .'

'And we wouldn't have managed it at all if you hadn't kept on shouting out . . .' added Shipshape.

'That's true,' said Shambles. 'Being able to home in on your voice was the one bit of good luck we had. But we could tell by the way you sounded higher and squeakier and more and more babyish exactly what had happened.'

'The almost impossible!' said Shipshape.

'And by the time we got to you,' continued Shambles, 'you'd already regressed to an age when you couldn't even understand our instructions.'

'We hung a rope down inside the Thought Box,' said Shipshape, 'but you were ignoring it completely. And even though we kept on shouting at you to take hold of it, you took no notice.'

'What *did* save me, then?' asked Neil.

'The Inkling!' they said in unison.

'The Inkling,' said Neil quietly. 'I'd forgotten all about it.' He put his hand into his pocket and pulled out the little, furry, grey animal.

'So you saved me did you?' he whispered to the creature, rubbing it against his cheek.

The Inkling only squeaked.

'How, though?' said Neil.

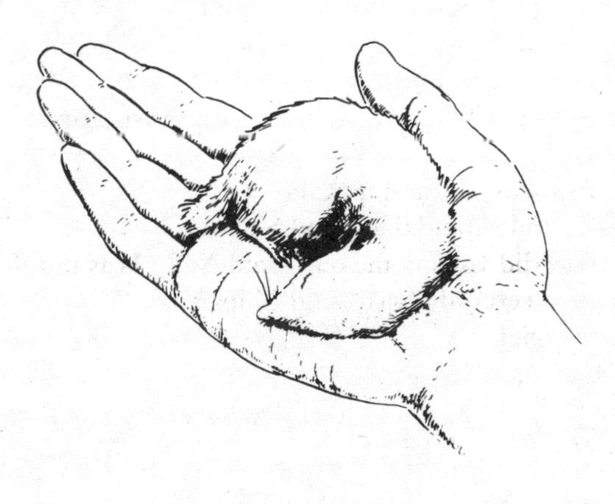

'The way inklings always have an effect,' said Shambles. 'Simply by whispering the hint of an idea.'

'One minute we saw it crawl out of your pocket and run up your sleeve to your ear and the next minute you reached forward and grasped the rope.'

'All thanks to you, little fellow,' said Neil. But the small ball of fur had gone to sleep again, and was whistling gently in Neil's hand.

Chapter 9
On the Ways of Thinking

It was impossible to tell how far they had come, how far they had still to go, as there was no way of measuring time or distance there in the Thought Domain. All they could say with absolute certainty was that they had come a long way and were all feeling totally despondent. No one had spoken for ages and the longer they remained silent, the more oppressive the silence became. Finally, it was Shipshape who spoke.

'This is hopeless,' she said.

'Don't say that,' said Neil.

'All is not yet lost,' said Shambles.

But basically Shipshape had only put into words what all three of them had been thinking.

'You're positive we're going in the right direction?' said Neil for the umpteenth time.

'As positive as I was the last time you asked,' said Shambles a little irritably.

If it had just been a matter of getting somewhere to have a picnic, or go for a swim, or feed the pigeons, or something equally unimportant, then they wouldn't have all been getting so tense. But knowing that the whole of the population of the world was depending on them put all three companions on edge. They were wasting so much time in travelling to their destination that by the time they arrived, it might already be too late. Occasionally, as if they had all heard a distant starter's pistol, they would break into a run. But it *was* hopeless, as Shipshape had said. They would end up doubled up, gasping for breath and seemingly no nearer their goal.

Neil wondered whether it was already too late.

'Hey!' said Shambles suddenly. 'Am I imagining it, or are there two people ahead of us?'

Neil looked up and squinted into the distance.

'I think you're right,' he said. 'Well, that's something, isn't it? Perhaps they know how far we've got to go.'

'We can but ask them,' said Shambles.

'I hope they're friendly,' said Shipshape.

'You mean they might not be?' said Neil.

'You never can tell,' said Shambles. 'You'd be surprised by the enormous number of unpleasant, vicious, mean vindictive, hateful and cruel thoughts that men and women have been responsible for!'

'Hmmm,' said Neil, feeling that Shambles was getting at him.

'We'll just keep our fingers crossed, shall we?' said Shipshape.

They approached the two thoughts in as friendly a manner as they could manage, while remaining on their guard. They looked harmless enough, Neil thought to himself. Both were dressed in jeans and a T-shirt; both were short and stocky; both had freckles and a crew-cut. In fact, apart from the different names printed on the front of their T-shirts they were completely identical. One was called Tyler. The other was called Lindle.

'Hello to you both,' said Neil, as chummily as he could.

'Hello,' replied Tyler and Lindle as one.

'My name's Neil and these are my two friends, Shipshape and Shambles.'

'Pleased to meet you, I'm sure,' said Tyler and Lindle, together again. They all shook hands and said how nice it was to meet one another and so on and so forth, until all the initial pleasantries were out of the way.

'I wonder,' said Shipshape, taking over, 'whether you two gentlemen could help us.'

'Most certainly, if we can,' said Tyler and Lindle together.

'The thing is,' continued Shipshape, 'we're heading for the Pillars of Reason and we wondered if there was much further to go. What would you estimate, Mr Tyler?' she said, turning to the one with TYLER printed on his front.

'Oh, I'm not Tyler,' he said. 'He is,' he added, pointing to his friend.

'But he's got LINDLE on his shirt,' said Shipshape.

'I know,' he said. 'We swopped shirts, you see.'

'Don't listen to him,' said the other one. 'Of course he's Tyler. I'm Lindle.'

'Well, why did he say he wasn't?' asked Shipshape.

'He's lying,' came the simple reply. 'He's always lying. It's compulsive. He is an obsessive prevaricator.'

'You LIAR!' screamed the one with the TYLER T-shirt. 'It's not me who's lying. That man there has never told the truth once in his life. I can tell only the truth. It is my fate never to let a falsehood pass my lips.'

'One hundred per cent inaccurate,' retorted the other. 'Certainly one of us tells only lies while the other tells only the truth, but I'm afraid he has got his facts round the wrong way. I tell the truth. He lies. He positively revels in mendacity.'

'Oh, good grief,' said Neil. 'Here we go again. I thought it was too good to be true to expect a simple answer in the Thought Domain. What a place!'

'We do seem to have a slight problem on our hands,' conceded Shipshape.

'Even if they do know how far the Pillars are, or whether or not we're going in the right direction, we don't know whose answer to trust, do we?' said Neil.

'Have we got far to go?' asked Shipshape.

'Yes,'
'No,' they answered in unison.

'Brilliant!' said Neil. 'Now who do we believe?'

'How strange to be so near and yet so far away from the truth,' said Shipshape.

Shambles, who had remained silent throughout the entire encounter so far, suddenly spoke.

'What would *he* say,' he said to the one with the LINDLE T-shirt, 'if I asked him if we were going in the right direction?'

'He would say that you weren't.'

'Thank you,' said Shambles with a smile. 'And what would *he* say,' he said, turning to the one with TYLER written across his chest, 'if I asked if it was still a long way to go to the Pillars of Reason?'

'He would say that it was.'

'Thank you so much, both of you,' said Shambles. 'You've been very helpful. Come along, Neil, Shipshape, I don't think we need to waste these two gentlemen's time any longer.'

'Bye, then,' said Neil to Lindle and Tyler.

The twins stood there looking quite bemused as the three companions departed, continuing their journey in the same direction as before. As soon as they were sure they were out of earshot both Neil and Shipshape started on Shambles.

'Come on,' said Neil, 'what was that all about?'

'How did your questions and their answers make you so sure we're going the right way?' said Shipshape.

'Not only are we going the right way, but we're almost there. Didn't you hear their replies?' said Shambles.

'And you're sure we're going in the right direction?' asked Shipshape.

'Most certainly,' said Shambles.

'And you're sure it isn't far to go?' asked Neil.

'Unquestionably,' said Shambles.

He fell silent. Shipshape and Neil looked at each other and shrugged. A few moments passed. Finally Shipshape couldn't bear it any longer.

'Come on then, you smug little piglet,' she said. 'Tell us how you know!'

'Oh, haven't you worked it out yet?' said Shambles with irritating mock surprise.

'No, we haven't!' they shouted.

'Quite elementary logic, I assure you,' he said. 'I asked them both to answer what *the other* would say. The truthful one truthfully admitted that the other would give us the false reply. The lying one meanwhile twisted the truthful answer of his honest companion into a lie. By reversing the answers given, we arrive inevitably at the truth.'

'Brilliant!' said Shipshape, staring at Shambles in awe.

Neil felt that it probably was brilliant, but he couldn't quite work it out. He kept going through Shambles's explanation, but somehow all the lies and truths kept getting confused: if Tyler didn't say what he hadn't meant, then the truth wouldn't be what Lindle might have said. Or not. Unless it was the other way round!

He was still letting the various possibilities play around his head when he noticed something in the distance. At first he dismissed the evidence of his eyes as an optical illusion: it was only perspective drawing the far-off roads together. And yet as they walked further, Neil became increasingly sure that they *must* be approaching the end of the Plains of Thought. Still, he wouldn't let himself believe it one hundred per cent. The disappointment if he was wrong would be too great. In the end it was Shipshape who yelled out.

'I can see the Ways of Thinking,' she yelled. 'Look!!'

They all gave a resounding cheer and Shambles was congratulated on having understood Tyler and Lindle's cryptic replies.

Neil looked at his map of the Thought Domain and confirmed that the pattern of roads they were approaching was indeed that of the Ways of Thinking.

The Ways were intricately arranged to enable the countless thousand roads separating the individual Thought

Boxes gradually to merge together to form the Right Track with the minimum of congestion. It had all been constructed in multiples of five. Along the length of the Thought Boxes every five of the roads would converge to form a single one. Then every five of the resulting roads would again converge, which in turn would also meet five more. And so on and so forth until, finally, the last five roads of the Ways of Thinking would come together as the Right Track, the mall which led directly to the Pillars of Reason and entrance to Chaos.

'At last!' thought Neil to himself. 'I just hope that there's still enough time left.'

As they finally neared the edge of the Plains of Thought, it became clear that Tyler and Lindle were far from being the only thoughts wandering around on their own. To the left and right, though still too far away to see their faces or forms clearly, hundreds of other thoughts were making their way in the same direction.

'Shouldn't they be under supervision?' asked Neil.

'Indeed they should,' said Shambles. 'Indeed they should.'

'I had no idea it had got so bad,' said Shipshape, shaking her head sadly.

'Look at the state of those,' said Shambles pointing down at the Thought Boxes. 'Quite disgraceful,' he said.

Neil looked and noticed that lots of the partitions between the boxes had collapsed. In some cases the walls had shifted, leaving some boxes too small and others half open. A couple of boxes had collapsed completely and the thoughts had all escaped.

'Oh dear, oh dear,' said Shipshape. 'This is chaotic. Nobody realized how far back the disorder had reached. That means that not only has the Right Track been affected, not only have the Ways of Thinking been disrupted, but that the Thought Boxes themselves are being thrown into turmoil.'

'What does it all mean for the people with these Thought Boxes?' asked Neil.

'Oh, it can have terrible repercussions,' said Shipshape. 'That one, for instance,' she said, pointing to an empty box with collapsed sides. 'That poor person will be suffering from amnesia. You know what that is?'

'Yes,' said Neil. 'It's when someone forgets everything.'

'Correct,' said Shipshape. 'And this is the cause. The walls break down. The thoughts break out. The person is left without any memories at all, and as soon as any new ones are made, they disappear as well. It's like pouring water into a bucket full of holes.'

'Gosh,' said Neil.

'And that there,' said Shipshape, pointing to a couple of boxes which had become one when the dividing wall had fallen down, 'that is how telepathy takes place.'

'But these two people may not even know each other,' said Neil.

'That's right,' said Shipshape. 'Maybe one of them lives in Africa and the other in China, but wherever they come from they are able to communicate with one another. It can be very confusing, hearing another voice inside your head.'

'I'll bet,' said Neil, thinking back to stories they'd done at school on Joan of Arc.

'And then there's *déjà vu*,' added Shambles. 'That's a bit similar.'

'Never heard of it,' said Neil.

'It's when you're doing something for the very first time and you have the weirdest feeling that it's all happened before and you know exactly what's going to happen next.'

'Oh, I know that feeling,' said Neil, excitedly. 'It's happened to me loads of times. So what is it exactly?'

'It's where there has been a temporary hole between your Thought Box and somebody else's and you share some of the other person's experiences, memories, conversations and so forth,' explained Shambles. 'So then, if you have a similar experience, it really does seem as though you are repeating something you've done before.'

Neil was interrupted in his thoughts about all the times *he'd* had *déjà vu* by the sound of someone or something counting.

'One, two, three, four, five, six, seven, eight, nine, ten, eleven . . .' came the voice.

The three companions all looked round to see where the numbers were coming from.

'Forty-two thousand and sixteen, forty-two thousand and seventeen, forty-two thousand and eighteen,' the voice continued.

Neil saw that the cause of the sequence of numbers was a curious object sitting cross-legged on the ground, if sitting is the right description for something with a carpenter's ruler instead of legs. Apart from its peculiar legs, it had slide-rule arms, a disc-like face similar to that of a clock, hair made up cf a bunch of tape-measures, hands consisting of calipers and feeler-gauges, and set into the place where its stomach should have been was a computer's digital display.

'Twenty-two, forty-four, eighty-eight, a hundred and seventy-six, three hundred and fifty-two, seven hundred and four . . .' the object reeled off with incredible speed.

'What on earth is it?' asked Neil.

'Seven, fourteen, twenty-one, twenty-eight, thirty-five, forty-two, forty-nine . . .'

'Can't you guess.' said Shipshape with a grin.

'Ninety-six, ninety-seven, ninety-eight, ninety-nine, one hundred!'

'No, I can't,' said Neil.

'It's the thought that counts!' said Shipshape, and both she and Shambles burst into howls of laughter.

'It's the thought that counts,' Neil repeated, and groaned. How many times had he heard his mother or father say that when he'd been able to afford only something very little for their birthdays. 'Never mind, Neil, it's the thought that counts!'

'I never thought it could be a real thing,' said Neil.

'Everything is here,' said Shipshape. 'Everything imaginable.'

And the nearer they got to the Ways of Thinking, the more chaotic 'everything' was becoming. Not only that, but there was an increasing tension in the air which was making them all more and more nervy. Although he couldn't actually pin the feeling down, Neil sensed an impending danger, an omnipresent fear, a nagging agitation which was mounting moment by moment. The strict order of the Thought Domain was breaking down here and the power of the Great Methodical was on the wane in this distant outpost. Chaos was visibly encroaching on the entire area, preparing the way for the final attack that would be launched by the evil Gander.

'Look,' said Shambles, pointing at the rows of broken Thought Boxes. This part of the plain looked as though it had been devastated by an earthquake. Row after row of the boxes had been twisted out of shape and now some had their walls crushed in together, while others had been stretched wider and wider.

'Both are fatal for any real thinking,' said Shambles. 'In those,' he said, indicating the reduced boxes, 'there isn't the room for decision-making, no choice the person makes has ever been thought out; and those other boxes are so wide that they're full of any number of useless, redundant thoughts.'

'So many,' added Shipshape, 'that a thousand sides to every argument can always be seen.'

'The narrow-minded and the open-minded,' said Shambles. 'Both as handicapped in different ways; both incapable of thinking rationally.'

'I thought it was a good thing to be open-minded,' objected Neil.

'Not always,' said Shambles. 'While it's wrong to be too dogmatic about anything, it's just as harmful to be too tolerant of everything.'

'I don't understand,' said Neil. It was meant to be good to be tolerant, wasn't it?

'You see,' said Shipshape. 'Some things *are* bad. Some things *are* wrong. And if they are bad, then it's wrong to tolerate them, isn't it?'

'But . . .' started Neil.

'It's been the Gander's greatest victory so far to convince people that they should be tolerant of anything which happens. Tolerating evil *is* evil!' said Shambles.

Neil couldn't think of anything to say. He'd always been taught to respect other people's ideas, even when he disagreed with them. And yet Shambles had a point. Neil thought of Barry Smedley from the class above him: he was a real bully, always picking on the smaller boys and stealing their pocket-money.

'Don't you agree?' said Shambles, looking at the confused expression on the boy's face.

'I think so,' said Neil, 'but I need a bit of time to think it over.'

Unfortunately, time was the one thing that was in very short supply. As they left behind the last remaining bits and pieces of the damaged Thought Boxes and came on to the Ways of Thinking, they came face to face with the full extent of the problem. The scene which confronted the three companions was completely chaotic. The wicked Gander had certainly been doing its work thoroughly and successfully.

More than anything else, the appearance, the atmosphere, the frantic activity reminded Neil of one of the Saturday street markets in town. Everyone (and everything) looked terribly busy and pushed for time, but nothing very much seemed to be going on. Some thoughts stood around chatting, while others sat patiently under make-shift shelters. Occasionally, a burst of singing or a peal of laughter would pierce the air, but despite the superficial good spirits, Neil sensed the prevailing mood of anxious anticipation. No one knew what was going to happen next and the uncertainty put the whole collection of thoughts on edge. The song or laughter could just as easily change as the tension brought on fits of rage and floods of tears.

'How long have you been here?' Shipshape asked a couple of depressed-looking thoughts huddled together under a tarpaulin.

'Don't ask me,' said one.

'Seems like for ever,' said the other.

'If only it would be over,' said the first.

'If only it would all come to an end,' echoed the second.

'I don't think I can take any more,' chimed in a third thought.

'My poor nerves,' said the first one.

'I'm at the end of my tether,' agreed the second.

'You should get a longer one,' said the first.

'A longer what?' said the second.

'A longer tether,' explained the first, 'if you've reached the end of the one you've got!'

All three thoughts began laughing uncontrollably.

'Nervous hysteria,' whispered Shambles to Neil as they left.

'It's hardly surprising, is it?' said Shipshape. 'Nowhere to go to, nowhere to return to and terrified the whole time by the lies of the evil Gander.'

As they continued their walk along the Ways of Thinking to where they would all converge on the Right Track, the atmosphere became increasingly bizarre, a complete mish-mash of emotions. It was like being at a festive funeral, or a mournful celebration.

Suddenly, from one of the parallel ways, they heard an uncharacteristically rowdy noise. There was something infectious about the obvious enjoyment of the thoughts there, and the three companiones were drawn over.

'What's going on?' asked Neil.

All the thoughts looked pretty much the same. They were dressed in harlequin costumes of multi-coloured satin diamond shapes. They were leaping around at their desks, slamming the lids and slapping their thighs, throwing ink pellets at one another while the teacher threw pieces of chalk at them.

'It's a school of thought,' said Shambles.

'A what?' said Neil, laughing at the antics of the clowns. 'You mean a place where thoughts learn?'

'No,' said Shambles. 'In fact, the opposite in a way.'

They had by now all formed a line and were doing flip-flaps round and round the class, up and down the aisles between the chairs. Hands. Feet. Hands. Feet. Over and over, their bells jingling with every landing. A couple of them picked up some balls and skittles and started juggling with them in pairs. Another grabbed the teacher's cane and this was thrown up to join the other objects flying through mid-air.

'What do you mean, the opposite?' asked Neil.

'Well,' said Shambles. 'They're all thoughts that occurred to different people at more or less the same time. Up here, they all become united.'

'But how do they teach *us*?' persisted Neil.

'Simple,' said Shambles. 'Let me give you an example. There was, some centuries ago, a school of thought which said that the earth was flat; another which maintained that the sun revolved around the earth; another which claimed that kings were chosen by God. At those times, the thoughts formed a school and influenced all the other thoughts around them.'

'But if the thoughts are in individual Thought Boxes, I still don't see how . . .' started Neil.

'I said "in a way",' said Shambles irritably. 'You really are becoming a most pedantic little boy!'

'Well, you taught me everything I know!' retorted Neil crossly.

'Hey, hey, hey,' said Shipshape. 'Calm down, you two. This isn't *you* talking, it's the atmosphere of this place. We're going to have to try to curb any negative feelings we may have, because they'll only do us harm in the long run. Okay?'

Neil and Shambles both looked sheepishly down at the ground.

'Sorry,' they both said together, then looked up and smiled.

'That's better,' said Shipshape. 'Now shake hands on it and we'll be off.'

They were just about to seal their apology with the handshake when a deafening whistle sounded directly behind them. It was a two-note whistle; one high, one low, and an instant later a whole column of speeding thoughts whizzed past them.

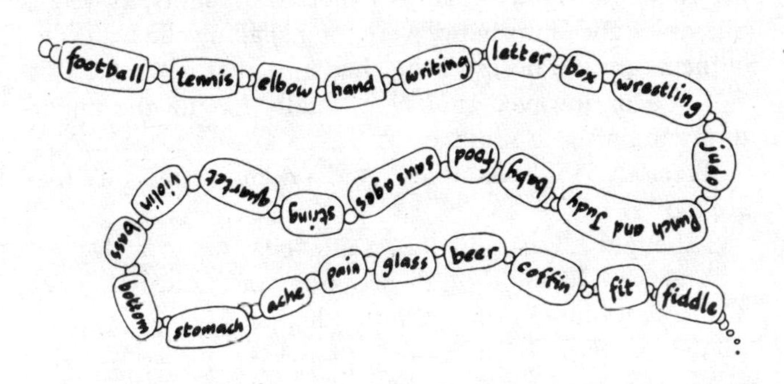

And so they went on, innumerable associations racing between Neil and Shambles's outstretched hands.

'Don't tell me,' said Neil, as the last of the thoughts sped past and disappeared. 'That just had to be a train of thought. Right?'

'Right indeed, Neil,' said Shipshape. 'You're certainly getting used to the way things work here.'

'The trouble is,' said Shambles, 'by the time he's learnt all about Order, it'll be time for him to go into Chaos.'

Neil felt his stomach churn nervously. The prospect of going to Chaos at all made him feel uneasy, but the fact that he had to go there alone . . . He refused to let himself think of it.

'And that,' he said, noticing a massive, curling arc of water that was sweeping about thirty squealing thoughts across the Ways of Thinking, 'must be a . . . Uh-oh!!' he yelled, as interest turned to alarm.

'Get down,' yelled Shipshape. 'Hold on to anything you can.'

The water had changed course and was heading directly at them.

'Hold on tight!' screamed Shipshape.

A moment later Neil felt the water rushing over him, drenching him to the skin. The incident had passed almost before it had begun and all the affected thoughts, as well as Shambles and Shipshape, were soon shaking the water out of their ears and noses (if they had any, that is!).

'. . . a brainwave,' said Neil, finally having the opportunity to finish his sentence.

'Precisely,' said Shambles. 'And a damned nuisance they are too.'

'I thought it was quite fun,' said Neil.

'You were lucky it didn't break on you,' said Shambles. 'Causes absolute havoc when that happens.'

'You were also lucky not to get swept away,' said Shipshape. 'Some thoughts have been known to go riding along on the crest of a wave for so long and so far that they get completely lost and never ever manage to find themselves again.'

'Just as well I managed to hold on, then,' said Neil.

'Good for you,' said a deep, grumpy voice, 'but why did you have to choose me to hold on to, huh? Nearly broken my leg, you have.'

'Sorry,' said Neil.

'Pardon?' said the thought, a metallic object with a large, circular grey head.

'I said I was sorry,' said Neil.

'Very nice of you, I'm sure,' said the metal thought. 'What for?'

Neil was beginning to feel confused. 'Because I was holding on to your leg,' he said.

'You were?' said the thought. 'I don't remember. What did you say your name was?'

'I didn't.' said Neil. 'But it's Neil. What's yours?'

'My what?'

'Your name!'

'My name? Hmmm. The tricky ones now, is that your game? My name? . . . pssshh. It's on the tip of my tongue. It's . . . it's . . . it'sssss.' Its eyes went vague. 'What did you ask me?' it said finally.

'Oh, nothing,' said Neil irritably. 'And what are you two standing there laughing about?' he snapped at Shambles and Shipshape.

'How would you describe the fellow you've been engaging in such a stimulating conversation with?' asked Shambles.

'Complete idiot,' said Neil. 'A memory like a . . .'

He looked back at the thought and its unusual shape suddenly looked terribly familiar. Neil burst out laughing.

'What are you laughing for?' asked the thought.

'Would you mind repeating that?' said Neil, trying to keep a straight face.

The thought looked puzzled. 'I don't know,' it said. 'Did I say anything, then?'

'Memory like a sieve,' said Neil. Looking closer, he saw the large round head was concave and full of tiny holes; when the brainwave had passed over, it had been the sieve's handle that he'd grabbed hold of.

'Bye bye,' said Neil, even though he knew that the poor thought would have forgotten him before he had even had time to reply.

As they continued walking past the odd collection of thoughts, Neil noticed that the roads on either side of them were visibly converging. They must be getting near to the

Right Track. He stopped to have a quick look at the map, but as the scale was all wrong, it wasn't possible to judge how far ahead the last stretch of their journey was.

Suddenly, as they were all clustered round the map, they began to sense something. Neil looked at Shipshape, who looked at Shambles, who looked at Neil! One thing was reflected in all their eyes. Fear. Neil felt goose-pimples rising all over his skin. His knees shook uncontrollably. His stomach turned and he gritted his teeth involuntarily. And inside his head . . .

'This is . . .' he started to say, but the fear was so powerful, so overwhelming, that it drove the words away. He felt his breathing turn to nervous gasps and heard the sound of his furiously racing heart pounding in his ears. Screwing his eyes tightly shut and clamping his hands over his ears, he attempted to keep the paralysing fear at bay. But to no effect.

And still the terror grew. It grew to the point where Neil was no longer even able to put it into words: a blinding, deafening, painfully indescribable fear!

'This *must* be the worst it could ever be,' thought Neil. 'Stop, stop!'

But still the screaming fear continued. Then, as Neil felt that he couldn't take another second of this intense horror, he heard a voice. It was behind all the other noise in his head, deep, distant but undeniable.

'You snivelling little worm,' boomed the voice. 'You will fail. YOU WILL FAIL! *YOU WILL DIE!!!*'

And as the words echoed in his head, Neil caught sight of a monstrous figure out of the corner of his eyes. If there can be black light, or white darkness, then that was the colour of the passing being. It was like looking at a black-and-white photograph and its negative at the same time, if that was possible.

His heart was beating so fast now that Neil could feel actual pain throbbing in his chest, and once again he heard the voice:

'DIE, WORM!' it said. '*YOU WILL DIE!!!*'

And then, as suddenly as the terror had come upon them it disappeared again. Neil looked at Shipshape and Shambles. The terror had gone, but the memory of it remained. Neil stood there trembling, too shocked still even to feel relief. That would come later.

'Are you all right?' asked Shipshape.

The boy remained silent.

'Neil,' said Shambles. 'Come on, now, don't let it get to you.'

'Chin up,' encouraged Shipshape.

Neil took a deep breath; finally his body was beginning to accept that it could relax.

'Something spoke to me,' he said quietly.

'What did it say?' asked Shipshape.

Neil swallowed. 'That I'd die,' he said.

'Well, that's optimistic,' said Shipshape, 'because the one thing you'll never hear from the Gander is the truth.'

'But it was so powerful,' said Neil. 'So . . . terrifying.' He shuddered at the memory. 'Why was it *so* bad this time?'

'You only came into contact with its evil helpers before,' explained Shipshape. 'You felt uneasy, of course, but the effect they cause is a mere fraction of what you've just experienced.'

'It was shattering,' said Neil, still dazed.

'For the first time since you arrived in the Thought Domain,' continued Shipshape, 'you've been confronted, not by any substitute or pale imitation, but by the lying Lord of Chaos itself: the Proper Gander.'

'The PROPER Gander, the proper GANDER,' Neil repeated, playing with the sounds of the words. All at once, they formed themselves into one single word that Neil had heard a thousand times over the breakfast table: PROPAGANDA!!

And everything suddenly clicked into place. Here in the Thought Domain his foe was a massive, dirty, wicked bird, but his mum and dad had described it as something altogether less concrete but infinitely more sinister: the deliberate twisting of the truth into evil lies designed to hurt as many people as possible.

'So that's what I've got to try and destroy!' said Neil, as the full impact of the task ahead occurred to him for the first time. 'But am I strong enough to take it on alone?'

'Of course you are, Neil, and not only strong enough but brave enough, cunning enough and clever enough too,' said Shipshape enthusiastically. But as Neil looked up, he caught Shipshape looking at Shambles and noticed the doubt in her face that the optimistic words couldn't hide. He felt utterly desperate.

'How can *I* ever hope to defeat the evil Proper Gander single-handed?' he thought miserably.

Chapter 10
On the Right Track

Slowly but surely, as his heart stopped racing and his knees ceased shaking and his tongue unglued itself from the roof of his mouth, Neil's confidence began to increase once again. Fear is a strange thing. Once the cause has been removed, you can only remember the fact that you were frightened; all the details disappear. That was what was happening to Neil. He remembered the feelings of utter terror and the words that the Proper Gander had whispered to him, but somehow the immediacy of the situation was gone and he was able to convince himself that things really weren't *that* bad.

'That was the most terrifying experience I've ever had,' said Neil finally, as soon as he could speak calmly again without stammering.

'It's unbelievable, isn't it?' said Shambles. 'And what's more, all the Proper Gander was doing was looking out from Chaos, through the Pillars of Reason, and that was enough to petrify all of us.'

Neil felt his lifting spirits slump again.

'Then how are we ever going to . . . ?' he began.

'STOP!' said Shipshape. 'Don't ever let yourself begin to think that. It's much too dangerous.'

'We must believe in ourselves,' added Shambles. 'And if we do, really do, then we cannot fail.'

Neil wanted to remain sceptical but he didn't want to

annoy the others, so he changed the conversation to something else he remembered about his first brief encounter with the evil Proper Gander.

'I think,' he said, 'I think I actually caught a glimpse of the Gander.'

'Did you?' said Shipshape. 'What was it like?'

'I'm not really sure I can describe it,' said Neil. 'It was all sort of black and white at the same time. And I could only see it, I don't know, when I wasn't looking at it.' He realized how stupid this must sound, but Shipshape seemed to understand.

'You mean out of the corner of your eye,' she said.

'Yes, that's right,' said Neil.

'That's the way it always is,' said Shambles. 'You cannot look the Proper Gander straight in the eye. It consistently defies all attempts at close analysis.'

'Hmmm,' said Neil, making a mental note of this new fact. 'I wonder if we could use that to our advantage somehow.'

Ordinarily, the Right Track would look quite different from the Ways of Thinking. While the Ways were narrow, curved paths which linked up with the Thought Box network, the Right Track was long, wide, straight and imposing. It was a spectacular mall which led right up to the massive Pillars of Reason, which stood there, tall, straight and white, emerging out of the flat landscape like two upraised arms reaching for the sky. Between them were the heavy and solid doors which separated Chaos from Order. Neil peered into the distance, but try as he might he couldn't see any fence or wall dividing the two aspects of the Thought Domain.

'It's difficult to explain,' said Shambles, in answer to his question. 'Chaos and Order exist at the same time and place, but you have to go through the Pillars of Reason to get from one to the other.'

Seeing that Neil still looked confused, Shipshape took over.

'It's a bit like your television,' she explained. 'It contains a completely different world. You can look to the side, above, below and even round the back of the set and you won't find that other world. You'd have to go through the screen to get into that television dimension. And it's the same with the Pillars of Reason. You could inspect them from all sides and wouldn't find Chaos.'

'And vice versa,' added Shambles. 'You could be in Chaos and walk round the Pillars of Reason and wouldn't find Order or the Thought Boxes.'

'It's only by going actually *through* the Pillars that you can pass from one side of the Thought Domain to the other.'

'I *think* I understand,' said Neil, finally.

'That's good enough,' said Shipshape with a smile. 'Let's keep going.'

As the three companions left the Ways of Thinking and stepped on to the Right Track, the change was far less impressive than it should have been. The road was obstructed by thousand upon thousand upon thousand of miserable thoughts. They shuffled about despondently like whole populations of homeless refugees. The market atmosphere the three of them had noticed on the Ways of Thinking was much more muted here, as if the day's trading was over but no one was allowed to go home.

The two white, vertical Pillars sparkled in the distance. But the sight of them made the assembled thoughts seem all the more dispirited, perhaps because they knew that on the other side of those pillars was Chaos, the goal which the Proper Gander was preventing them from reaching.

'This is really depressing,' said Shambles.

'You can say that again,' said Neil, glad that someone had spoken.

But the conversation didn't amount to much and soon they were trudging on silently again, picking their way through the sorry-looking collections of thoughts. A couple of times they felt the tell-tale goose-pimples up and down their arms, tingling at the back of their necks, and knew that the hench-geese were flying overhead in their V-shaped patrols looking for them. Each time it happened they had to hide themselves in amongst the waiting thoughts; each time it happened the close proximity of the evil geese drained a little bit more of their already sapping energy.

'They just don't seem to be getting any nearer,' said Neil, looking up at the distant Pillars of Reason.

'If anything, I reckon they've moved back a bit,' said Shambles, irritably.

'It certainly is a long track,' said Shipshape, the physically strongest of the three of them. 'But I'm sure we can all make it,' she added, encouragingly.

Shambles didn't look convinced. He was wheezing like an old man and his red, sweaty face clashed horribly with his lank, orange hair.

'I really am exhausted,' he said. 'Couldn't we just have a little sit-down. We'll feel fresher for it.'

'No,' said Shipshape.

'Oh, go on,' persisted Shambles. 'It'll speed us up in the long run, just a couple of minutes.'

'If we stop now, we'll never get going again,' said Shipshape ominously.

Shambles tutted his annoyance, but didn't say anything else. The walking became increasingly mechanical, one foot after the other after the other. Shambles stared unseeingly at the ground in front of him and his head was empty except for the thought 'I'm so tired, I'm so tired, I'm so tired!' And meanwhile Neil was thinking: 'It's so far away, it's so far away, it's so far away!' Even Shipshape was beginning to flag as the pervasive gloom of the Right Track affected them all in its insidious manner.

'This isn't *real* tiredness,' Shipshape managed to say. 'It's mental exhaustion. There *is* a difference . . .'

Before she had time to explain just what the difference was, another of the sinister V-formations of birds appeared in the sky. Neil and Shambles were too tired even to bother concealing themselves.

'Get down!!' screamed Shipshape, grabbing at both of them and pulling them down to the ground. She covered them all up with a stray thought of an old blanket and hoped for the best. She was quite certain that this time they would be detected, but once again they were lucky. The shadows passed over them and the geese were gone. She sat up and looked around. Neil and Shambles remained motionless.

'This is absolutely ridiculous,' said Shipshape to herself, feeling her own last remnants of energy dribbling away as she sat there. 'Good grief, am *I* being thick?' she suddenly yelled out.

It had dawned on her what the solution to the problem was. Of course, the answer was obvious, but when you are mentally tired even the simplest things seem difficult. She stood up and rolled Neil over so that she could get at the satchel.

'Here,' she said, breaking off a couple of pieces of the Food for Thought and handing it to the others.

The effect was instantaneous.

'Good old Great Methodical,' said Shambles.

'Well remembered,' said Neil to Shipshape. 'I don't know what we'd do without you.'

'It was nothing really,' said Shipshape, trying but failing to look modest.

They all felt as though an enormous weight had been taken off their shoulders and the relief, energy and excitement that they now felt overwhelmed them. It was as if they were just starting out afresh. So happy did they feel that without for a moment even considering the possible danger, they spontaneously burst into song.

We've lost our car
And we've lost our way,
We've lost some battles

And we've lost our say –
So we've nothing left to lose.
But if you think we're giving up,
Have we got news for you!
PROPER GANDER
We're coming after YOU!!

We'll win the war
And we'll win the day,
We'll win first prize
And we'll win the race.
You've got everything to lose.
So you may as well give up,
Have we got news for you!
PROPER GANDER
We're coming after YOU!!

Even the depressed faces of the desperate thoughts lining the Right Track seemed to brighten a little as the three companions passed them by. Perhaps it was light-headedness following their close encounter with the Proper Gander; perhaps it was the relief of knowing that their destination was in sight; perhaps they had simply eaten a little too much of the Food for Thought. It was impossible to say exactly, but whatever the cause of their present high spirits, it certainly left them dangerously vulnerable.

'Gentlemen, gentlemen,' said a tall, thin thought stepping out of the shadows to greet them. 'I can't tell you how pleasant it is to hear cheerful voices once more. One tires so of all these glum faces,' he added, with a sweep of his arm.

'We have good reason,' said Shipshape. 'We are on an extremely important quest.'

Neil had the feeling that Shipshape shouldn't be speaking to this stranger so openly, but when he went to tell her this the words came out all wrong.

'We're going to rid the Thought Domain of the Proper Gander,' he blurted out incautiously.

'And not before time, I should say,' said the newcomer. 'A bombastic piece of work if ever there was one.'

'And what might your name be?' said Shambles.

'Wishful,' said the thought. 'At your service.'

'Very nice to meet you,' Neil, Shipshape and Shambles all said.

'The pleasure is all mine,' said Wishful, beaming.

Neil looked at the newcomer more closely. Curiously, the more intently he observed him, the less he seemed to be able to say about him with any certainty. He was definitely tall, and yet there was a certain shortness about his height. And although you would describe him as slim, it was certainly a somewhat hefty slimness. And while thinking of Wishful as 'he', Neil was conscious of a very real 'she-ness' about him/her.

'But enough of me,' continued Wishful. 'Tell me, just how are you going to perform this mammoth task?'

'Oh, it shouldn't be too difficult,' said Neil, swaggering a little.

'A piece of cake,' said Shipshape.

'A doddle!' said Shambles. Even he seemed to be captivated by the charm of the smiling Wishful.

'A piece of cake, a doddle! Splendid, splendid!' he said, throwing back his head and laughing heartily. It was as though the three companions had just told him the best piece of news he had ever heard. 'Just walk in there and ZAP, THUNK, KAPOW! and the Proper Gander will bite the dust, right?'

'Right!' said Neil enthusiastically.

'Kick the bucket!' said Shambles.

'Snuff it!' said Shipshape.

There was something that Neil wanted to ask, but each time he tried to say the words they seemed to twist round into something else.

'And how long do you think this little venture of yours will take to accomplish?' asked Wishful.

'Two shakes of a cat's whiskers,' said Shipshape.

'We'll have done it before you can say Jack Robinson,' said Shambles.

Neil remained silent. He was struggling against the waves of optimism which kept threatening to make him give up with his question. He almost managed to ask it for the third time, but once again the jaunty voice of Wishful interrupted him.

'And what do you think your next task will be once you have disposed of the Proper Gander once and for all?' he asked.

Neil heard all sorts of vague promises whispering around inside his head: 'I could be champion of the world!'; 'Today the Thought Domain, tomorrow the Universe!'; 'I could be in total control!!!' But he knew it wasn't true, he knew that this newcomer was misleading them somehow. Before Shambles or Shipshape could come in with their glib platitudes, Neil finally managed to get out the question he'd been itching to ask.

'Just how,' he said, speaking so quickly that he wouldn't lose track of the question, 'how are you so happy when all the other thoughts here are so miserable?'

'Oh, I don't like things to get on top of me,' answered Wishful with a smile. 'I don't let things get me down!'

'Every cloud has a silver lining, eh?' said Shipshape.

'Exactly that,' said Wishful.

'Always look on the bright side of life,' suggested Shambles.

'You've hit the nail on the head,' said Wishful.

Neil had to concede that it was no good. He could not think straight, faced with Wishful's all-consuming optimism. But I'm sure that something's not quite right, he thought to himself.

Wishful was by now in full swing. 'My friends, my friends, my oh so valiant friends,' he was saying. 'I only want to inspire you with the courage you need to perform the feats and endeavours you have outlined to the best of your ability. I want to spur you on to achieve all that I am sure you can and will achieve, to boost your confidence, to raise you hopes, to lift your expectations and bless you with the strength of your resolve . . .'

'Yeah, yeah, yeah,' said a voice behind them. 'Pull the other one, it's got little silver bells on it.'

Neil felt himself being immediately brought down to earth from the lofty heights of self-confidence.

'And as for you lot,' the voice continued to Neil, Shipshape and Shambles, 'you all ought to be ashamed of yourselves, taken in by this simpering little creep!'

All three of them felt the spell Wishful had cast over them losing its power. The thought berating them for their gullibility was a well-built, blue character dressed in a grey track-suit.

'You really do need some sense knocked into you, and I, the Sobering Thought, am the one to do it!' he yelled.

Neil felt as if he was crash-landing after several hours' floating in mid-air. The light-headedness vanished completely. He felt back to normal and, looking round at Shipshape and Shambles, he could see that they felt the same. The biggest change of all, however, had occurred to Wishful. He looked completely different. The shine had gone out of his body, his tall handsome form had dwindled away and the voice sounded petulant and whiny.

'Oh!' he said dejectedly.

Looking at the thin, weedy figure in front of them, Neil, Shambles and Shipshape soon realized that Wishful was more miserable than all the other thoughts put together.

'What happened?' asked Neil.

'His bluff seems to have been called,' said Shambles.

'I'm going to be big and strong and handsome when I grow up,' said Wishful in his high-pitched whine. 'I am. Then you'll all see. Then you won't be able to treat me so badly. And I'll be really, really important, with loads and loads of people working for me, and a big desk with a leather top, and my name on the door in brass letters. I will. I will.'

'And it'll all take place on the 12th of Never in the Back of Beyond,' said the Sobering Through scathingly. 'Why don't you just go away,' it added.

Wishful remained there though, still trying to put his case:

'But . . . if you just . . . I mean . . . Just you see . . . Wait!!!'

But the others had all left him standing there.

'I have the feeling our little friend was more dangerous than we suspected,' said Shambles.

'You were *extremely* lucky that I happened to be passing,' said the Sobering Thought.

'Who was that, then?' said Neil.

'Well, his full name is Pointless Wishful-Thinking,' said the Sobering Thought. 'A double-barrelled thought. It was a sad day when the Thinkings married into the Wishful family. I always knew no good would come of it.'

'But he didn't really seem dangerous,' said Neil.

'No,' agreed the Sobering Thought. 'He's a tragic little figure. It's difficult to know whether he believes anything he says at all, either about himself or others. I suspect not. His strength, and his danger,' he added, 'is that so many of the people he encounters are willing to delude themselves.'

Neil, Shambles and Shipshape all looked down, feeling uncomfortable.

'He is an insidious little thought, capable of trapping anyone vain enough to believe his idle words,' concluded the Sobering Thought.

There was an embarrassed silence as the three companions contemplated how flattery might have undone all the trials and tribulations they had endured to get this far.

Neil looked round at the crowds of thoughts all milling about the confined area. It *was* just like the Saturday market in town. And then it occurred to him that just as you had to be on the look-out for all kinds of rascals, conmen and pickpockets in the real market, so here you had to be on your guard for the thoughts that were out to trick you.

'We really must watch how we go from now on,' said Neil. 'We can't mess it all up now. Not having got so far.'

'Very true, my friend,' said the Sobering Thought. 'And if you'd allow me, I should like to give you a few words of advice of my own before taking my leave of you.'

'Fire away,' said Shipshape.

But before it could say a word, a certain, and by now familiar, muttering passed through the crowd. It could only mean one thing: another of the goose-patrols was passing overhead. The three companions instantly scattered and hid themselves amongst all the other thoughts, and hoped they would remain inconspicuous.

Crouching down out of sight between two massive thoughts, a red and yellow combine harvester and a friendly-looking dinosaur, Neil thought back on some of the many curious things he'd seen since leaving the Thought Boxes: there was the memory like a sieve, the thought that counts, the school of thought, the train of thought and the brainwave, and now Wishful-Thinking and the Sobering Thought. And surrounding him now were untold thousands of still more bizarre objects, animal, vegetable and mineral. It all contrasted so starkly with the order and precision of the Great Methodical and his Memory Bank. In fact, the nearer Neil got to Chaos, the more chaotic everything was becoming.

'Y . . . y . . . you c . . . c . . . c . . . can ge . . . ge . . . ge . . . ge . . . get t . . . tup . . . up . . . n . . . n . . . n . . . now,' came a voice from beside Neil. 'The c . . . c . . . co . . . co . . . coast i . . . is cl . . . cl . . . clear.'

'Thanks,' said Neil.

The thought that had spoken was hunched and wizened and shaking almost completely uncontrollably. It looked so distressed that Neil couldn't help feeling sorry for it. Meanwhile, Shipshape and Shambles had also emerged from their hiding place.

'This is getting ridiculous,' said Shipshape. 'We seem to be spending half our time hiding from these flocks of feathered fiends. Surely we ought to be attacking them!'

'Ooooooooohhh w . . . w . . . w . . . what ta . . . ta . . . a s . . . s . . . su . . . suge . . . ge . . . a suggestion,' stuttered the old thought. It was shaking from head to toe so violently that Neil felt sure the set of yellowed teeth were bound to come tumbling out of its head at any moment.

'Who's your friend?' said Shipshape to Neil.

'You don't think we would be successful in a direct confrontation, then?' said Shambles politely to the shaking thought.

A convulsion of tremors passed through its body.

'N . . . n . . . n . . . n . . . n . . . oooo,' it said, every part trembling.

'I shouldn't waste too much time or effort on this one,' said the Sobering Thought approaching.

'What's the matter with him?' asked Shipshape.

'Ask him,' said the Sobering Thought.

'What's up with you?' asked Shipshape.

'I . . . I . . . I . . . I . . . shu . . . shu . . . shudder t . . . t . . . t . . . to th . . . th . . . th . . . think,' replied the thought.

Both Shambles and Shipshape stood there staring. Only Neil understood and burst out laughing.

'I don't believe it!' he said.

'What is it?' said Shambles.

'I don't get the joke,' said Shipshape.

'It's what my mum always says when someone asks her about something horrible,' said Neil. He looked back at the old thought and started laughing again.

'If I were you,' interrupted the Sobering Thought, 'I really would advise a speedy advance. So much still to do, you know.'

'Very true,' said Shipshape.

'We've still got to find you the key to get you out of Chaos again,' said Shambles. 'Remember what the Great

Methodical said, "Don't go in until you're sure you've got it!"'

'Oh yes,' said Neil, 'I'd completely forgotten all about the key,' he admitted and felt himself panicking.

'A thought for your pennies. A thought for your pennies!' cried a loud, clear voice. 'A thought for your pennies!'

'Is every single thing here topsy-turvy?' asked Neil.

'What do you mean?' said Shipshape.

'The wrong way round,' he explained. 'It should be "a penny for your thoughts".'

'No, it shouldn't,' said Shipshape. 'That doesn't make any sense at all.'

'Of course it does,' insisted Neil.

'How can it?' said Shipshape. 'Every thought has to be paid for in one way or another.'

'But . . .' started Neil.

'Now stop all this fruitless speculation,' said the Sobering Thought, 'and make sure you pick your thought carefully.'

The street vendor approached. He was wearing a baggy checked suit of red and yellow, a big, floppy bow-tie and a top-hat. A large tray of assorted odds and ends was hanging round his neck from a leather strap.

'Morning, ladies and gentlemen,' he said brightly, 'and what might I interest you in?'

Neil looked at the dazzling display of wonderful goods. Everything was interesting!

'I really don't know. I . . .' he started.

'What do you mean, you don't know?' demanded the Sobering Thought incredulously. 'Of course you know what you want. We've just been talking about it!' He turned to Shipshape. 'Cor, you picked a right one here!' he said.

'All right, there's no need for any of that,' said Shipshape, coming to Neil's defence. 'I'm sure he hasn't forgotten about the key. He just didn't expect it to be served up to him like that, on a plate.'

'Aah, so you're after a key, are you?' said the vendor.

'Yes,' said Neil.

'And what particular key might that be?' he asked. 'I've got all manner of keys here. Let me see,' he said, rummaging through the contents of the tray. He pulled out a small, ornate brass one and showed it to Neil. 'A key to unlock the secrets of any diary,' he said.

'I don't think so,' said Neil.

'No matter,' said the vendor, pulling out another. 'And this, the key to a treasure chest. And this, the key to a medieval castle. The key to a room left locked for a hundred years. And this,' he said, brandishing a curiously soft key, 'will unlock the hardest heart. And this is the key to the question that has puzzled you all your life.'

All of the keys seemed useful to Neil, but he wasn't *really* sure that any of them were the right one.

'You see,' he explained, 'what I'm looking for is the key that will let me return from Chaos, but I don't know what it looks like.'

'From Chaos, eh?' said the vendor. 'Don't get much of a demand for *that* sort of key. In fact I would say that you were my first ever customer. In fact, isn't there some kind of Thought Domain law about that sort of thing?'

'He's got special permission,' said Shambles.

'Special permission, eh?' said the vendor.

'From the Great Methodical,' said Shipshape.

'The Great Methodical, eh?' said the vendor.

'Good grief, man,' said the Sobering Thought. 'Are you going to repeat everything you hear or are you going to sell the boy the key he needs?'

'Keep your hair on,' said the vendor as he sorted through his tray again. 'This should do the trick nicely,' he said, handing Neil a leather thong with four short rods hanging from it.

'Is *this* it?' asked Neil dubiously. 'It doesn't even look like a key!'

'It is indeed the object you require,' said the vendor, 'and I claim my pennies.'

'Oh yes, your money,' said Neil, reaching into his pocket.

'Here you are,' he said, giving the vendor the money he had been saving for a bar of chocolate after school. How far away that all seemed now. The vendor clinked the coins into his little purse, tipped his hat and bade them all farewell.

'I don't get this at all,' said Neil, inspecting the bunch of keys. 'There are four rods, two of them are made of metal, one of wood and I think the other one is glass, but . . .'

'Let's have a look,' said Shambles.

He took the keys and, to Neil's surprise, instead of looking at the rods, he examined the leather thong they were attached to. 'As I suspected,' he exclaimed with glee.

'What?' said Neil.

'Here,' he said, 'can't you see the writing?'

Neil looked closely and there, in fine angular script, he saw a poem had been burned into the length of the strip of leather.

'Read it out,' said Shipshape.

When wood would fold,
When tin turns old,
The whole behold,
Through glass with gold.

Return, resound,
All else confound,
By beaten sound,
The key be found.

'And what's that all supposed to mean?' said Neil.

'All will no doubt be made clear when the time is right,' said Shambles, attempting to look confident. But Neil noticed Shambles and Shipshape exchanging nervous glances.

'Are you keeping anything from me?' he asked.

'No,' said Shipshape. 'But, well, to be honest, we haven't got a clue what the rhyme means . . .'

'But,' interrupted Shambles, 'it *is* designed to get you out of Chaos, so it is only in Chaos that everything will become explicable. I wouldn't worry about it at all.'

'Well, I hope you're right,' said Neil. 'For my sake!'

He tied the thong around his neck and tucked the rods inside his shirt.

'If I might hurry you all along,' interjected the Sobering Thought quietly. 'I really think you should . . .'

'Yes, yes, I know,' said Neil. 'It can't be much farther to go now,' he added, looking at the white pillars looming up in front of them. 'Why don't we try running the last bit?'

'Good idea,' said Shipshape enthusiastically.

'If we must,' said Shambles, somewhat less enthusiastically.

'Come on then,' said Neil.

And with their eyes all fixed on the Pillars of Reason ahead of them, they started to run. At first it was easy. Knowing that he was now fully prepared for Chaos, Neil was eager to get there as soon as possible, and he hopped, skipped and jumped energetically over and around the many thoughts still cluttering up the Right Track. He could hear Shambles puffing away at the back.

'Nearly there,' Neil called out encouragingly.

'Ah . . . ah . . . are we?' wheezed Shambles in reply.

Gradually, as the pillars stubbornly refused to get any nearer, Neil felt his own energy draining away. Just ten more paces, he kept promising himself. And when those ten had been done, just ten more. And still the pillars didn't seem closer. Even Shipshape was beginning to flag.

'Ooooh, oh!' yelled Neil, suddenly doubling up.

'What is it?' asked Shipshape.

'I've got a stitch,' said Neil. 'I'll have to stop for a couple of minutes.'

'Well, you know what they say,' said a voice behind them. It was the Sobering Thought again.

'I didn't know you'd followed us,' said Shipshape.

'I couldn't let you go without saying goodbye,' it said.

'Wh . . . wh . . . what *do* they say?' puffed Shambles.

'Pardon?' said the Sobering Thought.

'You said, "you know what they say",' said Shambles. 'Who and what?'

'Oh yes,' said the Sobering Thought. 'Young Neil here said that he'd got a stitch and it just reminded me of that little proverb. I mean, all that racing about and where has it got you? And yet, a stitch in time, saves nine!'

Neil was suddenly overcome with the weirdest sensation of flying through the air. He heard the Sobering Thought calling out: 'Goodbye, good luck and don't think anything I wouldn't think!' And the next thing he knew, the three of them were sprawled out under the towering columns of the Pillars of Reason, next to the two massive wooden doors which divided the Thought Domain into two.

'How on earth did we get here?' asked Shipshape.

'Don't even ask,' said Shambles. 'We are, and that's all that matters.'

And so there they were, on the boundary between Order and Chaos at last. Neil felt strangely calm. Everything he had ever done had been leading up to this point, he felt, and as he looked up at the massive marble pillars, all the words of advice he had received in the curious Thought Domain echoed round his head.

SEEING ISN'T BELIEVING . . . NOTHING IS WHAT IT SEEMS . . . IF YOU THINK SOMETHING IS DANGEROUS IT WILL BE . . . NEVER TAKE ANYTHING FOR GRANTED . . . and now the latest from the Sobering Thought: DON'T THINK ANYTHING I WOULDN'T THINK, which presumably meant keep a clear head!

'Are you okay?' asked Shambles.

'I'm fine,' said Neil. 'Just thinking,' he added and smiled.

'You're on your own from here,' said Shipshape sadly, 'though I would love to fight beside you, Neil.'

'We'll be thinking of you the whole time,' said Shambles. 'Take care.'

Neil felt tears welling up in his eyes and the sight of his two friends blurred. He swallowed back the painful lump in his throat.

'Now, have you got everything you need?' said Shambles.

'I think so,' said Neil.

'Better make sure,' said Shambles.

Neil looked in his satchel. The Inkling was there, fast asleep as usual. The map of the Thought Domain was there, but it wouldn't be of any use from now on as no one had charted the area beyond the Pillars of Reason and returned. There was the remaining half bar of Food for Thought. There was also the little glass disc which the Great Methodical had given him to help keep everything in perspective. And wrapped up in his handkerchief was the Seed of an Idea which the Great Methodical had asked him to use wisely.

'Do you know what?' said Neil.

'What's that?' said Shipshape.

'Well, I don't know why exactly,' he said, 'but I'm sure that this would be the best time and place to plant the seed.'

'And why do you think that?' asked Shambles.

'I don't know,' said Neil. 'I just feel it.'

'Incredible,' said Shambles.

'Do you think I'm wrong, then?' asked Neil.

'No, no, not at all,' said Shambles hurriedly. 'I'm sure you're right. I was just marvelling at that element of Chaos which is in every human being. That's why the Great Methodical had to get the help of a human child. No one here could possibly have any intuition: we're all too logical.'

Neil bent down and scraped a small hole in the dry soil exactly midway between the two pillars below the dividing doors.

'I hope it grows,' he said.

'I'm sure it will,' said Shipshape.

'Bound to,' said Shambles.

Neil turned round to get one last look of the ordered part of the Thought Domain. He saw the miserable rows of lost thoughts standing about on the Right Track; in the distance he caught a glimpse of the Thought Boxes and remembered the state of disrepair they were in; and he thought back on those never-ending arguments his parents had and knew it was time to enter Chaos.

'See you soon, Shambles,' he said.

'See you,' he said.

'And look after yourself,' said Shipshape.

'I will,' said Neil. 'I will.'

Then he turned, patted his satchel, checked the keys were still round his neck and walked solemnly towards the heavy wooden doors which kept Chaos and Order separated. Looking up, he saw the fluted pillars towering above him and felt smaller than he had ever felt before. But there was no turning back now. He sensed the fear in the air that was keeping the thoughts from stepping into Chaos, but he was not so easily dissuaded.

As he got right up next to the doors he discovered that their solidity was only an illusion. There was nothing

there. It was like looking through into nothing; not into a foggy landscape, nor into darkness, but truly into nothing at all. And still he kept on walking. For a moment he was dimly aware that the white pillars were to his left and right. An instant later, and everything changed with a sudden jolt.

He twisted round. Shipshape and Shambles had vanished. The illusion of the doors had disappeared. The very Pillars of Reason themselves were no longer there. Neil found himself standing on a wide plain, bathed in the luminous lights of a green sun down near the horizon.

'So *this* is Chaos,' he whispered. 'Chaos!'

Chapter 11
Chaos

Neil had heard so many stories about Chaos, ranging from the terrifying to the ludicrous, that now he was actually standing in the place itself, it was something of an anti-climax. He was completely alone in a vast, barren expanse without the slightest idea about where to start looking for the Proper Gander. Apart from the fact that the green light made everything look quite eerie, the landscape reminded him of photographs he'd seen of the Sahara Desert. Mile after mile after mile of not very much at all!

Peering into the distance, he fancied that he could see mountains far away on the horizon, but this could equally well have been a mirage effect caused by the shifting layers of light and shade. In fact, the more intently he looked into the distance, the more unsure he was not only of what he *could* see, but also what he *couldn't* see. Or to put it in other words, his eyes started to play tricks on him.

'I don't think I like this,' he muttered nervously to himself. It was all too bleak, too forbidding, too unknown for him to know what to do. And as his unease grew, all the tell-tale signs of nervousness switched on, one by one. His palms began to sweat; his teeth began to chatter; his heart began to pound.

'Calm down, calm down,' he instructed himself, trying to take long, deep breaths.

He kept his eyes peeled for any landmarks he might have

missed, but there were none, and as he surveyed the flat terrain massive areas of sliding darkness seemed to form themselves into moving figures. Tall ranks of marching shadows sped uniformly over the increasingly rugged earth. Massive, menacing, imposing, Neil listened in terror as their huge boots crashed down to earth with every step.

But then, just as he became conscious of the strict rhythm of the marching, it immediately changed and the rigid columns turned into a liquid formlessness which coiled and squirmed.

'Ugh!' Neil uttered involuntarily. The movement reminded him of snakes, a million slippery zig-zag snakes rearing up at him. And as he looked down, the ground had become a writhing, seething mass of red, green and orange serpents, intertwining and hissing hideously. Neil recoiled in horror as they wound themselves around his legs, up his body and flicked their darting red forked-tongues closer and closer to his face.

'I hate snakes!! I HATE THEM!!!' he screamed, struggling to free himself from their tightening grip. But the words merely disappeared into the endless plains, leaving him with the crush round his body, the shiver of icy scales against his skin, the taste of bile.

The more the pressure increased, the more confused the situation became. All Neil's senses seemed to get jumbled up. It was as though he could hear the touch of their snakey bodies, taste the sound of his own shaky voice, see the smell of their stinking, carnivorous breath and hear, with crystal clearness, the screeching discord of their dripping, venomous fangs. He looked up to avoid the nightmare, but even the sky seemed to be squirming. The sun was like an orbitting apple riddled with worms.

'That can't be right,' said Neil to himself. 'The sun is simply *not* an apple, and if it isn't an apple, then it can't have maggots in it.'

And the maggots duly disappeared.

'It's just my imagination,' he said. 'There is no apple. There are no maggots. And there are *no snakes*!'

But he didn't dare look down yet, just in case. Instead, he concentrated on the beautiful sun, which could do him no harm. And yet, as he looked, a new problem arose. The longer he looked into the fiery brightness, the less sure he was of the colour. When he had first entered Chaos he would have answered, with complete certainty, that it was green. But now it seemed to be red, or perhaps yellow, or white. And then again, it inverted itself to resemble an endless, black tunnel reaching back into the depths of space. He realized that now, if anyone were to ask him what colour the sun was, he would have to say . . . He would have to say . . .

But the words wouldn't come.

At home, at school, with friends, the one thing he had learnt never to say was 'I don't know'. You *had* to know, and if you didn't, then you were expected to hide your ignorance behind a show of brash self-confidence. But here it was impossible. And anyway, there was no one to show off to, no one to try and impress. Just himself.

And he couldn't tell what colour the sun was! It seemed so stupid. How could he *not* know what colour something was? Having set himself the task of identifying the colour, the pressure to find an answer built up and built up. He felt his pulse racing.

'What colour is it?' he yelled. But there was no answer other than the one he now called out: 'I DON'T KNOW!!'

His voice circled round and round like the echo in a deep cavern. And with his final admission came instant release. The sun continued to shine, but it didn't matter what colour it was or wasn't. The snakes had also disappeared.

'It really doesn't matter if you admit that you don't know sometimes,' Neil realized happily. 'It doesn't matter at all.'

He looked around him to make sure that the vile, slippery slimy snakes hadn't returned. Thankfully they were nowhere to be seen, and even better was the fact that nothing else had appeared to take their place. He remembered the words the Great Methodical had said, but now they assumed a much more significant meaning: 'nothing is what it seems.' That's what he had to remember. Nothing is nothing – nothing more, nothing less!

Whether the snakes had been a result of his nervousness or merely a trick of the light, what they certainly had not been were real snakes. On the one hand, the thought was comforting, especially as he had managed to dismiss them relatively easily. On the other hand, it was alarming to discover how quickly he could be taken in.

'Seeing isn't believing,' he reminded himself.

This was undoubtedly the case, but if Shambles had been there, he would have reminded Neil that 'sight' is only one of our senses. He would have pointed out that if seeing isn't believing, then neither is hearing, feeling, nor any of the others. But Shambles was not there and Neil found himself shockingly ill-prepared for the sudden rasping, jarring cacophony of sounds which seemed to pierce through the pores of his skin and scrape along the bones. And even if he had realized in time that hearing isn't believing either (which he hadn't), how can you convince yourself that you're *not* hearing what you *are* hearing once you've actually heard it? Is it possible to 'unhear'? Neil was to discover that once you let go for a moment, your imagination takes over, for better or worse. And at this particular moment, it was definitely for the worse.

The noise was increasing in intensity to such a degree that Neil was sure that either his eardrums would burst or that his bones would rattle to bits. And the thought of his body falling apart only made the rattling all the more severe.

'What is it?' said Neil. 'WHAT'S THERE?' he shouted. But no matter how loud he called he couldn't hear his own voice above the deafening din. And then it occurred to him that if there was such a terrifying noise then there must be something out there making that noise. Something immeasurably massive, inconceivably huge, undeniably out to get him was lurking in the shadows.

'Stop it!' screamed Neil. 'LEAVE ME ALONE!'

And then the impossible happened.

The volume and pitch of the sound had reached such a level that, just as a glass will shatter if an opera singer hits a certain note, so the entire landscape surrounding Neil broke into a million and one pieces. For a split second they remained there, suspended in the air, interlocking pieces like the most gigantic jig-saw the world had ever seen. And then they collapsed, each piece taking its own small segment of the weird world of Chaos away with it as it fell, clattering down into nothing. Then there was silence, and Neil found himself back in the void.

Nothing, he thought to himself. Nothing at all.

The mysterious, lurking presence had certainly disappeared, but so had everything else, and Neil didn't like it. No people, no trees, no grass, no sky, no ground . . .

The panic Neil felt when he realized that he couldn't even see himself was more intense than anything he had ever before experienced. No feet, no legs. He held his hands out in front of where his face should have been, but there was nothing to be seen. And there was worse still to come. When he went to feel his hair, touch his cheeks, it was as though his absent hands were passing through air.

I'm not here either, he thought. I don't exist!

His mind started playing all sorts of games with him. Memories of all the things he had been told came back to him, but they refused to make sense. If seeing wasn't believing, did that mean that *not* seeing was believing? And if nothing was what it seemed, did that mean that if it seemed like nothing, it wasn't what it seemed to be at all? He found himself getting all tied up in logical knots. But then, if he didn't exist, just what was doing all the thinking now?

If I'm still able to think, then I must exist, Neil concluded proudly. And although he wasn't a hundred per cent convinced, it was something to hold on to.

But what if he were wrong? With this terrifying thought he felt a slight increase in his heartbeat.

If I've got a heartbeat, then I must have a heart, he reasoned. Sure enough, when he looked down he saw a soft red object pumping blood through a series of tubes and pipes leading in and out of it. Neil had always felt a bit sick in biology lessons when he'd had to dissect bulls' eyes and dead mice, and yet here, as he watched the minute details of his own functioning heart with its veins and arteries, chambers and valves, he felt only fascination.

Well, if I've got a heart, then I must have lungs, he deduced, and indeed, on checking, he saw two large triangular bags of air steadily inflating and deflating. The lining of the lungs trembled lightly like butterfly wings delicately fluttering in the wind.

And if there are lungs, he thought, then there must be a way for the air to get down to them. He felt around his face and found his mouth and nose, just where they ought to be!

And if I can see my heart and feel my nose, then I must have eyes and fingers, he concluded. And they too returned.

It looked too strange to see the familiar fingers flashing disconnected through the air and so logic dictated that they be connected to hands, and hands to wrists, wrists to arms, arms to body and so on, until piece by piece his entire body returned.

'I am myself again,' said Neil to himself proudly. 'I'll never take you for granted again,' he added, addressing the assortment of parts which comprised himself.

The sight of the bones dancing round and round him set his heart off frantically pounding all over again.

'I forgot the bones!' he said with alarm. 'Does this mean I'm going to fall apart like a jelly-fish?'

Even as he said the words, his legs began to wobble, his fingers took on the consistency of rubbery Frankfurter sausages and his face felt like plasticine.

'This is crazy!' he yelled as he collapsed on to the ground.

He watched, awestruck, as the bones put on a dancing display of incredible detail and intricacy. One after another they span through the air like drum-majorettes' batons, then they lined up in order of size and did a rat-ta-tat tap-dance until the skull came rolling along towards them and knocked the first, which knocked the second, which knocked the third, until, like a row of dominoes, they all fell down. They didn't stay on the ground for long, though. A second later and they were flying through the air in ever more complicated sequences of movements: loop-the-loops, figures of eight, somersaults and cartwheels, and every one executed perfectly by all the bones except for two. They were the two smallest bones there and, no matter how they tried, they were incapable of getting the movements right. Time after time they messed everyone up and got in everyone's way.

Neil stared, totally enthralled, and the more his interest in the stunts grew, the more his fear subsided. The long left thigh-bone was just about to attempt a double-somersault back flip with anticlockwise twist when the two little bones tripped it up, causing it to come crashing down heavily on its ball-and-socket joint. Neil burst out laughing, and at that instant every single one of the bones disappeared into thin air.

'Oh!' said Neil, disappointed that the display had come to an end. It occurred to him that if letting your mind wander could sometimes be a bad idea, it could also be more fun than just about anything else. The important factor to remember when he came face to face with the Proper Gander was that he had to keep his thoughts away from the negative and destructive areas.

The landscape had returned to the featureless state that Neil had encountered when he'd first entered Chaos. The stupid thing was that he wasn't sure that this, rather than anything else he'd seen, was Chaos as it *really* was.

'Well, I haven't got very far, have I?' he said to himself.

'If only I could see the place as it really and truly is!' he said.

'Your wish is my command,' came a voice from right next to him, and instantly the whole view transformed itself into something quite different. There were fields and trees and fluffy white clouds scudding across a deep blue sky. Further away were lakes, with flocks of pink and grey birds fishing in them, and beyond these, ranges of snow-capped mountains to the left and the silver stripe of a coast fringed with palm beaches of pure white sand to the right.

'This is more like it,' said Neil.

'You only had to ask,' said the voice.

'I didn't know it would be so easy,' he said.

'The best things in life always are!'

Neil pulled himself away from the beautiful panorama in front of him to see just who was responsible for the trite little comments he kept being answered with.

'My name's Neil,' he said. 'What's yours?'

'Wand,' said the man.

'That figures,' said Neil.

'Wand by name, wand by . . . well, appearance,' he said.

The small figure was as thin as a rake and dressed in jet-black, all except for a white drummer-boy's hat. He looked for all the world just like a conjuror's magic wand. Neil looked back at the new vision of Chaos.

'You know,' he said, 'this is more what I thought it would look like.'

Running around the meadows, jumping over the streams, rolling playfully down the hills were the freed thoughts. Millions of them. Gambolling like spring lambs, glad to be rid of the constraints of the Thought Boxes, content to live in harmony and happiness for ever and ever. It reminded Neil of the Sunday School pictures they'd drawn of heaven.

Lions and lambs, promises and lies, a snowflake and a flame, anger and love, every possible type of conceivable thought was here, playing together without any conflict.

Neil couldn't help being a little suspicious. It suddenly all seemed far too good to be true.

'So this is *really* how it is, is it?' he said.

'Indeed!' said Wand. 'That was what you wanted to see, wasn't it?'

'Yes,' said Neil, nodding.

'And if there is any other little matter I might oblige you with. Your wish is *still* my command!' said Wand.

'Any wish?' said Neil.

'I think I've already proved the efficacy of my powers,' said Wand a little curtly. 'Wish away!'

Neil stared at the stick-like figure. He knew he had no reason to be suspicious of the little man, other than the fact that he'd learnt *always* to be suspicious. However, *if* Wand was genuine, *if* he could wish for anything and *if* there were no strings attached, then it was just too fantastic an offer to pass up. Surely he could destroy the Proper Gander and complete his task with one single wish.

He wasn't quite so gullible though. As a child Neil had read quite enough fairy-tales to know that there was usually some sort of catch to them. As a rule, you were allowed only three wishes and the people who got them generally messed them up so badly that the last wish had to be wasted undoing all the harm that the previous two had caused. Dealing with something as wicked and dangerous as the Proper Gander, he knew he'd have to be very cautious with his wishes. Any careless slip could be fatal.

'Ready?' asked Wand.

'Hang on,' said Neil. 'I'm just thinking. How many wishes can I have?'

One thing Neil had often wondered when reading the fairy-tales was why wish number one was never: 'I wish I had a million wishes.' It would have solved so many problems. But then, perhaps that simply wasn't allowed.

'You can have any number of wishes you like,' said Wand.

So that answered that. No matter how he looked at the

offer, Neil had to concede that it definitely looked like a good one. Just to be on the safe side, however, he decided to wish for something quite small at first, rather than leaping in with the Proper Gander biggie.

'Okay,' he said. 'I wish I had an apple.'

Instantly a red and green apple appeared in his hand.

'Yum!' said Neil, biting into it. He spat out the sour fruit immediately.

'You must be specific,' cautioned Wand.

'Hmmm!' said Neil. 'I'd hardly wish for an unripe apple, would I?'

'You might,' answered Wand, a trifle huffily.

'All right,' said Neil. 'I wish I had the sweetest, ripest, juiciest apple from a Cox's Orange Pippin tree.'

Again, no sooner had the words left his mouth than the wish came into effect and, to his horror, Neil found himself at the top of a thirty-foot tree, his hand resting against a huge apple. Without any doubt it was the sweetest, ripest and juiciest apple there!

'Very funny,' Neil called to Wand. He picked the apple. 'I wish I was back down again.'

He found himself hurtling to the ground.

'Gently!!!' he screamed, and the plummet changed to the gentle see-sawing descent of a falling leaf in autumn. When he landed he realized that, like the tree, the apple had also vanished into thin air.

'This is pointless,' said Neil irritably.

'I told you,' said Wand. 'You *must* be specific!'

'Okay,' said Neil, trying not to lose his temper. 'I wish I had a million pounds.' Surely this couldn't cause confusion.

Instantly, with the efficiency of all the other wishes, there he was sitting on the top of a 1,000,000-lb weight. It was made of lead and iron and was freezing cold.

He jumped down off it and laughed.

'I suppose that was a bit obvious,' he said. 'A million pounds of money, sterling,' he explained, 'not weight!'

The weight disappeared and Neil found himself clutching

a crisp banknote. He inspected it and, just like the £5, £10, £20 and £50 notes, it was decorated with whorls, spirals and intricacies of colour to deter forgers. And there, to the left of the picture of the queen, was the familiar sentence 'I promise to pay the bearer on demand the sum of', and underneath this, 'one million pounds'.

It looked like the real thing, but Neil knew that he would never be able to spend such a note: nobody would have enough change!

'This is hopeless,' he said.

'Still not satisfied?' asked Wand.

'Of course not,' said Neil. 'All this is doing is wasting my time.'

'But just think of it,' said Wand. 'Anything you want. It's too good an opportunity to miss, isn't it?'

'All right,' said Neil sighing. 'I wish I was taller.'

Hardly had the words been spoken than he started to regret the wish. A curious itchy feeling made him scratch at his neck as he felt the skin grow taut. To his horror, it extended out like a telescope. He felt taller. His eyes told him that the ground was farther away, but the thin, ostrich-like neck swaying in the breeze was hardly what he'd had in mind.

'Back to normal,' he shouted, terrified that the willowy neck might snap completely.

'Be precise,' said Wand.

'Well, what should I have said?'

'Search me,' said Wand with a shrug 'They're your wishes.'

'I wish I was bigger, then,' said Neil.

And the inevitable happened! He felt himself being blown up like a balloon. Rolls of fat flowed over the top of his jeans, the buttons on his shirt burst open, his cheeks puffed out and his neck grew so fat that he could hardly turn his head. 'I must look like Fatso Newman in 3B,' he thought to himself. And still he was growing.

'Bloob bloob,' he said, trying to reverse the wish, but it

was as though even his tongue had grown fat and the words wouldn't come out properly.

'Bli blish bi boz back bo blormal!' he finally managed to utter and, like an airbed being deflated, Neil felt himself shrink back to his old, familiar size.

'This can be dangerous,' he said to Wand angrily.

'"Bigger" obviously wasn't the right word for what you wanted,' said Wand sanctimoniously.

'Well, I wish I could get the hang of all this wishing!' said Neil.

He didn't actually mean it as a wish but it must have come out like one, because the next thing he knew he found himself hanging by the neck from a hangman's noose. Above the gibbet he saw big, black birds circling slowly through the air. The pain behind Neil's eyes was excruciating as the blood pounded inside his skull. The rope was so tight around his neck by this time that he couldn't speak no matter how hard he tried. All he could do was 'think' the wish, and hope that it would work.

I wish I was safe, he thought. But nothing happened. I *wish* I was safe! he thought again. But still he remained suspended from the rope. He thought he was going to black out. 'I WISH I WAS SAFE!!!' he thought as loudly as he could.

This third attempt was successful and he fell down to the ground. The gibbet disappeared. Neil sat there rubbing his neck, which was extremely sore (as he hadn't wished that it wouldn't be), and feeling very, very frightened. In a way it was a good thing to be able to wish for things, but it was terrifying to know that anything at all he might inadvertently think of might come true. Especially if he didn't want it to.

'Are you all right?' said Wand.

'Why didn't you help me down?' said Neil crossly.

'Can't interfere in the wishes of another person,' said Wand. 'That's most definitely not allowed.'

'Well then, I don't want any more wishes,' said Neil.

'The whole thing is too dangerous. I don't believe that any good can come of it at all.'

'Perhaps the problem is that you keep wishing for yourself,' said Wand.

Neil realized that there was some truth to this. Of course, he hadn't wanted to use his very first wish on trying to destroy the Proper Gander in case something had gone wrong. But having said that, he had to agree that he'd become rather carried away with irrelevant things like trying to become taller and richer. He decided to give it one last try and this time to make the wish more selfless.

'And you're sure that I can wish any wish I want?' he checked.

'Just wish away,' confirmed Wand, 'and it shall be granted.'

'I wish, then,' said Neil, choosing his words carefully, 'that I could see the Proper Gander but remain in safety, with the Proper Gander unable to see me!'

From his vantage point at the top of the massive, grubby, feathered monster Neil had time to reflect on his predicament. Once again the wish had tricked him, although this time he really didn't seem to be in any immediate danger. The Proper Gander was *so* gigantic that it hadn't noticed the appearance of a little boy on its head. But looking down, Neil felt increasingly nervous. Not only did the height make him feel dizzy but it also made him horribly aware of the daunting task he had facing him. How could he, little Neil, destroy this winged dinosaur? It seemed impossible. He looked down at the Gander to see if he could detect any signs of weakness. But as he looked from the massive feet striding over Chaos to the solid toothed beak which opened to let out a hideous, echoing cackle, from the impenetrable bulk of its folded wings to the armour-plated covering of feathers, he had the horrible feeling that the Proper Gander had *no* weak points.

'Oh dear,' thought Neil to himself.

What was more, the close proximity to the evil Proper

Gander was rapidly draining Neil of his energy. He could feel his hair standing on end as the goose-pimples covered every last square millimetre of his body. He would have to wish himself away again or risk slipping and being snapped up by the Proper Gander's savage beak. It was at that moment that he suddenly remembered one of the main pieces of advice he had been given. NEVER TAKE ANYTHING FOR GRANTED. And what had Wand said? 'Wish away and it shall be GRANTED!' No wonder he'd ended up in such a pickle.

'What an idiot I've been,' said Neil to himself. 'What a complete and utter dimwit!'

And now he had no alternative but to take one more wish for granted to get out of the present situation. All he could do was hope for the best.

'I wish I was back where I was before,' he said.

Nothing happened.

'I WISH I WAS BACK WHERE I WAS BEFORE!' he repeated a little more desperately.

Still nothing happened, and then the awful truth dawned on Neil. Having discovered that he shouldn't take *anything* for granted, the wishes had stopped working. It couldn't have happened at a more inconvenient time.

'Now what?' he wondered. He could feel himself becoming more and more nervous; his hands were beginning to shake badly, but he couldn't take the chance of releasing his grip. 'What on earth do I do now?' he said.

The decision was made for him. At that moment the Proper Gander suddenly flexed its wings, beat them a couple of times and soared up into the sky. All Neil could do was clutch precariously to a feather on the top of its head. And pray.

'Where are we going?' Neil asked no one in particular as the Proper Gander rose higher and higher up into the air. Below him, Chaos extended as far as he could see. There were mountains, rivers, seas and islands down there, yet it wasn't like looking at the TV satellite pictures they used for weather forecasts, because nothing in Chaos stayed still. The land-masses and areas of water constantly shifted in size and shape, so that whatever Neil looked at slid away out of view.

It beats a Boeing-707, he thought. Neil's only other flight had been to Spain a couple of years previously; this was certainly infinitely more spectacular.

There was only one problem, and as the journey continued it became more acute. The nervousness brought on by the presence of the Proper Gander was no longer restricted to goose-pimples. Neil's whole body was shaking uncontrollably. His hands were clammy and slippery and it was as much as he could do to hold on to the little feather. And with the shaking came an increased weakness. He felt the power in his hands gradually going.

'If only the bird would land,' he said with chattering teeth, but the time for making wishes had definitely passed now.

Occasionally, Neil caught sight of the V-shaped formations of the Proper Gander's flocks of wicked geese flying to the right and left of them. They would dip their wings as a sign of respect, but the Proper Gander ignored them. And still they continued on to the Gander's destination.

If we don't land soon . . . , Neil thought, stopping himself before he could complete the sentence.

Then, just as he was about to give up all hope, just as his tired, shaking arms were about to give up, just as he was about to slide off the bird's head and tumble down, down through the air to certain death, he saw something in the distance which gave him just the necessary amount of encouragement.

Over on the horizon was a massive edifice. It was a brown and silver construction which, as they approached, resembled a cross between a castle and a nest. The walls were tall, with turrets and crenellations. But out of the cracks between the stones were countless thorny bushes which softened the edges of the stonework. The nearer they got to the Proper Gander's home, the more Neil shook.

'You can do it!' Neil encouraged himself.

The Proper Gander was coming in to land. Lower it flew, across a forest of the same thorny shrubs which encircled the Castle-Nest. Neil looked ahead and saw, half-way up the stone ramparts, the dark entrance that they were headed for. The Proper Gander let its legs swing round to prepare for the landing, but the jolt this caused proved to be the last straw for Neil. The feather slid out of his slippery grip, he rolled back head-over-heels down the back of the bird, flicked off the end of its tail and into mid-air.

Over and over and round and round he turned. The sharp spines of the thorny bushes got nearer and nearer. All Neil could do was cover up his eyes and hope that he wasn't hurt too badly. A second later and he landed with a jarring, though surprisingly painless, thud on a springy mattress of fine webbing.

'Phew!' said Neil, checking that no bones were broken. Everything seemed to be all right. 'PHEW!!' he repeated.

He looked up and just caught sight of the Proper Gander disappearing into the entrance of its Castle-Nest before the portcullis slammed shut.

Chapter 12
Through the Forest

'OH NO!!' yelled Neil.

Relief at not being skewered on the thorny bushes turned into dread as he realized what was standing in front of him. With blood-red eyes the size of soup tureens, mandibles rasping like chain saws and thick black hairs on eight multi-jointed legs slowly advancing on him, Neil found himself confronted by the biggest spider ever. And if he hated snakes, then he loathed and detested spiders!

As the beast got nearer he could smell its stinking breath and if he hadn't studied spiders in biology, he would have sworn that the massive specimen in front of him was licking its lips in anticipation of the tasty morsel it was about to enjoy. And that tasty morsel was *him*, Neil Davies.

He tried to slide out of the web, but the same strands which had saved him from his fall now threatened to lead to his death. He wriggled and shook desperately to free himself, but it was hopeless. It was like trying to get rid of a piece of chewing gum: as soon as you got it off one finger, it stuck to another one. By using all his force he managed to get one arm free, but to release his leg he had to put his hand down, and it was trapped again. Neil's panic soared as he noticed just how near the spider was. He shook the sticky strands of the web even harder, but although they twisted and bent, they refused to break.

'No, no, no!' he screamed at the petrifying sight of the spider's gaping mouth.

He could hear the sound of the Inkling squeaking frantically from inside his satchel. Obviously, it had sensed the presence of the spider and knew that it would be next on the menu.

'What do I do?' he yelled. 'There must be something . . .'

But his mind remained a blank. And still the Inkling kept squealing.

'What is it?' said Neil. He tore his wrist free from the web and opened the satchel. Inside, he saw the little Inkling sitting up on its hind legs.

'There's nothing I can do,' he said miserably. 'Nothing.'

But the Inkling only squealed all the louder. A glint of light caught Neil's attention and he saw that the Inkling was holding something up in its tiny paws. It squeaked encouragingly.

'What is it?' said Neil. He reached into the satchel and took the small, round glass object away from the animal.

'Well, what am I supposed to do with this?' he asked, turning the lens over in his hand. And then he remembered the Great Methodical's words. It will help you to keep things in proper perspective, he had said.

'Of course!' Neil exclaimed.

He held the glass lens to one eye, shut the other one and looked at the giant arachnid just as it was about to sink its teeth into his left leg. The effect was immediate. It was like holding the wrong end of a telescope up to your eye. Everything around Neil regained normal proportions, including the slavering beast, which was reduced to the eentsy-weentsy spider it should have been all along. He hardly dared to take the lens away again just in case. But when he finally did so, the spider remained small and insignificant, a common-or-garden spider which scurried away from the boy who had destroyed its web.

'All thanks to you,' said Neil to the tiny Inkling as he stroked it behind the ears.

Characteristically, the Inkling had fallen asleep again. Neil gently replaced it in his satchel, along with the life-saving glass disc, and wiped the dusty cobwebs from his clothes and out of his hair.

He could see the uppermost parts of the castle silhouetted against the bright yellow sky ahead of him, while all around him were the thorny, brown bushes. They formed a thick and, when he wasn't careful, painful obstacle, but if he stooped, it was possible to get through. It reminded him of the story of the Sleeping Beauty: he was the prince trying to hack his way through the forest, even though the wicked Proper Gander was hardly a beautiful princess.

He was just setting off, roughly in the direction of the Castle-Nest, when he heard a blood-curdling scream.

'Waaaaahh!'

The sound sent shivers up and down his spine. And again,

'Waaaaaaaaagghhh!!!'

Neil stood stock still, wondering what on earth could be screaming so horrifyingly. It was a strange noise, like the cry of a baby, or the screech of a seagull, or Neil's cat when he accidentally trod on its tail.

'Waaaaaaaaaggghhhh!!!' it came again.

This time it was from a different part of the forest, although the echo around the woods made it difficult to pinpoint the noise exactly. Whatever it was, it definitely sounded like a cry for help. Neil was in a quandary. His natural instinct was to go to the aid of whoever was calling for help, but then again, it could just be another ploy to keep him from the Castle-Nest.

'Waaaaaaaaaaaaagghhoooo!' came the scream again. This time it sounded much nearer and Neil crawled through the thick, thorny undergrowth towards it.

Suddenly he emerged in a clearing where a gnarled and warty old woman was hacking at something in a bowl. He decided it was best to remain hidden.

'Our hearts, our hearts,' came the plaintive cry. 'She is cutting out our hearts!'

'Be quiet with you,' snapped the old crone.

Neil looked on in disgust as the red liquid dripped from the blade down over the dusty ground and settled in tiny droplets.

'Save us from her wicked knife,' came the voices again.

Good grief, thought Neil, what on earth is going on and what can I do to help? Before he could do anything at all, there was a sound of pounding hooves behind him, the swishing of a sword cutting through the brambles and the abrupt appearance of a knight in somewhat tarnished shiny armour.

'Do I hear the sound of damsons in distress?' he roared.

That doesn't sound quite right, thought Neil to himself.

'Sir Prize, Sir Prize,' screamed the old hag in terror. 'You've found me out.'

She dropped the knife and cowered down behind the bowl of fruit.

'So,' called Sir Prize, 'Miss Chief, accurséd witch, we meet again. I bet you weren't expecting me to spoil your dastardly deed.'

'Spare me,' she whimpered. 'Spare me!'

'Spare you?' he mocked. 'Spear you, you mean,' he said, raising his lance and running it through her heart.

Neil watched, horrified and perplexed, and certainly glad that he had remained hidden.

'Wherever there is Miss Chief in the forest,' he proclaimed hammily, 'I, Sir Prize, shall come to put an end to her!' And with that the horse reared up and galloped back off into the depths of the dark woods.

Neil looked around nervously. However macabre the scene had appeared, the old woman and the knight had seemed to recognize each other. And then . . . It had all happened so swiftly. Cautiously, Neil emerged from his hiding place and walked over to the bowl. Inside it was a heap of damsons, half of them already stoned.

'Was it you calling for help?' asked Neil, feeling somewhat daft talking to a bowlful of damsons.

'Of course it wasn't them,' came a hoarse voice.

Neil turned and saw the old woman standing up.

'You're alive!' said Neil in amazement.

'Indeed I am,' she said, 'and no thanks to you, I might add. You seem to be more concerned with fruit!'

'But the knight . . . I saw him . . .' said Neil, confused and embarrassed.

'Pah!' said the old woman and spat. 'That conglomeration of old tin cans couldn't hurt a fly. Interfering old goat. He's absolutely desperate to prove his worth and rushes around attacking any old woman who happens to be unfortunate enough to have a couple of warts on her face. It's coming to something when a person can't even make herself a little bit of jam without some loonie Knight-in-Error running her through with a lance. I mean, really!'

'So who was calling for help?' asked Neil.

'Don't ask me,' said Miss Chief. 'I thought it came from over there,' she added, pointing. At that moment they both heard a petrified scream from the opposite direction. She shrugged.

'And now, if you don't mind, I've got work to do,' she said and, picking up the huge knife, resumed her damson stoning.

As he was heading off, Neil thought he heard a little voice calling out 'damsons have feelings too!' But he couldn't be sure.

A couple of hundred yards further on, he saw a spiral tower coiling its way up into the sky.

'Help,' he heard, and this time there could be no doubt what the voice had called.

Looking up at the tall tower, it reminded him a little of the fairy-tale he'd read years earlier, Rapunzel, where the prince had had to climb up the imprisoned girl's long golden hair. But here there was no need. The spiral staircase around the tower would take him right up to the room at the top.

'Hurry! Help!' came the cry again, this time more urgently.

Round and round he ran, up the spiralling stairs to the top. There, a small gold plaque on the oak door announced that this was the residence of one Amelia Taken. Neil knocked politely and the door was opened by a small, hunchbacked old woman, not dissimilar to the old woman with the damsons.

'Good morning,' said Neil, looking round the room.

'What do you want?' snarled the old woman.

'Errm, nothing really, I . . .'

'Well, you'll get none of that here,' said the old woman. 'We've got lots of things here, fat things, round things, soft things, sharp things, red and blue things, all manner of everythings. But no nothings! So if that's all you wanted, then I'm afraid I can't help you. Goodbye!'

'No, I don't think you understand,' said Neil. 'I thought I heard a scream and I wondered if there was anything the matter.'

'The matter? The matter? Of course there's something the matter.'

'What?' asked Neil.

'YOU! You horrible little wretch!' she screeched. 'You're the matter, now be off with you before I decide to eat you!' she screamed.

'Okay, okay,' said Neil. 'Don't worry, I'm off.'

But just as he was leaving there was a clattering, clanking sound behind him, something like a cross between a laden milkfloat driving over cobblestones and a box full of spanners being shaken.

'What the . . . ?' said Neil, looking back through the door and down the spiral staircase. He turned back and saw that the old crone was hiding in the corner behind a tall, dark wardrobe.

'Shut the door and slide the bolt across,' she hissed.

Neil did as he was told and a moment later recoiled as a massive axe splintered the door. Again and again the vicious, glinting edge of the axe pierced the door, sending chips and chunks flying through the air. Finally, unable to withstand the battering it was getting a moment longer, the door flew completely off its hinges. A second knight in somewhat less than shining armour was standing there in the doorway holding the halter of a bedraggled old nag.

'Sir Ender!' he boomed.

'I do,' whimpered the old woman pitifully.

'No, hag, *I* am Sir Ender.'

'You surrender?'

'I AM Sir Ender,' he roared, spelling it out.

'Ah,' she said. 'I am Miss Taken.'

'In what way, pray?' asked the knight.

'Epithetically speaking,' said the old woman complicatedly.

'What?' yelled the knight. 'If you think you can pull the wool over my eyes with your long words, you are very much mistaken.'

'I am,' she replied.

'Are what?'

'Miss Taken. Miss Amelia Taken, witch of this parish.'

This has got to be a joke, thought Neil to himself. And he couldn't help laughing at the idiocy of these two geriatrics, one a wrinkled old woman in tattered robes hiding behind a wardrobe, the other a doddery old man in rusty armour sat upon the mangiest excuse for a horse he had ever seen in his life.

'Enough of this claptrap!' said Sir Ender. 'Where is the sweet maiden, the fair damsel in distress?'

'What damsel?' asked the old woman craftily.

'I definitely heard a young woman scream,' he said. 'And the sound came from this tower.'

'Yes, so did I,' agreed Neil. 'That's why I'm here.'

'And who might you be?' asked Sir Ender.

'Neil,' said Neil.

‘Are you on a quest, boy?’

‘Of course,’ said Neil smugly.

‘So am I,’ said the knight. ‘Fun isn’t it? Been on it for years.’

‘What sort of quest?’

‘Oh, you know, the usual. Saving sweet, innocent girls from dragons, crones and ne’er-do-wells.’

‘How long for?’

Sir Ender’s eyes glazed over.

‘Dashed if I can remember,’ he said. ‘I must have been younger when I started though, what?’ he added with a laugh.

‘And you still haven’t achieved what you set out to do?’ said Neil, growing somewhat panicky and trying to imagine himself as an old man hobbling around Chaos still in pursuit of the Proper Gander.

‘Well, I’ve got bits and bobs sorted out, you know. Trouble is, there’s always *someone* worse off than someone else. You never really get finished. Still,’ he said brightly, ‘it’s a living!’

At that moment they all heard a scream coming from the bottom of the tower and looking out they saw a dragon racing past with a fair maiden clutched tightly to its scaly chest with savage claws. A third knight on horseback was in hot pursuit.

‘Pfa!’ exclaimed the knight. ‘Never a dull moment, eh! Tally ho!’ he whooped, turned the horse round and without any warning he drew his sword and sliced off the old woman’s head.

‘And let that be a warning to you,’ he yelled as he clattered and clanked his way back down the stairs.

Neil stood there in stunned silence.

‘Stupid old fool,’ said the head from its position over by the back wall. The body wandered over to it, picked it up and screwed it back into place.

‘What are you staring at?’ shouted the woman, now back to her normal self.

'Nothing,' said Neil.

'I told you before,' she said. 'There's no nothing here.'

'I suppose I'd better be going, then,' said Neil.

'I suppose you better had!' said the woman, bolder again now that the knight had departed.

'This is really peculiar,' Neil thought as he walked down the stairs. 'Everything in the Thought Domain was so logical, even the things which went wrong, somehow. But here . . .'

And yet he had to concede that though Chaos *was* chaotic, just as it should be, there was something curiously familiar about it all. Like dreams he'd had and fairy-tales he'd read. And it occurred to him that as it *was* familiar to him, then maybe, just maybe, the Great Methodical hadn't been entirely correct in saying that Chaos had nothing to do with the way that people think. For the time being at least, however, the puzzle would have to remain unsolved. The sight of the beautiful princess tied to a rock behind the battling knight and dragon drove it instantly from Neil's head.

The fight in progress was certainly ferocious, with both combatants seemingly intent on carrying on to the death. The knight was flailing away valiantly in an attempt to pierce the dragon's scaly hide. The dragon, for its part, was slashing out with its razor-sharp claws and firing jets of sulphurous flames at the knight's visor. The princess jeered and cheered alternately as first the dragon and then the knight seemed to get the upper hand.

Parry and thrust!

Attack and retreat!

Lunge and yield!

The battle continued and the dust kicked up by the horse's hooves and the dragon's claws swirled menacingly around the duelling duo.

'Oh, Victory to my Valiant One!' screamed the fair princess. 'Down with the Dastardly Dragon! Away with the Awesome Animal!'

Neil remained hidden as the protagonists continued their struggle, each trying their best to win the hand of the stunning princess, who was still calling out from her hapless vantage-point on the rock.

'Exit, Evil Entity! Leave, Loathsome Lizard!'

'Oh, shut up!' roared a voice. Neil had the impression that it had come from the dragon. But now the princess was in full swing, there was no stopping her.

'Desist, Dark Demon! Recoil, Repulsive Reptile!'

And still the fighting continued. The amount of dirt and sand surrounding the struggling knight and dragon had by now become so thick that Neil could see nothing except the occasional glimpse of a weapon, talon or flame which penetrated the moving dust-ball.

'Fly, Foul Fury! Vanish, Vile Vagabond!!' yelled the princess.

The battle continued a while longer and then Neil heard a rather pathetic voice coming from the centre of the thick fog.

'Where are you?' said the voice. 'Stand still and be slain, damn it!' A moment later and out of the swirling dirt trotted the distraught and dishevelled knight. Both he and his horse were covered from head to food in thick, brown dust.

'Good Lord!' said the knight, lifting his visor and flicking some of the powdery earth from his bushy moustache.

'Aaah! I thought you'd been killed,' screeched the princess. 'My hero!'

'Killed?' said the knight. 'But I am Sir Vive!'

'I'm so glad you did,' said the woman. 'You may have my hand in marriage.'

'Just the hand?' said Sir Vive.

'All of me, you wonderful dolt,' said the princess. 'Take me away from this wicked wood and let us live happily ever after.'

'You know, I do declare, the dragon just upped and ran away,' said the knight as the dust settled to reveal that there was nothing there. 'Cheek of it!' he exclaimed. 'I'm meant to slaughter it. That's in the rules!'

'Oh, never mind all that,' shouted the princess. 'Untie me. Take me away. I shall be your queen.'

'Oh, all right then,' said Sir Vive.

He leapt off his horse and sliced through the ropes binding her to the rock with his sword. Just as the princess was about to climb up into the saddle, however, Sir Vive seemed to notice something about her. He looked more closely at her face.

'Wait a moment,' he said sharply. 'You're not a beautiful princess, a damsel I've saved from sore distress. You're . . .' And with that he pulled the long blonde wig from her head and ripped the smooth, creamy-skinned mask from her face. Underneath was another of the hideous old hags, warts and wrinkles and all.

'True,' she conceded sadly. 'I am Miss Leading, but couldn't you take me away anyway. I'm so sick of it here.'

'Certainly not, treacherous old bag,' said the knight rather unkindly. 'I must leave, to save the day!'

And he leapt back on his horse and galloped off.

'Blast!' muttered the old crone.

It seemed to Neil that the series of events he had just witnessed was likely to repeat itself *ad infinitum*. It was like watching a group of old-age pensioners reliving countless childhood games. Whatever the explanation for the curious drama, there didn't seem to be any point in staying around. He still had to rid the world of the evil Proper Gander, and having got his bearings from the turrets peeking out above the thorny forest, he set off for the Castle-Nest once again.

He hadn't got more than a hundred yards when he found his way barred by the dragon. It was as if the whole of Chaos was conspiring to prevent him from ever reaching his destination.

'Oh no,' said Neil quietly as the dragon reared, roared and sent a jet of fire straight at him.

Neil leapt to one side and stood mesmerized as the

thorny bushes where he had been a second before burned to the ground. Both dragon and boy remained motionless. Some time passed and Neil became conscious of a sound, something like laughter. It seemed to be coming from *inside* the dragon!

'I gave you a fright, though, didn't I? Go on, admit it!' came a familiar voice, as the dragon struggle to pull off its hideous head. Neil recognized the figure inside the costume instantly.

'SHIPSHAPE!' he exclaimed, rushing towards his friend. 'What are *you* doing here? Why are you dressed up like that? Who were those strange, old people back there? Where's Sham . . .?'

'Whoa! Whoa!' said Shipshape. 'One thing at a time. Now, first of all, far more importantly, how have *you* been getting on?'

'Oh, I don't know,' said Neil. 'I don't think I've got very far. Although I have seen the Proper Gander at last. In fact, I've been for a ride on its head. But as for destroying it . . .'

'You haven't actually been inside the Castle-Nest, then, I take it?' she said.

'No, I haven't,' Neil had to admit, a little shamefacedly.

'No matter, no matter at all,' said Shipshape encouragingly. 'Masses of time to go!'

As his conversation with Shipshape progressed, Neil found it increasingly difficult to hear what was being said because of the frantic squeaking of the Inkling. Awake for once, the little, furry animal was making its presence known in the noisiest way it could.

'What is it, then?' asked Neil, taking it out of his satchel and stroking it. 'Calm down. Ssshhhh! There, there.'

But the anguished yelps and squeaks continued.

'Don't worry about that little thing. It's probably just had a bad dream,' said Shipshape and laughed. She stepped out of the dragon's costume and hung it on a tree. 'Now, you've got to tell me all your adventures, Neil.'

And so he did.

Perhaps Neil should have been more suspicious of this new character than he was. After all, everyone, including Shipshape herself, had told him that it was impossible to pass from Order to Chaos and back again without the one special key. So what was Shipshape doing here? Common sense should have told him that this couldn't really be Shipshape. Unfortunately, common sense doesn't play much of a role in Chaos. And anyway, the coming into contact with a familiar friendly face after all the ups and downs he'd undergone since stepping through the Pillars of Reason was such a relief that his guard had temporarily dropped a little.

Shipshape certainly seemed flatteringly impressed with Neil's many tales.

'Well done!' she said when Neil explained how he'd come to understand that the snakes were all a figment of his imagination.

'A mistake anyone could have made,' she commented sympathetically as Neil told her about his getting carried away by making wishes.

'Brilliant deduction!!' she marvelled when Neil let her know how he'd managed to keep things in proper perspective when faced with the monstrous spider. And as Neil concluded his account, Shipshape could only stand there with her mouth open.

'Incredible!' she said at last. 'Quite incredible! The Great Methodical certainly did well in picking you.'

'Oh, I haven't done all that much,' said Neil modestly.

'But you have. You have,' said Shipshape. 'And after all those adventures, you must be absolutely famished.'

Neil realized that indeed he *was* hungry.

'But the Great Methodical said that I couldn't get hungry here,' he said.

'That was in Order,' said Shipshape. 'Here in Chaos everything is possible. Now, what would you like to eat most of all in the world?'

Even as Shipshape was asking the question, Neil thought he could smell the faintest aroma of sizzling bacon wafting through the woods.

'A bacon sandwich,' he said slowly, savouring the words, licking his lips and feeling his mouth water.

'A bacon sandwich it shall be,' said Shipshape. 'Follow me.'

The Inkling let out a terrified warning screech. But Neil, following a vision of rashers of crispy bacon nestling between warm bread, dripping with golden butter and topped with just a smidgen of tomato ketchup, had no ears for the little animal.

'I know a tree near here where the most succulent bacon of all grows,' said Shipshape.

'A tree?' said Neil.

'Of course,' said Shipshape.

'I didn't know that bacon grew on trees.'

'Well, where did you think it came from?' she asked.

But Neil couldn't remember.

'Straight ahead and follow your nose,' said Shipshape, which was exactly what Neil was doing.

They trudged on through the woods, but Neil, mesmerized by the promise of his favourite snack, was oblivious to almost everything around him. Blind to the increasing density of the woods, deaf to the imploring cries from the Inkling and insensitive to the thorns which scratched viciously at his face, he was aware only of his sense of smell. And this dragged him relentlessly towards the delicious fragrance of the frying rashers of bacon.

'There it is!' he shouted with delight.

Just in front of him, near the base of the grey walls of the Castle-Nest, was a tall, rounded tree with branches stretching out over the ground. It looked quite like a horse-chestnut tree, but instead of leaves, every twig was decorated with a strip of sizzling red and white bacon.

'Mmmmmmmmmmmmm!!' said Neil.

'So here we are,' said Shipshape. 'But I'm afraid I have something to tell you, my little friend.'

Neil felt an icy chill run down his spine as Shipshape's familiar voice suddenly changed to something altogether more cold and sinister.

'This is not a bacon tree,' came the new, harsh voice. 'It's an *'am-bush*!'

And with these words, the so-called Shipshape disappeared completely and seven wild geese emerged from their hiding places and ran hissing and cackling at Neil.

It had all happened so quickly that at first Neil couldn't make head nor tail of the situation. And then the joke clicked.

Not a bacon tree, but an 'am-bush?

And what a joke. Probably the worst joke he'd ever heard. And he realized that the whole episode – thinking he'd met Shipshape, imagining the smell of the bacon sandwich, seeing the bacon tree – had all been leading up to that one ridiculous punchline. It could only happen in Chaos!

If it had all been an intricate way of trapping Neil, though, it had sadly backfired. The situation struck Neil as being so ridiculous and so contrived that he simply couldn't take it seriously. Instead of rushing terrified from the geese, as they expected, he started to laugh. And he laughed and laughed and laughed and laughed. And his laughter must have been contagious, because the geese started laughing too, in the hissy, goosy way that geese do! Soon all seven of the birds were rolling around on the ground in hysterics, while Neil moaned, doubled up and clutched his stomach.

'It hurts, it hurts,' he said laughing all the more.

The Inkling tried to urge him to escape with its insistent squeaking, but catching sight of the geese rolling about in the dirt only sent Neil into new fits of giggles. He realized, however, that if he was going to escape from the geese then this would be his only chance, so, still laughing, he dragged himself up and was off.

The geese saw that they had been given the slip at once. They ordered one another to 'pull yourself together' and began to chase after the boy.

'Ssstop! Ssstop!' they hissed. 'You're under arressssst!'

Luckily for Neil, the dense thorn bushes prevented the geese from taking off, and a goose on foot is not the swiftest of animals. It's a bit like running a race wearing flippers. The distance between Neil and the geese soon increased, but as he belted along the side of the Castle-Nest wall, he turned and saw them divide into two groups. Presumably they were going to try and head him off. Faster and faster he ran, his heart beating frantically as the wild-goose chase got more and more desperate.

'I've got to find somewhere to hide,' he thought to himself. 'I can't let myself get caught now!'

Slipping round the corner of the ramparts, he noticed a small hole in the wall some ten yards or so ahead of him.

'It's my only hope,' he thought, and prayed that the geese wouldn't get round the corner before he could hide himself. As he approached the hole, he fell and rolled in. A couple of seconds later the webbed feet flapped past him, and as he sat, head down, trying to regain his breath, he heard their hissy dismay at losing sight of their quarry.

'That was certainly a close shave,' said a voice from the back of the hole.

'Who are you?' said Neil, nearly jumping out of his skin. He had the horrible feeling that it was one of the geese lying in wait for him. But it didn't sound like a goose's voice and that was reassuring.

A minute but impeccably dressed man appeared from the shadows and marched up to Neil. He was wearing a red and blue uniform with gold piping around the sleeves, collar and down the outside of his trouser legs. He twisted his waxed moustache ostentatiously and saluted.

'General Knowledge, at your service,' he announced.

'Pleased to meet you, sir,' said Neil to the little man,

who, even though Neil was seated, barely came up to his knees.

'And what can I do to help you?' asked the General.

'I'm not sure you can,' said Neil. 'I want to get inside the grounds of the Castle-Nest without being noticed.'

'Then you've come to exactly the right place,' said the General. 'There is a secret entrance at the end of this tunnel and all you have to do is answer a couple of simple questions, and then you may pass.'

'Are they easy?' asked Neil.

'How can I say?' said the General. 'The definition of an easy question is one that you know the answer to, and the definition of a difficult question is one you don't. How much do you know?'

'I'm not sure,' said Neil, wishing he'd paid attention a little more closely in school.

'Number one,' began General Knowledge, 'Which planet did William Herschel discover in 1781?'

'Ooh,' said Neil. 'Pluto?'

'Wrong. Neptune,' said the General smugly. 'What a pity. You could already be going through that door by now if only you'd known. Now you have to answer two correctly.'

'What are the seven virtues?' he asked.

'Errm. Faith, hope, err, charity,' said Neil getting stuck after three of them. 'Hoovering the carpet? Helping old ladies cross the road?' he suggested tentatively.

'Wrong,' barked the General. 'Faith, hope, charity, fortitude, justice, prudence and temperance.'

'Can't I have a half for the first three?' said Neil.

'Certainly not,' he answered, 'and now you've got to get four questions right.'

'Four? Not three?' said Neil.

'That's correct,' said the General. 'It's a geometrical progression, you understand. Now, approximately what percentage of her weight is a nine-year-old girl?'

Well, if it was Janice Basin, thought Neil, one hundred

per cent. Surely she couldn't ever get any fatter. But a normal nine-year-old girl.

'Oh, I don't know. Twenty-five per cent?' he said.

'Wrong,' shouted the General again. 'Fifty per cent. Eight questions to answer. Which female swimmer won the hundred-metre freestyle at three consecutive Olympics?'

'No idea,' said Neil angrily. 'Who?'

'Dawn Fraser. In 1956, 1960 and 1964,' answered the General. 'Sixteen questions to answer. Which tree is also called the Scots Mahogany?'

'Pine?' offered Neil.

'Wrong!' answered the General, gleefully rubbing his hands together. 'You're really not very good, are you? The answer was the alder and you've now got thirty-two questions to get right. What nationality was Dame Nellie Melba?' he asked.

'Who?'

'Dame Nellie Melba,' he said.

'Sounds like an ice-cream,' said Neil.

'Nationality is all I'm interested in,' snapped the General.

'English?' said Neil.

'Wrong,' said the General. 'Australian.'

'But I don't even know who she is,' said Neil.

'Irrelevant,' said the General.

'But this is pointless,' said Neil.

'Precisely,' he replied. 'Absolutely useless. Utterly futile. Completely profitless, valueless, senseless. In short, a waste of time. But curiously compelling, wouldn't you agree?'

Neil looked at the little man and suddenly saw General Knowledge in a completely different light. It had always seemed something important to have, but at the moment at least it just seemed a way of keeping you from getting down to more important matters. But how to get past the little General, that was the problem. The sword he was wearing looked extremely sharp.

'I've got a question for you,' said Neil. 'If that's allowed.'

'Fire away!' said the General.

'What *is* when it *isn't*?' asked Neil.

'Oooh, a riddle,' said the General. 'I'm not so good at riddles. What *is* when it *isn't*? Now let me see.'

He scratched his head, sat down, frowned, stood up, tweaked his moustache, closed his eyes.

'Hmmm. Tricky. Very tricky indeed, I must say. No, don't tell me. What *is* when it *isn't*?'

And he paced up and down the little tunnel with his brows knitted in deep thought, wavering, wondering, pondering, poring over the right reply.

'It's no good,' he conceded finally. 'I give up. Tell me.'

But in the meantime, while the General had been busy racking his brains, Neil had slunk past on tip-toes and hurried to the end of the tunnel. There he had found a door, turned the key and cautiously peered through into the courtyard of the Castle-Nest.

'Okay! You win!' called General Knowledge, his voice

echoing round the darkness, 'but *please* don't go without giving me the answer. I couldn't stand that.'

Neil ignored him and slipped into the courtyard. He locked the door behind him and pocketed the key, but even with the door shut, the sound of the General's voice still resounded.

'Tell me! Tell me! Tell me!' he demanded.

Frightened that the troubled voice would alert the guard-geese, Neil turned and called through the key-hole.

'You want to know what *is* when it *isn't*?' he said.

'Yes,' shouted the General.

'ABSENCE!' he called back, and heard his answer echoing down the tunnel behind him as he hurried off to explore the grounds of the Castle-Nest.

Chapter 13
The Final Confrontation

At last! Inside the grounds of the Proper Gander's stronghold. Of course, strictly speaking, there shouldn't have been any fixed buildings within Chaos; it showed just how strong the Proper Gander felt itself to be that it could flout the rules of the Thought Domain so blatantly. The Castle-Nest was a curious assembly of constructions, as strange from within as they had looked from without. Walls, pillars, walkways, porticos and winding staircases seemed to have been erected without any plans, one built on to the next as the fancy took the builders. And the higgledy-piggledy haphazardness of it all was emphasized the more because of the thorny bushes which sprouted from every crack and crevice in the stonework.

'Where to look?' said Neil quietly to himself. If it was possible, the Castle-Nest seemed even bigger now that he was inside it than it had before.

Walking cautiously over the cracked paving-stones of the courtyard, Neil realized that it would be a process of trial and error to try to find the Proper Gander. It could be hiding out anywhere in the massive sprawl of buildings. Keeping an eye and an ear out for the guard-geese, Neil took a sloped walkway down to the left which led over to a small, tiled landing and a second set of stairs. Everything was cracked and crumbling and weeds had pushed their way up wherever possible.

With one hand on the wall to help him keep his balance as the pathway darkened, Neil descended a third staircase which brought him down into a catacomb of small rooms with barred doors.

'Dungeons,' he whispered, and heard the Inkling squeak in agreement.

There were rusty chains fixed to the walls, leg-irons and arm-clamps bolted to the floor and neck-braces suspended from the ceilings. Over in one corner was a rack for stretching bodies and a small cage for enclosing them. There were thumbscrews and tongs, tongue-presses and knuckle-crushers, and standing near the door like the tomb of an Egyptian mummy was an iron-maiden with its cruel spikes fixed to the inside of the door.

'A real chamber of horrors,' said Neil, almost hearing the cries and screams of the unfortunate victims who had been tortured there.

He shuddered and turned to leave. Emerging into the brightness of daylight outside, he found that he had taken a different set of stairs, as he was somewhere quite unfamiliar.

'Damn it!' he said.

The task of finding the exact whereabouts of the Proper Gander seemed more and more daunting as he realized that from this small courtyard alone there were fifteen separate exits, or sixteen if you included the well in the middle. He went through a nearby door on the left and found himself in a long banqueting hall with a vaulted ceiling. A carved, black oak table ran the length of the room and had been set for a gigantic feast. Silver goblets, soup tureens, bone-china plates, gold knives, forks and spoons, jade cruets, lace napkins: the overall impression the spread made was one of immeasurable wealth. But the guests had evidently never arrived: the bottles of wine remained unopened and the boar's head centrepiece had been eaten away by time and was now just a grinning skull. Everything was covered in a thick layer of dust and cobwebs. A chandelier had fallen from the ceiling at one end of the table and lay, like a thousand frozen tears, across the abandoned banquet.

It all made Neil feel unbearably sad. He wondered if the castle had been lived in by a king and queen who had been savagely deposed by the evil Proper Gander and its cohorts. He imagined all the song, dance, music and laughter which must have echoed round the hall before. Now, the only movement came from the particles of dust sparkling like fireflies in the shafts of light pouring in through the windows. Neil walked to the far end of the hall and left by a high arched door into the square.

'Left . . . left . . . left, right, left . . . left . . . left, right, left . . .' echoed across the square.

Neil was so lost in his own thoughts that he'd forgotten completely about the geese. He ducked down behind a pillar as two goose-stepping goose-guards passed him by. Only when he could no longer hear their footsteps did he dare to breathe again.

'Idiot!' he said to himself. 'You must be on the alert at *all* times!'

He ran over to a door at the bottom of a tower and tried the handle. It opened and Neil found himself on another spiral staircase. Round and round it went, up and up. He was just beginning to flag, wondering if it was a good idea anyway being in such a confined space in case anything came down in the opposite direction, when he noticed that it was getting lighter above him. A moment later he was standing at the top of a crenellated turret.

The view across the plains of Chaos was magnificent, and from his vantage point, he realized just how huge the Castle-Nest itself was. Somewhere in this vast complex was the Proper Gander itself. But where? He climbed down a small rickety ladder on to the battlements below him and taking care not to be seen from the bottom, he ran along the narrow pathway at the top of the castle ramparts.

'I'm sure it knows I'm here,' thought Neil suddenly.

The certainty hit him with such force and such abruptness that he almost fell down. He looked around half-heartedly for any concealed cameras, knowing deep down that he wouldn't find any, because the Proper Gander wasn't looking *at* him. It was looking *inside* him.

'Perhaps I can feed it some false information,' thought Neil, but immediately realized that the Proper Gander had just read that proposal too. It was certainly a tricky situation to be in. Even though the Castle-Nest was so big, Neil felt very claustrophobic knowing his every step was being monitored.

Filling up his thoughts with a nonsensical nursery rhyme in an attempt to keep the wicked Proper Gander's prying mind at bay, Neil took a turning on the left which went down three steps and led into a square, echoing hall with wooden bars running the length of one wall. He knew, of course, that the Proper Gander knew where he was, but what else could he do? It was no longer a case of searching for his adversary but rather of waiting for it to show its face.

'Oranges and lemons . . .' Neil sang to himself, quickly looking back over his shoulder to see if any possible danger might be following him.

He didn't see anybody or anything there, but what he did see was that where his shoulder had brushed along the wall, it had wiped the dust away and revealed a shiny area of mirrored tiles.

It was then that Neil had THE IDEA!

But before it could formulate itself in his head properly he stopped himself thinking about it. If the Proper Gander saw the plan in his head, it could never work. Still singing the nursery rhymes which he hoped would conceal any other thoughts he might have, Neil set about cleaning the walls. It was a slow and draining task as he only had his shirt to use as a duster and the room was immense. Even stretching up high from the parallel bars, he still found it difficult to get the uppermost parts of the walls completely spotless. Finally, however, the whole room was reflecting in on itself and Neil stood there fascinated by the countless images of himself which repeated back and forth between the opposite walls.

If the banqueting hall had belonged to a king and queen, then this room must have been set aside for their princesses to practise ballet movements. Neil imagined them carrying out their graceful pirouettes and spins. One or two of the tiles had come unstuck from the wall and now lay on the floor, but nevertheless Neil had no difficulty in picturing the entire hall in its former glory.

A deep and throbbing rumble interrupted his daydreaming. At first, he thought Chaos must be undergoing a major earthquake, but as he listened, Neil realized that the vibrations were forming themselves into words.

'How dare you?' came the voice. 'How dare you challenge my might?'

And Neil knew he was being addressed directly by the evil Proper Gander itself. He found himself trembling once again. It was inevitable, but then, hadn't other experiences he'd had in Chaos shown him that the Proper Gander was not infallible? Hadn't it mistakenly led him to its lair? Or had that been a deliberate trap? No, Neil wouldn't allow himself to believe that. The Proper Gander could and would be destroyed.

'Destroyed?' boomed the voice. 'And by a worthless little toad like you? You're deluding yourself. I am the most infinitely superior being in the Universe. I am 'OMNIPOTENT!' it roared. 'I am OMNISCIENT!!' it bellowed. 'I am,' and its voice suddenly changed to a low, evil hiss, 'omnivorous!!! And if you don't know what that means, I shall tell you. It means I eat EVERYTHING – and I am particularly partial to meddling little boys!'

Neil heard the sound of a beak opening and shutting noisily, of a giant stomach rumbling hungrily.

'Where are you then?' shouted Neil as boldly as he could.

'You have the audacity to ask ME questions?' countered the Proper Gander.

'Why not?' said Neil.

'Why not? I shall show you why not. I could clap you in irons!' it roared, and Neil found himself back down in the gloomy dungeons. His arms and legs were clamped by the iron rings and he was chained to the wall. Looking around for help, he saw only skeletons of previous victims, draped in cobwebs. A rat ran from a grinning skull and scurried across the stone floor.

'I don't believe it!' said Neil. 'I DON'T BELIEVE IT!'

Instantly, the dungeon disappeared and he found himself back in the banqueting hall, clutching a turkey drumstick and a glass of red wine.

'I could poison you!' screamed the Proper Gander. The turkey turned at once into a foul-smelling, maggot-ridden piece of rotten meat; the goblet was filled with effervescing green slime.

'IT'S NO GOOD,' shouted Neil out loud. 'I SIMPLY DON'T BELIEVE ANY OF THIS!'

'I shall crush you away to nothing,' came the voice again, as Neil found himself back in the hall of mirrors again.

'The power of lies is in their being believed,' shouted Neil. 'AND I DON'T BELIEVE THEM ANY MORE!'

He felt the whole building tremble and shake.

'What did you dare to say?' thundered the Proper Gander.

'You heard!' Neil yelled back.

A hundred-foot serpent rose up out of the floor, venom dripping from its needle-sharp fangs, eyes flashing green and yellow, tongue darting out at him.

'I DON'T BELIEVE IT!'

Blue flames suddenly filled the hall, engulfing the boy as he stood there.

'I DON'T BELIEVE IN ANY OF THIS!' he yelled again. 'HOW CAN I BELIEVE IN SOMETHING I CAN'T EVEN SEE?' he added cunningly.

The fire disappeared.

There was silence.

'I mean, if you were actually here, standing in front of me,' said Neil, 'perhaps I might possibly consider acknowledging your greatness. Maybe,' he added as evasively as he could manage.

'But I am . . .'

'Then prove it!'

The room quaked and quivered, shivered and shook. As if echoing from the belly of the earth came a bellowing roar which set Neil's stomach churning. He stood there terrified, knowing it was too late to undo what he had done. Any second now the Proper Gander would be standing in front of him, and he had asked for it, literally.

When it did appear, it was even more massive than Neil had remembered, towering above him monstrously. Taller than the room, it was forced to stoop, which brought its savage beak swaying down close to Neil. It was bedraggled, it was filthy and it stank of rotting vegetables and sour milk. Eyes black as bottomless pits stared expressionlessly out from above its cruel beak, razor-sharp and lined with teeth. A little trickle of dried blood stained the feathers by its gaping mouth ominously.

'But I've already told you,' said Neil, trying to keep control over his quivering voice. 'I don't believe any of this. It's just one more deceit. I want to see you as you *really* are.'

'You must believe,' screeched the Proper Gander petulantly and stabbing at the boy.

'If I shut my eyes, you're not there,' said Neil. 'If I think something is dangerous, it will be. But you're not! Seeing isn't believing and I certainly don't believe what I see in front of me now. Nothing is what it seems,' he continued bravely, 'and it seems to me that you are nothing.'

'You . . .'

'Just take a look at yourself,' commanded Neil, refusing to give the Proper Gander the upper hand for a moment.

'You're afraid, aren't you? The oh so wonderful Proper Gander can't even maintain the delusion to itself. It's pathetic!'

The bird looked away and squawked in what sounded like alarm. Just for the briefest fraction of an instant its outline tremored and Neil thought he could see right through the immense repulsive form. A second later and it became solid again. But Neil knew that he was getting warm.

'You don't even believe in yourself, do you?' he persisted. And once again, the monster lost its solidity for a wavering moment.

Neil had one last weapon up his sleeve. It was a long shot and if it failed, then he had lost. But it could just conceivably work . . .

'BOO!!!' he yelled at the top of his voice. The sound echoed round the entire mirrored hall and the outline of the Proper Gander trembled and flickered.

'BOOOOO!!!' he shouted again, and the entire form took on the flimsy consistency of knitted fog.

Summoning up all the longest words he knew, Neil drew a deep breath and bellowed with all his might:

'To one fat, fraudulent, garrulous goose, I say BOOOOOOO!!!'

And with a sound like someone clicking their fingers, the Proper Gander disappeared. In its place was a pale, wiggly maggot wriggling around on the floor.

'I *am* great. I *am* almighty. I *am* all-powerful,' it squeaked.

But now that Neil had seen the wicked Proper Gander for what it *really* was, there was no way it could ever exert any power over him again.

'Of course you are,' he said, humouring the little worm.

He took two of the loose tiles from the side of the hall and laid one on the floor in front of him. Then he gently laid the wriggling maggot on it.

'What are you doing?' it squealed.

'You're going on a trip,' said Neil, carefully positioning

the second mirror. He lined it up above the other one, so that the repeated reflections between the two multiplied themselves smaller and smaller down to infinity. Then slowly he brought the two mirrors together.

'Can you see a long, long corridor leading back behind you?' he asked. 'That's where you're going. For ever!!'

'No, no, no,' squeaked the maggot as the two mirrors were laid flat against one another.

'Let me out!' it called plaintively.

'Not likely!' said Neil.

'Please, let me out,' it called again, more faintly now. 'Let me oou . . . ou . . . oou . . .'

The sound grew more and more distant as the actual maggoty form of the banished Proper Gander tumbled down the endless tunnels towards infinity.

Gone!

The Proper Gander had finally been destroyed and he, little Neil Davies, had been the one to do it. At the same moment that the last echoes of its pleas for help drifted away into oblivion, so the entire Castle-Nest disappeared and Neil found himself kneeling on a grassy ridge somewhere on the plains of Chaos. He scarcely dared to close his eyes, in case when he opened them again the monstrous bird had returned. He blinked once, twice, three times. Everything seemed to be all right. And he knew that he had sent the Proper Gander packing, once and for all.

Even if his eyes had played any more tricks on him, Neil could never have mistaken the sudden change in the atmosphere. It was altogether lighter, friendlier and less threatening. He heard a commotion behind him, and looking round, saw thousands of thoughts with smiling faces and opened arms rushing towards him. They hoisted him high up in the air and carried him off on their shoulders.

'Three cheers for Neil. Hip hip!'

'Hooray!' came the response.

'Hip hip!'

'HOORAY!!' The tumultuous roar echoed all round Chaos

'Hip hip!'

'*HOORAY*!!!' It was the loudest cheer that Neil had ever heard, and he knew he'd never felt happier or prouder before.

And as they bounced along over the meadows carrying the small boy, the thoughts sang *For He's a Jolly Good Fellow*! over and over.

In the distance, Neil saw two shiny white columns and realized that the thoughts were taking him back to the Pillars of Reason. He felt both excited to be returning to Order again and saddened to be leaving Chaos, where he had learnt so much and which he was still only just getting to know.

As the pillars loomed above them, the thoughts placed Neil down on the ground.

'Speech! Speech!' they demanded.

'Oh, I can't,' said Neil bashfully.

'Come on,' they encouraged. 'Speech!!'

'Well,' said Neil, realizing he wasn't going to get away without one. 'I'd just like to say that I'm so glad I've been able to get rid of the Proper Gander. And I just hope it'll never return!'

The thoughts roared their unanimous approval.

'And I'd like to thank all of you who helped to prepare me for my final confrontation with the beast, although, of course, at the time I hated you for it!'

He looked down at Wand, the dragon and the various knights and damsels in distress, and smiled.

'I'd like to stay here a lot,' he said, and a cheer of support went up 'BUT,' he continued loudly, causing the crowd to groan 'but, well, Chaos really isn't the place for me, at least, not yet, although I'll be sending you loads of my own thoughts when I get back!'

Once again a rapturous cheer filled the air.

'And so now,' he said, 'I'm afraid it's time to say goodbye

to all of you. BYE!' he yelled, and waved both arms at the crowd so that even the little thoughts at the back who hadn't heard his speech could see him.

'If I can ever make heads or tails of this riddle,' he muttered under his breath, looking at the little verse on the leather thong.

When wood would fold,
When tin turns old,
The whole behold,
Through glass with gold.

Return, resound,
All else confound,
By beaten sound,
The key be found.

But what does it all mean? Neil wondered. He remembered Shambles assuring him that everything would become clear when the time was right. Well, it hadn't become clear. Did that mean that he had to stay in Chaos longer?

Then, as he was wondering whether to simply postpone his return for a couple of weeks and take a holiday, something started happening to one of the rods. It was the wooden one. Without his even touching it, the wood turned all soft and curled up like an autumn leaf which fell to his feet.

'When wood would fold,' Neil muttered.

A moment later, the tin rod changed to a bright orange and crumbled away to rust.

'When tin turns old,' said Neil. He kept watching, but nothing else seemed to be happening. 'Now what?' he wondered.

'By beaten sound, the key be found,' he said, pondering over the words. 'By beaten sound . . .' he repeated. 'Perhaps if I . . .'

He took the two remaining rods and struck them together. It produced a pure, resounding note which filled the air.

'That's it!' he said excitedly. 'By beaten sound, the key be found, of course!' And with the glass rod in one hand and the gold rod in the other he beat the two of them together. Louder and louder the sound became, one crystal-clear tone which pulsed and resonated throughout the Thought Domain. Neil didn't know this, but he was producing a chord in the key of A, the sound at the beginning of the music of the universe. And as the notes reached every last corner of Chaos and Order, the massive gates between the Pillars of Reason slid effortlessly open.

'Don't forget us!' cried the thoughts as Neil stepped forwards.

'I won't,' he promised. He stopped for a moment to look back and wave, and then walked through the gateway and out of Chaos for ever.

The first sight to confront him was a gigantic tree, growing on the dividing line between Chaos and Order and with its branches reaching into both sides of the Domain.

'NEIL!!!' shouted Shipshape and Shambles in unison.

'You did it, didn't you!' said Shipshape.

'Everything suddenly changed here,' said Shambles. 'All the waiting thoughts stood up and cheered!'

'And then we heard the most incredible sound echoing through the whole area,' said Shipshape.

'We didn't know what it was,' said Shambles.

'But it was beautiful,' said Shipshape.

'That was the key,' explained Neil.

'It certainly was,' said Shipshape. 'You're back here with us, and look!'

She pointed down the Right Track. Neil turned and saw the column of thoughts which had been so desolate and fearful before all beginning to march happily through the unlocked doors into Chaos. The fear generated by the wicked Proper Gander had gone and the thoughts were all on the move again.

'Soon clear up this backlog!' said Shambles.

'Hurry along there, mind your backs,' Shipshape called out cheerfully.

'What do you think I ought to do with this!' asked Neil, taking the two sandwiched mirrors out of his satchel.

'What is it?' asked Shambles.

Neil explained all about how he had called the Proper Gander's bluff and then managed to banish it to eternity, and, after praising his cleverness, Shipshape and Shambles both agreed on the ideal place to secure the mirrors.

'Just up there,' said Shipshape, indicating the cleft in the giant tree, where it divided up into the two halves shared by Order and Chaos.

'But what is this tree?' asked Neil. 'It wasn't here when I left, was it?'

'You planted it,' said Shipshape. 'Don't you remember?'

'The Seed of an Idea!' said Neil.

'Precisely,' said Shambles, 'and now, to keep ignorance and fear from separating the two lands, it has grown into the Tree of Knowledge.'

Neil climbed up the thick, gnarled trunk and, using a knotty foot-hole to pull himself up, managed to reach the cleft. He slipped the two mirrors carefully into the gap, which instantly sealed itself up without a trace.

'Encased in the Tree of Knowledge,' Shambles called up, 'the Proper Gander will never have any power over us again.'

Neil looked down as the rows of thoughts continued to pass happily between the Pillars of Reason.

'I did it,' he whispered softly to himself. 'I really did it.'

'Come on,' called Shipshape, 'we've got to report to the Great Methodical. He'll be expecting us.'

'It's going to take ages,' said Neil, climbing back down. 'It must be miles away!'

'No problem,' said Shipshape. 'Not only have we

recovered the car but it's working like never before. Like a jet-propelled rocket it is now!'

'Climb in,' said Shambles, and with Shipshape at the wheel they sped off down the Right Track, along the Central Way of Thinking and back on to the narrow roads between the perfectly ordered Thought Boxes.

'Bit more speedy than before, eh?' said Shipshape.

'I'll say,' said Neil.

'Bit *too* speedy, if you ask me,' said Shambles.

'We didn't!' replied Neil and Shipshape together and laughed.

As they raced past the thousands of Thought Boxes something that had been bothering Neil since before he'd got into the Castle-Nest occurred to him again.

'Shipshape?' he said.

'Yes?' she said.

'There's still one thing I don't understand. How did you manage to get into Chaos and back out again?'

'What?' she said.

'I saw you there,' said Neil.

'You couldn't have,' said Shipshape. 'I was with you the whole time, wasn't I?' she said to Shambles.

'Indeed you were,' said Shambles. 'But I bet I know who you came into contact with, Neil,' he said.

'Who?' asked Neil.

'CAREFUL!' screamed Shambles as Shipshape swerved to miss one of the helpers taking a fresh load of used thoughts away from their boxes.

'No problem,' said Shipshape. 'Keep your hair on!'

'Who *did* I meet then?' asked Neil.

'When they made the batch of helpers that look like Shipshape,' Shambles explained, 'they made one who went a bit wrong. She thought she was greater and more methodical than the Great Methodical himself and tried to bring a little bit of Chaos into Order when she was thwarted. Her name was Slipshod.'

'Slipshod,' repeated Neil.

'They tried to reprogram her, but it didn't work. In the end she was banished to Chaos.'

'So you've seen my Chaotic double, have you?' said Shipshape. 'And which one of us do you prefer?'

Neil thought back to the look-alike in the dragon suit. He remembered the endless retellings of the fairy-tales and legends with ridiculous battles and tricks. And as he recalled the punchline of the worst-joke-in-the-world he couldn't help laughing all over again.

'That's the thing,' he explained. 'You're two halves of the same person. It's just like . . .' he paused.

'What?' said Shipshape.

'Nothing,' said Neil. 'I was just thinking of something I want to say to the Great Methodical when we get back.'

'Well, you won't have long to wait,' said Shipshape. 'We're nearly there.'

And sure enough, in the distance, Neil could already make out the imposing Memory Bank looming up above the checkered patterns of the Thought Boxes.

A few minutes later and they pulled up in front of the building. And there, surrounded by a welcoming committee of helpers, was the Great Methodical.

'Well done, my boy,' he said shaking hands with Neil. 'Very well done indeed.'

'Thank you, sir,' said Neil. 'Of course, I couldn't have done it all on my own.'

'But without you, it couldn't have been done at all,' said the Great Methodical, still pumping Neil's hand up and down. 'And on behalf of all of us here, not to mention the people of the world, who certainly should be grateful, I would like to extend my warmest thanks and sincerest gratitude.'

The Great Methodical certainly hadn't lost any of his pomp or formality, Neil realized, but despite his outward ceremoniousness, he knew that the old man was elated underneath. He simply found it too embarrassing to display his emotions.

'So once again, thank you, Neil. I regret that the time has come for you to return to your own world once again. It is not good, after all, for anyone to dwell *too* long in thought.'

'But I . . .' Neil tried to say.

'So if there's nothing more that you wish to say, then it . . .'

'But there *is* something I would like to say,' said Neil firmly.

'Oh!' said the Great Methodical looking a bit taken aback. 'And what might that be?'

'I think I've learnt a great deal on this quest,' started Neil, sounding almost as pompous as the Great Methodical himself, 'but the most important thing I've learnt is this: Order and Chaos cannot be separated. Both of them are vital to mankind. When I first came here I thought that the Thought Domain just meant Order, but I have discovered that Chaos is the other side of the same coin.'

'Well, I . . .' blustered the Great Methodical.

'What's more,' continued Neil, 'it is beause Chaos was seen as something separate from and not a part of the Thought Domain that the Proper Gander was able to gain such a stronghold.'

'If I could just . . .' started the Great Methodical. But Neil was not to be put off.

'There is always a little Chaos in the most ordered of minds,' he said, quite determined to finish his speech, 'and a certain Order to the most chaotic of situations. The important thing is getting the balance between them right.'

'But you don't . . .' tried the Great Methodical, to no avail.

'What I suggest,' said Neil, 'is a closer link between Order and Chaos. Regular communication, as it were, and I think I met just the right person for the job in Chaos. Her name is Slipshod.'

'WHAT?' bellowed the Great Methodical. 'That young upstart! That little, meddlesome bounder! That . . .'

'That young upstart understood the link between the two halves of the Thought Domain,' said Neil. 'If there isn't any meeting-point between Order and Chaos, you're bound to end up with thoughts so bland and regimented that they'll be dangerously receptive to any future attack on the way people think. And next time it might not be possible to destroy any evil influence!'

The Great Methodical went silent. His helpers all took one step back. Then another. His face turned white. Then red. Then purple. Then white again. Neil wondered if he hadn't gone too far, whether, having destroyed the Proper Gander, he wasn't now going to be struck down by the Great Methodical himself.

The old man took a deep breath, fixed his eyes on the small boy and spoke.

'You're right,' he said gently. 'I must take some responsibility for the situation. You *are* right.'

The helpers all breathed a sigh of relief.

Shipshape let out a loud whoop of delight. The assembled

crowd cheered noisily and happily. Even Shambles allowed himself a smile and a moderate round of applause!

Neil, embarrassed now, smiled and looked down at the ground.

'Things are going to be very different from now on,' said the Great Methodical. 'Very, very different. Yes, they most certainly are. Of that you can be sure. Oh yes, very different indeed.'

As Neil looked around him, the Great Methodical seemed to become enveloped in fog, and the Memory Bank grew hazy and disappeared. Shipshape and Shambles melted into the same mist and, as they did so, their cheering and the Great Methodical's voice grew less and less distinct.

'Very different indeed. Oh yes, very difff . . .'

Conclusion

The World Starts Thinking Again

A familiar room with blue and yellow patterned wallpaper appeared. It was his bedroom, and looking up, Neil saw five big, concerned faces looking down at him: his mum, his dad, a policeman, Dr Grady and Miss Beale. And as his eyes focussed on them, one after the other, they all smiled at him.

'What happened?' he asked, and winced in case they all told him not to worry his head with silly problems.

'You were playing in that old wood and a rotten branch landed on your head,' said Mr Davies.

'I saw you through the railings while I was taking my Alsatian for a walk,' explained the policeman.

'I examined you and found you to be suffering from mild concussion,' said Dr Grady.

'I phoned your mother at work when you disappeared from school,' said Miss Beale, 'and I decided to come and visit you when I heard you'd been found.'

'We've all been waiting for you to come round,' said Mrs Davies, stroking his forehead.

One question and five answers! Now that *was* a change. The Great Methodical's last words echoed in his head. Things certainly did seem to be different and hopefully this was just a start. Neil smiled up at them.

'I think what he needs most of all now is rest,' said Dr Grady.

'I agree,' said Mrs Davies.

When they had closed the door Neil turned over to go to sleep. The sudden pain he felt made him yelp loudly as he rolled on to the bump at the side of his head.

'It must look a terrific size,' he thought, feeling the tender skin gently.

He climbed out of bed and, by using the mirror on the table in conjunction with the mirror on the wall, he got a view of the back of his head. The swollen bump where the branch had hit him looked angry and sore.

Really horrible, he thought proudly. The skin had broken and you could already see the purple bruising, even through his hair. Having satisfied himself that the others would be impressed with the wound when he got back to school, he took the desk mirror and held it up in front of the other one. He saw the mirror reflecting the other mirror reflecting the other mirror, time after time, until the long corridor of mirrors gradually curved away out of sight. And he knew that right at the end of that infinitely repeating set of reflections was a little banished maggot which had nearly destroyed the world as the Proper Gander.

'Neil,' said his mother. 'What are you doing out of bed?'

'I just wanted to see the bump, mum,' he said.

'Well, into bed with you now. The doctor said you're to rest until tomorrow afternoon at the earliest.'

'Okay,' he said, and climbed back under the duvet.

'Oh, and by the way,' she said, just before closing the door. 'Where did you get that hamster from?'

'What hamster,' asked Neil.

'The one in your satchel. Don't pretend you don't know anything about it.'

Neil smiled.

'It's not a hamster,' he said. 'It's just a little Inkling.'